About th

Anne-Louise Quinton lives and works in Leeds and Yorkshire. Following an accomplished career in art and design education, a persistent idea for a great story led her to write her debut novel *On Hold* while her life was very much on hold with a broken leg. Used to inspiring and entertaining her students with tall tales, now she keeps readers rapt with the same energy and experience. Drawing on a lifelong love of classic ghost stories and a strong belief in practical skills and creative thinking, her writing captures both the wit and wickedness of the north in equal measure.

On Hold

Anne-Louise Quinton

On Hold

Vanguard Press

A CIP catalogue record for this title is available from the British Library.

ISBN 978-1-83794-510-8

This is a work of fiction. Names, characters, businesses, places, events and
incidents are either the products of the author's imagination or used in a
fictitious manner. Any resemblance to actual persons, living or dead, or actual
events is purely coincidental.

*Vanguard Press is an imprint of
Pegasus Elliot Mackenzie Publishers Ltd.*
www.pegasuspublishers.com

First Published in 2025

**Vanguard Press
Sheraton House Castle Park
Cambridge England**

Printed & Bound in Great Britain

Dedication

This book is dedicated to the memory of David Coates,
my wonderful, kind and generous neighbour.
3rd December, 1935–27th December, 2021.

Acknowledgements

I would like to thank the legendary Carol, Amanda and Karen for being so constant. To Sarah Hyndman, for showing me that when you have an idea, you must trust it and stick with it. I would like to thank every member of my sixth form tutor groups throughout my teaching career who sat and hung off my every word when it was a story telling time. A huge thanks to the inspirational Jeremy Dyson, whose path I crossed at the age of eighteen and who has ever since blazed a trail for the ghosts among us. Jim and Angela, thank you for showing me that age is irrelevant, and how to master growing older with hilarity and a very sharp wit. A massive thanks to all my friends who supported me and didn't say I was mad when I leapt out of the teaching boat and into the life raft. Big thanks go to our "Ian" and his love of little eats. And the biggest thanks to Beck, for first telling me to just write my memoir, and who then told me to turn my little idea into this story. Your blind faith in my ability has been incredible. I would also like to thank Mother Nature for all the magic that is happening above and below the surface of this earth that we have yet to fully understand…

Chapter One – The Call-up

Elinor stared out of the kitchen window and looked at the big old house opposite. It used to be gorgeous to look into Tom and Lynne's back garden. Tom had trained the roses across a network of posts, creating a wonderful circle of blooms that lasted from late spring to early autumn. Nearly every year there would be a strong storm with high winds that would pull and damage the rose frame. The following day Tom would be out with hammer and nails, fixing the posts and the struts. He would do everything possible to avoid getting someone in and paying for more sturdy repairs. Elinor fixed her gaze through the window, plunged her hands into the washing-up bowl and grabbed a plate. Now, she stared at the side wall of a kitchen extension of bricks. It sat on top of that rose garden patio now. All visual memories of Tom, Lynne and the roses were gone. The variegated green colours and leaf shapes, interspersed with the delicate colours of roses had been replaced with the hard solid terracotta vertical plane of cheap bricks. She used to wave at Lynne through their respective kitchen windows, almost daily. The food from last night's dinner was stubborn on the ceramic surface and she scrubbed harder. The lasagne didn't want to budge, so she took off her marigolds and decided to let the plate soak a while.

Deciding to retire early had turned out to be a stroke of genius for Elinor on many levels. No longer caught up in the machine, days were now incredibly long and mentally peaceful. No stresses and deadlines. The morning alarm never went on for anything other than an early morning holiday getaway. She never had to wake up in the dark again. Elinor knew she was lucky that she didn't have to try and work through the chaos of COVID and lockdowns either. She felt blessed to have made the right judgement call at the right time. Any time that she did feel annoyed, overwhelmed, stressed or angry about anything; she could just tell herself that at least she was no longer trying to manage it with a full-time job too. No more 5.40 a.m. alarm. No standing at the bus stop in the pitch black, freezing cold and rain for a start. That was luxury enough. The only thing she did miss was getting that sunrise all to herself. There was a sweet spot in the year when waiting for the bus completely alone, coincided with the dawn chorus and a sunrise that burnt into her retinas like she was looking at highly polished gold. However, she wouldn't swap her lifestyle change just for that. She took her freshly brewed mug of tea into the sitting room and plonked herself down happily onto the sofa.

Trying to keep up with all the latest news and technology could have felt like a full-time job in itself; so after opening her laptop, Elinor scrolled through the online news, gathering the latest doom and gloom and mulling it all over. It had been a definitive choice to never watch the news on the TV ever again. The thumping heart beat music leading into a seriously toned newsreader delivering every worst-case scenario from the day or week of world and local hardships, had become too much for her. Just scanning and choosing what to read, in silence, without the soundtrack, was far less stressful. It was easier to digest the written word than the intonation and gravitas of Fiona Bruce or Clive Myrie.

The art, design, and culture sections offered brevity, colour and hope. She enjoyed all of the amazing photography portfolios and liked to see them on the "big screen" rather than on her phone. Then an article caught her eye "The big switch off". All landline phones will be switched off by 2026. The end of an era. She scrolled further into the story and digressed her attention to the phone boxes around the UK. Apparently, five thousand were to be kept in remote areas for emergencies. On a train journey, she remembered seeing the phone box graveyard. Hundreds of red telephone boxes squashed together in a yard somewhere near Stalybridge if she remembered correctly. She still had a landline phone. When it rang it was usually a telemarketing sales pitch and she really didn't have time to listen to people trying to con her out of money. There were a few ways she would approach her call and response when this happened. Depending on her mood, she could be incredibly friendly and polite and graciously say "thank you but no", when the sales pitch finally came to an end. If this was met with continued harassment, then as far as she was concerned, they deserved her far more harsh response. She never swore at them but would make it incredibly clear that they had pissed her off and really should just stop there. It amazed her when some actually tried to carry on talking past that point. If it wasn't telemarketing it would be Tom, asking for help with something, usually a little job like getting something from the shops or posting a letter. He would always start by inviting her round for a cuppa and a biscuit, but Elinor never begrudged his requests; he was adorable. After Lynne had died, all of Tom's close friends and neighbours kept an eye on him and kept him company. After Tom had died, the phone was pretty much silent. That is, apart from the strange little chimes that it made for no reason at all. Elinor joked with friends that it was as if someone was calling from the past. 19.47 p.m., was a regular time for it to "ping" to life. Although the times did vary from about seven thirty p.m., to ten p.m. Naturally, she just attributed the random chime to an electric pulse in the network system, what else could it be?

Elinor was not bored in her new life. She did work part-time and was keen to keep fit and healthy by walking everywhere and going swimming, but there were the occasional days when all the jobs were done, everything had been ticked off the list and she couldn't quite settle herself to just sit and read. This was a throwback to the fact that there was always something more important to do than read a book for pleasure. Consuming books on holiday, on the beach, was easy and very enjoyable, but sitting at home, it just never felt like time well spent, it felt like time squandered. It felt like she really had retired and there was absolutely nothing else to do. If it was research and factual that was a different kettle of fish altogether. If it sparked her interest and was intriguing, then she could get lost down the rabbit hole of Google information cave systems and struggle to find her way out. She was about to fall down a very deep rabbit hole into a huge cave system and it was about to consume her. She didn't know this yet of course.

She slurped on her tea and scrolled further. Many small communities and villages were purchasing their old phone booths for one pound and turning them into little libraries, plant swaps and other twee alternatives to the original use. Those that were still connected were in places where wi-fi and any other form of internet connection was patchy at best.

As she shuffled herself round on the sofa for a more comfortable position, mug in one hand and laptop on her knees, the landline phone rang loudly. The internal bell had no softness to its sound as the metal hammer clattered inside the hard plastic. The house was silent in the mornings and this was a jolt. The bell was louder than her iPhone by quite some decibels of course and couldn't just be turned down, or set to vibrate. Thankfully, the tea splashed away from the keyboard, but a jumpy "fuckin' hell" still came out on autopilot as the tea splashed over her jeans. This was going to get her back up now; whichever roofing, insurance, or accident claim company it was, was not going to get polite, Elinor. She made for the phone in the study. It was still attached to the wall socket by a relatively short cable. Grumpily, she called, 'Hello?' as she picked up the receiver. It had been getting increasingly more static disturbance over the past year and she moved it away from her ear a little to avoid the crackling that made her initially wince. It was not a telemarketing call.

'Hello, Elinor, it's Tom. I wondered if you wanted to come round for a cuppa and a biscuit? I wonder if I could ask you to do a little job for me?'

Ed and Pat both took a deep breath, then breathed out slowly at exactly the same time. Staring out from the top of Warrendale knots and Attermire Scar, they looked across the Settle valley and at the massive majestic sky. In the distance was the domed roof of Giggleswick school chapel. Over to the right up the valley, was the formidable shape of Pen-y-Ghent, one of the three peaks they had walked countless times. The hard part of their walk was done and this view was the payoff. The lapwings and curlews sang their Spring songs on the breeze and in this exact moment everything was just how it should be. They loved this place and as they turned to continue their walk, the sun broke through and the light on the limestone was stunning. As a couple they had considered themselves very lucky to have found each other when they did and never bothered with children to get in the way of their enjoyment of each other's company. When both sets of parents had died not too long apart from each other, four funerals in two years had been the hardest of times; they found themselves with two houses and two substantial – in their minds – inheritances, so they both retired in their forties and never looked back. Never wanting to succumb to spend, spend, spend living, they had spent a great deal of time looking at their finances and once the two houses were sold, they knew exactly how much they could spend each year until they both expired. They had no one to leave any money to and had no intention of squirrelling anything away that was unnecessary. Various charities could share whatever was left.

As they strolled through the scars and past Victoria cave, they chatted about anything and everything and what they would have for tea back at the hotel. Tea was really dinner, but it was never supper and it was always hearty, especially after this walk. The menu had always been old school, out of time, nothing fancy. The classics were still there for those who wanted them, and they did. Yorkshire boasted Michelin-starred chefs, exquisite food and of course, Betty's was to be worshipped by all who wanted afternoon tea or a "Fat Rascal" slathered in butter. Towns like Malton were dedicated to food and drink artisans, but any Yorkshire town worth its salt also knew its stick-in-the-mud clientele, who needed pies, mushy peas and lots of gravy. Back at the hotel, it had been a surprise for them to see a menu including some "fancy" foods, but thankfully pies, meat and burgers along with a fruit crumble were still the favourites of the regulars. Gravy and custard, not jus and coulis.

They tried to make this little trip a yearly occurrence. It rebalanced them. A short mini break away, not far from the city, but a world away mentally and visually. If you passed anyone up here, it really would be just one person, especially mid-week and that could still be the mole exterminator man in his van. On the final walk back into the town they walked through the main market square. The town had bought the two old BT red telephone boxes for one pound each back in 2017. Cleverly, they had rigged one up to tell the stories of the town and local area. The other phone box was decked out as a miniature art gallery, just a short walk away too. The stories phone box was open twenty-four hours a day, but they had never gone in to listen. They had seen day trippers and parents holding up children to let them grasp the big old black handset and hear the voice on the other end. By now, they were both quite exhausted and looking forward to the large bath tub that they could soak their aching bones in. With faces tightened and flushed from the exposure and freshness of the early Spring weather, their lungs full of the freshest air and their limbs stretched from the climb and descent, Ed and Pat got to their hotel room and flopped onto the sofa at the side of the bed and stared at the painting of a friendly horned cow on the opposite wall.

After bathing and soaking they got themselves to "dinner-ready" presentability, which wasn't very fancy at all, just tidy and presentable, but still comfy. Life was all about comfort for Ed and Pat. They liked to eat early, so that tea had a chance to settle. It was five p.m., when they wandered downstairs and feasted on a classic dinner of pie, mash and gravy, followed by a sticky toffee pudding for

Ed and the blackberry and apple crumble for Pat. Of course, they stuck a spoon in each other's dessert just for quality control purposes. After this feast, they knew they needed an evening stroll to give them time to digest, otherwise, they would never sleep, and headed to neighbouring Giggleswick to walk round the very quaint streets, even if they were filled with far too many teenagers. The mild early Spring evening was calm and the light was accenting the limestone and Yorkshire stone buildings with warm sunsetting tones. The school seemed to own most of the village for teaching and accommodation spaces. Instead of an old place filled with old people, it was full of youthful chatter and was in some ways rather delightful. Watching the gangs of friends obsessing over their phones and using the current slang way of talking just cemented their correct decision to not have children, but they didn't mind seeing young lives just getting on with living. They overheard conversations and laughed at the chasm of difference in their lives compared to the youth of today.

They often talked of moving here, in fact, they had that very conversation on today's walk, again. It had a Booth's after all. That was one up from Waitrose as far as they were concerned. As they strolled back into town and through the square, they eyed up any for sale signs. Dusk had sneaked up on them and sunset orange became street lamp orange. Ed took his phone from his pocket and checked the time, 19.48. He glanced at the phone box, still lit up. Then it rang. Was it rigged to a sensor, so that when

19

someone walked by it would activate the phone to call the passer-by over to listen? What a hoot. They walked towards it; Ed pulled the door and propped it open for Pat to listen in too. Pat leaned in so that the phone was between them both. Ed picked up the black plastic handset and instantly moved the ear piece away from his head as the static surged through the receiver. 'Hello!' said Ed, grinning slightly at the potential prank of the phone. Then came the reply that was about to change everything in their lives.

'Hello, Ed, it's your dad; is Pat with you? It's been a while. I need you to...'

Harry was in the kitchen, filling bowls with "little eats". He loved little eats; they were timeless. When they were just kids, Mam had them all arranged in her different coloured bowls on the sideboard. Crisps were rarely part of the selection, but there were always little mini square crackers, cheesy balls, twiglets, salted peanuts, and those flattish corn wheels that he loved. When Mam had first experienced a Tupperware party, she was beside herself at the prospect of keeping everything airtight, neatly stacked in the pantry. No more of those twisty ties. She had bought the full range and enjoyed telling them that you had to "burp" the lids for a complete seal. Harry knew that babies were "burped" so the idea of doing this with a plastic container had been very funny when he was five. It still made him laugh as an adult. As Harry had grown, there never were leftovers that needed to be kept in airtight conditions, he scoffed the lot. Edie was in the sitting room plumping cushions unnecessarily. The house was spick and span though it would be carnage by the end of the day. A large quantity of those little eats, would be squashed into the carpet and other fabrics there would be little sticky finger prints everywhere. The experience meant they never put out Wotsits ever again.

The twins were like whirling dervishes or the cartoon Tasmanian devil. Had he and Edie been quite so energetic and full of beans when they were both five? Harry didn't think so. He had played out in the street from dawn until dusk, using up every morsel of energy, but once indoors he had to follow strict rules. Only indoor voices, no running, and indoor games only. Bedtime was bedtime, no screaming ab-dabs or tantrums, just routine and lights out. Not following the rules had consequences. The twins went into meltdown regularly and as cute, delightful and good as they could be, when they were bad they were horrid. Harry and Edie would be exhausted after a day and overnight stays required military planning.

When the doorbell rang too many times, they knew their daughter Olivia was at the other side with the twins, and one of those girls seemed to have their finger welded to the bell button. They were greeted with hugs, squeezes and big sloppy kisses. Harry and Edie hid their paranoid "home-wrecking" concerns as the two five-year-olds ran about the house, smearing sticky grime everywhere, onto everything as they played. Olivia had enough on her plate without her parents wincing about volume, behaviour, touching and breaking things and they knew it. They could spend the evening and tomorrow tidying up and wiping down.

Now the twins were five, they seemed to run on Duracell batteries, but Harry had made the most incredible play area in the back garden that was up against the back fence as far away from the patio doors as possible. As a child, Harry had been helped by his own father to make a bogie. The low go-kart was made with old fruit boxes and pallet wood, pram wheels and rope. Harry felt like Steve McQueen. The value of being able to make things with your hands and share that with your children and grandchildren was priceless. The love and enjoyment he received when the twins saw what he had made for them was etched onto his heart forever. There was a tree house, about five feet off the floor and a slide, soft bark surrounding it and inside were soft cushions, torches, books and the old telephone, which was a tin can fitted against the wall and a length of string which was pulled tight across the garden to near the patio door. There it was held on a hook, with the other tin can at the end. There was enough space inside for two small children to make their den adventures come to life. The adults could sit at the dining room table, facing the garden and keep an eye on them, with the patio door almost completely shut. He was a genius and Olivia was very grateful too. The best thing about being grandparents was being able to play and make things magical for the children for a set amount of time and then hand them back.

Nel and Erin shot out through the patio doors and disappeared up into the treehouse. They appeared down the slide and repeated this an impressive number of times. Olivia's face relaxed as she stared out at them and slid her arm around her dad's waist and gave him a massive squeeze of thanks. Harry beamed and felt that warm glow of satisfaction. Edie looked over and beamed too. The girls were hard work for sure, but there was enough combined love to deal with all that energy and she knew that as soon as they became teenagers, they probably wouldn't move off the sofa for good few years. It was all about front-loading the effort right now.

Harry picked up the tin can and pulled the string tightly. Then he made his pretend ringing noise. 'Brring brring, brring bring,' he called loudly into the can. There were squeals and giggles from the other end.

'Hello?' they both yelled together.

'Time to come in for some lunch ladies,' said Harry in a posh voice. There were more squeals and giggles.

'Ok.' They chuckled and the line went dead as the sound changed direction and the yelling shot out down the slide, as fast as the girls. Lunch for them would be a selection of sandwiches, little eats and a soft drink. They could take these back over to their tree house in Mam's Tupperware bowls if they wanted, and more importantly, the adults hoped they would. They appeared one after the other and raced to the house. Thankfully, Harry spotted them and opened the patio door just in time to avoid a full face plant on the glass. Harry had kept Mam's sideboard

23

as well as Tupperware because it made him happy. His parents' furniture had gone to charity, but this piece was special. It wasn't too deep, so it sat neatly against the wall, not jutting out too much. This was handy as the girls were head height with most sharp and hard edges at the moment. That wasn't the problem of course. Not looking ahead of them, or around them was the problem and cause of most accidents, bruises and tears. The sideboard still had lots of internal storage and there was space for the old telephone at one end, magazines, *Radio Times* and Mam's old sewing box at the other. On the top, of course, there was enough room for a line of bowls of little eats. Tradition. The girls took their plastic dishes of sandwiches, that were cut small and dainty to make them more fun and then worked the bowls like professional buffet users, filling up every available space with crunchy nibbles.

Just as the girls took their first fistfuls of snacks to their mouths, the landline phone in the left side cupboard began to ring. Harry had kept it plugged in, in case of emergencies, but as it was inside the bottom cupboard of the sideboard, it sounded like the bowls of little eats were ringing. Nel and Erin looked around at Harry. How was he making that noise, when there was no tin can or string? Nel opened to cupboard door.

'Go on then, pick it up,' said Olivia to Nel. Nel and Erin had played with real old phones in the Discovery Centre and knew what to do. Nel picked up the phone. It crackled loudly, like someone was emptying little eats from a packet.

'Hello, who's speaking please?' She listened attentively and then relayed the message. 'Gramps, it's for you, it's your mam.'

Elinor had been stunned into silence. Hearing Tom's familiar voice was enough to freeze her on the spot. The crackling sound was loud again. 'Tom? Tom? Where are you?' There was no response. The static stopped dead and Elinor could only hear her heartbeat pounding through her ears. She put down the phone timidly and stared at it.

What had just happened? That was Tom, that was his voice and it sounded like all the other times he had rung to invite her round. But Tom had been dead for well over a year. She had been to his funeral for heaven's sake. Who on earth could she tell this to? She couldn't believe herself, so why would anyone else? When the phone had made its evening pings and chimes, she had found it funny and had told Twitter all about it. She thought that the static noises and the pings were the death throes of the whole system being uncared for or poorly maintained. She remembered that some people had responded to her tweets and said that their old landlines did the same thing. So, Elinor decided to tentatively tell Twitter what had happened, kind of, anyway. With a limited number of characters, composing the words would be vital to getting interested not weirdo responses, but this was a weird tweet and she knew it.

Just got a phone call from the other side. Not sure how science works, but surely only posts get delayed by years, not phone calls. Does anyone else have a landline that

25

seems to be a law unto itself or sentient in some way? #HauntedLandline

She pressed "tweet" and then decided she should tell someone she actually knew in real life, who didn't live purely in her phone. *Are you free for a quick phone call? Something really weird has just happened.* Elinor had just texted her old school friend, Amanda. The phone rang almost instantly.

'Hiya, what's up? Is everything OK?'

'Mand, I know you won't believe this, but I have to tell you what's just happened. I've just had a phone call from my old neighbour Tom.' Amanda was about to ask what was so unusual about that and then she remembered.

'Tom's dead, what are you on about?'

'I know Mand. I'm freaking out a bit here. He just invited me round for a cuppa and a biscuit, like he used to.'

'And what did you say?'

'I asked him where he was, but the phone went all crackly and he never replied and then it went dead.'

'It's got to be a sick prank El, that's all it can be.'

'But it was definitely his voice, right down to the intonation and everything.'

'It can't have been him love, you know that. Someone, for whatever reason, is winding you up. Finding out who and why, is going to be the hard part. Make sure you record the conversation if it happens again.'

'Mand, it was him; I'm telling you, no word of a lie.'

Regardless of what Amanda thought, she knew Elinor was indeed completely freaked out, so whoever had done this, needed finding and made to explain themselves. Amanda liked the challenge too and so proposed a get-together at the weekend, so they could find out more about setting up a listening and recording device on the old phone. Then she had a brain wave.

'1471,' she shouted all of a sudden. 'Dial 1471, do you remember El? It lets you know the number of who's just called. Call it back now.'

Elinor picked up the receiver and the static crackled so loudly that Amanda could hear from her end. It was a button phone not a circular dial. There was a feint hum of a signal and so she pressed the numbers with precision.

'Sorry, the number you have dialled no longer exists, please hang up and try again... sorry, the number you have dialled no longer exists.' That familiar posh female voice was still as condescending as it always had been.

Amanda had heard it too. They agreed to meet up on Saturday and have a think.

In the phone box in the market square, Ed and Pat looked at each other as if they had both been sworn at for no reason at all. Puzzled and disconcerted, Ed finally managed to reply. 'Dad? Dad?' The phone crackled loudly again, but there was no reply. He placed the receiver back on the hook, looked at it, and then as if he might have just imagined the whole thing, lifted up the receiver once more. This time the hum was as clear as a bell. The Yorkshire voice began speaking; 'Settle has been a market town since 1249 when it was granted a Charter from Henry

27

the IIIrd.' The booth telephone was working perfectly. Pat felt a very cold chill run up her back and pressed into Ed for warmth as well as comfort.

'OK, Pat, what the hell just happened there? We both heard that didn't we? Bloody hell, I need a drink, a proper drink.'

'Ed, that's just put the wind up me, what the heck? We're just normal people; this doesn't happen to us. We don't believe in stuff like that. We haven't both imagined that have we? We both had the pie though.'

They looked at each other intensely. Lit by the street light and the low glow from the phone booth, Ed reached out and clasped Pat's hands together.

'I don't believe in ghosts Pat, but that was my dad's voice, wasn't it?'

'How did he know we were here? In Settle? In this exact spot? Right now?' questioned Pat, totally baffled.

'Never mind that detail Pat, how did he call when he's been dead for ten years? And what did he want me to do?'

As they walked back into the hotel in silence and straight towards the bar, the young man behind it, saw their faces. 'Crikey, you two look like you've seen a ghost. What can I get you?'

'Pat?'

'Gin and tonic please, Ed, double, with ice and a slice.'

'And a Remy brandy for me please, double as well, no ice, thank you.'

Harry leaned down towards the cupboard and took the receiver from Nel and cradled it gently. With the short lead, he was bent down and then on his knees, which he knew he'd regret very soon.

'Mam?'

'Harry, listen to me, you need to find Elinor Coates, on Twitter.' It was Mam's voice for sure.

'What, Mam? Where are you? I don't know what's happening. How are you? No that's ridiculous. Why do I need to find Elinor Coates? I don't do Twitter. Mam – *eh?'*

The static on the line intensified and Harry had to pull it away from his ear. 'Mam? Mam, are you still there?'

There was no response just noise, and Harry put the receiver back on the hook and closed the cupboard door. He then held onto the side of the cupboard and one knee to hoist himself back up and groaned the inevitable old person groan of stiff joints and weak muscles.

The girls burst out laughing as if a magic trick had happened. 'Can we go and eat in the treehouse please?' yelled Erin. Olivia nodded and smiled and they shot off, leaving a trail of little eats across the lawn, that the birds and squirrels would enjoy later.

Edie closed the patio door and there was silence. Olivia and her mother stared at Harry.

'So, that is some crazy voodoo, Dad. What just happened really? Have you been doing some tinkering with some recordings or something?'

Harry was clearly shaken and Edie went over to him and put her arm around his shoulder and then began rubbing his back lightly.

'What's the name of the person she told you to find Harry?'

'Er, Elinor Coates, I think she said. I haven't got a clue what to think. It can't be real. Mam died in what, 2003? That was before Twitter was invented. She wouldn't know what it was. That couldn't have been her, but it sounded like her. But what was the point of it? Why is someone pretending to be her and why use the landline?' A stream of questions flowed from his mind. He knew he had no enemies who would want to trick him in this way. Absolutely nothing made sense. He knew he was beginning to ramble.

Olivia could tell that this bizarre call had really unnerved her father, although her mother didn't seem quite so, well, scared. Heck, even Olivia herself was experiencing the heeby jeebies.

'Right, well, I'm on twitter, so the first thing we can do is try and hunt down this woman, yes?'

Olivia clicked on her Twitter app hit the search button and typed in the name, Elinor Coates. Nothing came up. Elinors were highlighted, and Coates were highlighted, but no singular name. This was going to take some time. If this person existed, they didn't need to use their actual name, so this may be completely impossible. There was no telephone directory anymore. That could have been very useful right now. An old-fashioned A to Z of home telephone numbers. Now that suddenly seemed like it would be the best possible thing to have. Google was a failure.

Edie made a suggestion, 'Do we need to find a clairvoyant? Should we have a seance?' Edie had always enjoyed ghost stories and films. She had seen every B movie, Boris Karloff, Bela Lugosi film and all the rest too. She had enjoyed all the Hammer House of Horrors and had developed a bit of a thing for Vincent Price. Peter Cushing was a bit wet and Christopher Lee always seemed too glam. When it had all become a bit too 1970s blood and guts slasher horror, she had given up on it. Edie had always secretly wanted to see or experience a ghost, or at least an unexplainable phenomenon and this might have just happened. Her husband, however, was knocked for six and Edie knew she had to rein in her excitement.

Olivia decided to try the hashtag approach to sifting the endless content. #telephones, nothing, #landline, nothing. #ghostsinphones, nothing, #hauntedtelephones, nothing. Olivia was already frustrated and knew she was clutching at straws. She pushed her phone away and tutted. Then she picked it up again and had another go inputting random hashtag sequences. Repeatedly, dead ends followed after each try.

Suddenly, a massive banging noise came from the patio window and they each gasped in shock. Olivia jumped and dropped her phone. Harry held his chest and Edie swore loudly, 'Christ on a bike!' Erin and Nel grinned from the other side of the glass. 'Can we come in? We need

31

a wee.' Harry slid back the door and the pair of them shot through and clattered up the stairs. 'Thank you.' They hollered throughout the house.

'If we've got a haunted landline, perhaps we need an exorcism,' offered Edie.

Olivia typed into her phone again #hauntedlandline. Up came Elinor's tweet.

Just got a phone call from the other side. Not sure how science works, but only post gets delayed by years, not phone calls. Anyone else have a landline that seems to be a law unto itself or sentient in some way?

#HauntedLandline

The tweet came from @LinoCoat66 and Olivia pressed "follow".

Chapter Two – Connecting

By the time Amanda had arrived, Elinor had already made a start on her gin and tonic, but the food was in the oven and she was ready for some very interesting conversation. Prepping the lasagne before she had started on the drink was a wise move. Amanda was staying over, she was bringing prosecco and would be drinking it like lemonade, so things could get messy. As long as all she needed to do was crawl into bed, that would be fine. Not long after dinner, they would change into their elasticated pyjamas and that would make things even easier. There was never any pretence or ceremony; Elinor and Amanda had been mates forever and there were no secrets or lies between them. Elinor knew she was bloody lucky to have Amanda as her friend and she was going to be testing their honesty this evening, trying to work out what that phone call was all about. Amanda would call her a crazy lunatic if that's what she thought. No holding back.

After a big hug, Amanda dumped the Prosecco on the kitchen table and put the first bottle in the door of the fridge, she put her overnight bag in the spare bedroom and came back into the sitting room.

There was a full cold glass already bubbling away, waiting for her. After the usual pleasantries of asking each other how their days had been, Amanda went straight in with the big question.

'So, you're convinced you're not going mad, you weren't hallucinating, you're not winding me up and you think it really was dead Tom speaking to you?'

'I know it sounds like a total wind up Mand, but that's how I feel too. Either this *is* a wind-up and I don't know what the point in that would be, or it's bloody real and my dead neighbour has phoned me up for something. What the hell am I meant to make of that?'

'I don't know love, I really don't. Ooh, that reminds me, hang on.'

Amanda went off into the spare room and came back with a cardboard box the size of an old biscuit tin and pulled out an old answer machine. Then she got out a small white plastic box the size of a packet of tissues.

'I got it off Amazon Prime, it was the easiest one I could see to understand how to set it up and record. It's a telephone recorder for landlines and it saves it to a memory card so we can put it on the computer if we need to, as evidence.'

By now they were both a few glasses in and had not eaten. Sensibly they decided to wait and fit the devices when they were in a better state to follow the instructions, and in the light of day would be able to see what they were doing. As they were about to move to the kitchen table for food, the landline pinged in the study. Elinor looked at her phone, 19.47. She smiled. Had this been Tom all along?

34

For the rest of the evening, they ate and drank more and talked more and laughed more.

Amanda was still working at the school that Elinor had left five years ago. The madness of the job, the system, the expectations and the data just seemed to be getting worse. Many of the colleagues Elinor liked had left and so less and less resonated with her. The biggest loss was not having that amazing rapport with her classes and tutor group anymore. She had kept up to date with young minds by asking them regularly about what they were into and asked them to explain terminology and slang. It kept her finger on the pulse, but when she realised that not a single child would know who she was anymore, it was the final uncoupling of Elinor from being a classroom teacher. For Amanda though, she still had to deal with it all. They poured another drink. Working in the school office was chaos. Despite Elinor becoming bored of the same old problems and rants, she let Amanda get it all off her chest. Amanda needed to vent her spleen and knew that Elinor was the only one who really understood. In turn, Elinor knew she had to be the friendly ear to listen and help her offload the stresses and the strains. Time for another glass. As Amanda recounted another ludicrous situation, Elinor once again thanked her lucky stars that she had got the hell out of Dodge, in the nick of time. They moved on to discussing their own school days and the pain from laughing made their faces ache. At some point in the small hours, they sensibly downed a pint of water each, clumsily headed to their rooms and hit the pillows heavily.

When they both began to stir in the morning, they were each surprised by the lack of severe headaches or stomach-churning consequences of overindulgence. The lasagne and later carb snacks as well as the water had actually been a very good judgement call. It wasn't even that late in the morning. They were still sluggish and slow of course, but that was nothing new. Long undisturbed sleep was non-existent for both of them these days. In youth, they could sleep for England, but now it was as if the body just refused to let them waste time asleep. Amanda was in the kitchen first and got the kettle on. Then Elinor appeared and reached for the bread. Toast and tea and coffee brought them both round and they discussed what to do first.

After breakfast and then a shower, Amanda and Elinor set out the voice recorder instructions near the landline phone and gradually added all the right bits to the cable and answer machine in the right order and had a test run. The line was still crackling. Amanda called the landline from her mobile and they let it ring. First of all, they tested the answer machine. Elinor had recorded her message. It clicked into life. 'Hello, you've reached Elinor, I'm afraid I can't get to the phone right now, please leave your message and number and I'll get back to you.'

'God, I hate the sound of my own voice,' she said. 'It's like listening to Vera Duckworth, Jesus!'

'Well it hardly matters, so don't let it get to you. There's nowt ye can do about it.' Amanda was taking the mick and upping her own accent by dropping an octave as well as lots of consonants.

Then Amanda rang the number again and this time Elinor picked it up. The small box had a green LED light that began to flash to indicate it was recording the conversation. 'Hi El, it's Mand, am I dead yet?' She laughed and put down her phone. Holding onto old bits of technology for a good reason, was not something that Elinor was good at. Being lazy and not throwing stuff away though, was something she was very good at. Sure enough in the very back of the study table drawer underneath generations of her old phones and chargers, was an SD card reader with a USB cable. She slotted the card into the reader and connected everything up to her laptop and the icon appeared on screen. She clicked on it and there was an MP4 file. She double clicked, it played and Amanda's voice was as clear as a bell. 'Brilliant.'

They decided to head out for the day. A good walk up through Valley Gardens out to Harlow Carr and some treats from Betty's would be the perfect way to get rid of the last fug of alcohol. Amanda nipped back inside for one more trip to the loo. It was a chilly day and she would never pass up a loo stop. Elinor scanned her phone and saw she had some notifications on twitter. She was about to take a closer look but Amanda appeared and off they went.

Ed and Pat had finished their drinks in a very subdued manner in the big armchairs in front of the fire of the hotel. They both noticed how the dimmed lighting and the low warm colours glowing from the fire, made the whole scene look like a Rembrandt painting. They had discussed the phone call a great deal and gone round and round in circles. Slowly they made their way back to their room and settled down. Despite the relentless questions swimming around in their minds, the physical exhaustion of the walk, the fresh air, food and strong alcohol night cap, knocked them out quickly and they slept like logs. The next morning after one more ridiculously large Full Yorkshire breakfast, they would both be back on the bran flakes tomorrow, they checked out and headed home.

Pat had got a little exasperated with Ed with his lack of focus to act and make choices about what to do. She had never seen him at such a loss, as he was always the decisive one, practical and logical. As a local councillor he had always been the go-between and negotiator, working out solutions to best satisfy a situation. He had been very good at it. Nowadays his negotiating skills were used over a shop counter to try and get a better deal, or schmoozing a builder to do a few extra jobs at no extra cost. Faced with the complete opposite of logic, he was incapable of deciding what he wanted to do next. She knew him inside out, back to front and upside down as she always enjoyed saying, but his dithering was something new. Pat needed to take things into her own hands. The problem was that she wasn't really sure what to do either. She didn't believe in ghosts and suchlike. She could hardly hold a seance in a phone box, let alone one in the middle of a town square with locals walking past, but she could at least do some research and hunt down a clairvoyant or two and see if anyone sounded remotely sane or anywhere near credible. Did happy customers write reviews online for good clairvoyants? Well, she was about to find out.

Ed had gone out for lunch; offering an ear to one of his old colleagues, who was still on his way up in the Council. Actually, Joel wasn't that old either, and that's why Ed had offered to listen. On the corridors of local power, there were some really out-of-touch, beer bellied blokes stuck in their 1970s arrogant sexist ways. He felt guilty liking pie and peas when those dinosaurs liked the same. He never wanted to be associated with that brigade at all. So when Joel called him up to ask for advice, Ed was more than happy to oblige and know that his experience still counted for something. When Joel had called Ed "woke", he had felt quite proud and relieved to be seen differently.

The problem with googling for supernatural services was the sheer quantity of choice. Never mind trying to sift through the madness of it. Those that seemed to promote themselves online suddenly seemed very expensive. Pat realised that she had to narrow her search. To begin with she had found some amazing and effusive reviews and then realised they were from South America. Hardly available for a quick trip to Settle town square. She wouldn't be offering to pay travel costs. Some were just far too religious. If she had to choose, she would believe in ghosts before a god. Even by selecting "UK only" businesses, it was still too broad. It was quite a revelation to see how many people were peddling their psychic skills. It was not a surprise to see that the majority were women. Pat even guessed that they would probably be as mad as a bag of frogs and wear interesting fabric choices. She thought it would be tie-dye fabric sheets, stretched out on walls or Laura Ashely vibes as the dominant choices. Although she knew she was stereotyping, she was also putting a mental bet on some pink or purple-dyed hair – with grey roots, and the whiff of patchouli. She wondered if she should just go to Yell.com. Was anyone promoting themselves like a plumber? And she started singing out loud as she typed, 'If your mansion house needs haunting just call, Rentaghost.' She scrolled and scrolled. 'Oh for God's sake, this is bloody ridiculous. What on earth am I doing?' She went into the kitchen and made herself a cup of tea and paced around the house a bit, before sitting back down in front of the screen and muttering to herself. 'This is bloody ridiculous.'

Finally, Pat typed in, *Clairvoyants, psychics, West Yorkshire.* There were nine in total, but the top five would be the only ones she would explore further. There were some men on the list, that would teach her to be so presumptuous. Judging by the excessive amount of brown clothing and bald heads, she felt safer with the velvet brigade. Then she saw one in Hebden Bridge, of course! She told herself off for being so terrible and then found one in Leeds that sparked her interest, there was no photo and it sounded, well, sane.

I can help you make connections with lost souls and decipher psychic happenings. No nonsense and very practical. If there's a more logical answer I will find it. Karen Wilsden. Call 07111 2093019. Based in West Yorkshire and available throughout Yorkshire. Will consider travelling to Lancashire. Pat copied the number into the contacts on her phone, and then saved the website address. Should she call or send a text? She wouldn't do it straight away; she was going to have to think about what she wanted and she was going to have to tell Ed first anyway. Then she went and got the clothes out of the dryer.

Olivia had sent a tweet to @LinoCoat66 and hoped it was OK. *'Hi, will you follow me back, so I can DM you about this please? @OvJo89.'*

Amanda was just dropping Elinor off after their very enjoyable day out. They were now both feeling the effects of a very late night and then a day of fresh air and walking. Both just wanted to crash on their sofas at home alone. Elinor still invited Amanda in for a cuppa, which she gratefully declined, but would use the loo, before setting off home. While Amanda had disappeared, Elinor scrolled through her phone and saw her notifications on twitter. Then she got to Olivia's reply. 'Mand!' She was aware this yell was a little too dramatic and hoped Amanda had pulled her knickers up by now. Amanda appeared sharpish back in the kitchen. 'What? Bloody hell, what?' She saw Elinor staring at her phone. 'I thought you'd injured yourself or you'd been burgled or something.'

'I've got a reply to that tweet I sent about the phone. But I need to follow them to find out more. What should I do?'

'Er, follow them. You can always unfollow and block them if they're psycho.'

This was very true and Elinor had done this countless times already with people who first seemed friendly but rapidly began to give her the creeps. The blocking function was brilliant.

'Look I've got to head off El, keep me posted and phone me later if it gets interesting. Love ya.' Amanda gave Elinor a big hug and headed out with a loud "bye!"

No sooner had Elinor pressed follow back, there was a message. It was very tricky trying to say the right thing in a direct message. It wasn't like writing an email and it felt ridiculous to try and say so much in a long narrow text space.

So, Elinor just typed: *Hi, I don't want any hassle with time wasters, as I am trying to work something out. Where are you based? Could we meet somewhere public or can I phone you?*

The reply was swift; Olivia could type quickly. *'Based just outside Harewood, in West Yorkshire, where are you? It's not my phone; it's my mum and dad's. I'm Olivia by the way.'*

Elinor replied, *Hi, Olivia, I'm Elinor, we're really close, I'm in North Leeds. Are you available tomorrow, either to meet up or by phone call?*

Olivia said she would contact her after she had spoken to her parents and the DM conversation stopped. Elinor didn't know that Olivia had suddenly had to stop her daughters from running round the house with a pair of knickers on their heads, unable to see where they were going.

Elinor switched on the kettle, grabbed a notepad off the table and got her favourite pen out; she missed Paperchase. The evening crept up on her and she realised she was hungry.

Ever the researcher, she had written down everything, so that she could cross-reference it later and refer back to it all as she went. Time ticked away from her as she scrolled and scribbled. Writing things down would give her prompts and questions to ask this Olivia and her parents when they got back to her. She also knew that her memory had decided to be far more selective these days. Now she was really hungry and berated herself for not getting something out of the freezer earlier. It would have to be toast. She had a good lunch and treats with Amanda, so unfulfilling toast would be perfectly acceptable. As she tried unsuccessfully to avoid getting crumbs in her laptop keyboard, she started to research the history of the landline telephone and got lost in the unexpected facts that she began to read.

The lovers' telephone was the thing she had played with as a child. Two tin cans and a piece of string. She had probably made one with Amanda back in Middle school. *'The gourd and stretched-hide version resides in the Smithsonian Museum collection and dates back to around the seventh century AD,'* said Wikipedia. That really did surprise her. A landline phone was an electromagnetic device and although she half remembered some of the details, she laughed to herself realising that learning had gone in one ear and out of the other, similar to being on the phone in a boring conversation.

Harry was out earning his pocket money. When he was a full-time electrician, he ended up working twelve-hour days and sometimes that was seven days a week. He never liked to say no to people, especially when he knew they were struggling. He couldn't retire fully because people still called him up with odd jobs. Edie had managed to get him down to a maximum of three jobs a week. It kept his hand in the business, brought him extra cash and he loved knowing that he was still useful. Edie used to work at Edmunson's in Harrogate. It was there that she spotted the young Harry when he came in for supplies as an apprentice to his dad. Edie didn't know anything about electrical goings on, she was just doing her best to get a Saturday job and the owner had been a very forward-looking man called Mr Marcham. After a year she had absorbed a great deal of knowledge of what bits and pieces were used for many electrical jobs. This caused some moments of profound sexism and hilarity. Old curmudgeonly types not wanting to ask her for anything, presuming she was a clueless female, and the ones who were gobsmacked when she offered correct suggestions for what was needed. Harry had been seduced by her knowledge of all things electrical and how much wattage something would need and also that he thought she was beautiful.

Olivia called in at her parents' house shortly before going to pick up the girls from their reception class. She barely had time for pleasantries and Edie was surprised that she didn't get her usual big hug. No sooner was she through the door and Olivia was telling her mum that she thought she had made contact with the right Elinor.

'What are you both doing tomorrow morning?'

'Why?'

'We can meet up with her, she's local, North Leeds.'

They discussed locations and times and then waited for Harry to come home and tell him the latest. Then Olivia remembered she had children and shot off to go and collect them. She couldn't forget, again.

Elinor picked up her mobile and spotted more twitter notifications. There was a new DM from Olivia. *'Do you know the Muddy Boots cafe? Could we meet you there at ten-thirty a.m.?'* Elinor had replied with a "yes" before even thinking about if it was a safe thing to do. However, it was public, and in the daytime, there would be staff around too. Then she texted Amanda, to see if she could join her, forgetting that it was a working week day.

The reply came back quickly. *'Have you forgotten that I have a full-time job, or do you want me to play truant?'*

'Sorry, Mand, can you play truant?' This was followed with the grinning emoji and a thumbs up and crossed fingers.

'Dream on,' was Amanda's response.

'Bugger!' was Elinor's response to that.

Elinor, Harry, Edie and Olivia too, spent their respective evenings thinking about the other's phone call. What would Elinor look like? Were Harry and Edie normal or would they be bonkers? How old were they? And if this was all real, what on earth would all of them decide to actually do about it?

After Ed had got back from his lunch meeting with Joel, which had gone very well and made Ed feel like he momentarily had a son, Pat said she had something to discuss with him as an idea about the phone call from George, Ed's dad. He realised that while he was helping Joel to work through ways of dealing with the old farts on the Council, he had forgotten about the phone call. That had been a very positive respite, but now it was at the front of his mind again. So he mentally girded his loins, sat down and listened to Pat's idea.

She had found a clairvoyant in Meanwood. After looking through the top five suggestions, this was the best one, or least worst, or less crazy, or most normal advert she came across. Pat brought up the details on the laptop and let Ed take his time. He was very good at smelling out a rat from documentation, but as this seemed like it could be a pile of rats, distinguishing a good one from a bad one, was an impossible task.

'I know it's a daft idea and it's expensive for what it is, but why don't we just give it a go and put it down to experience if we think it's total bollocks?' Ed was as surprised as Pat that she had recently started swearing more. 'Sorry, but it's an easy way to let out the stress, so it's better that I just become sweary Mary rather than Punching Pat, don't you think?' Ed agreed, especially imagining that he would be the most regular recipient and could already imagine a line of bruises up his arm. Pat was not a violent person, but he knew she would still surprise him if she needed to.

After clicking on the contact email request form, Pat filled in the details as simplistically as she could. She inputted her mobile number followed by her email address. They were both well aware of the easy way basic information was twisted and used to create supposedly random genuine contact. The first thing she did was tick the "yes" box for contacting a dead relative. Then the box for wanting a question answered. Yes, they would come to the clairvoyant's home, especially as it would mean the clairvoyant couldn't scope out the nicknacks and photos and work out who they were and all those clues lying around.

'Ed, when should we go? There are slots we can choose from. It's a bit like picking a delivery from Waitrose.' Ed leaned in and looked at the screen. There were no morning slots, two afternoon and two evening slots. 'Well, it will have to be that first evening slot don't you think? Then we've had our tea and it still won't be too late.'

'Hmm,' wondered Pat, out loud. 'That makes sense, I'll check out exactly where it is so we know where to park.'

They clicked the seven thirty p.m., slot for the following evening. Payment details came up next, cash only forty-five pounds, to be paid at the start of the session. They already felt like they were about to be had. In the grand scheme of things, although forty-five pounds was a heck of a lot of money, for an hour maximum, they could afford it. They both knew this was a one off. She typed in her mobile number, then pressed send. The laptop mailbox chimed almost instantly with an automated response confirming the appointment.

'What do you wear to a seance, Ed?'

'Comfy layers, they could try every trick in the book to unnerve us and make us feel weird, so we may as well be as comfortable as possible. Turn the heat up, or have it freezing, so we shiver. My bullshit detector is going to be in overdrive. I didn't think that I would be needing it after retiring.' They both laughed, both at the truthfulness of Ed's remark and the stupidity of this unfolding scenario.

On the morning of meeting up with Olivia, Harry and Edie, Elinor had texted Amanda and been told quite seriously to make sure she was always within earshot of other people, just in case. Elinor had replied saying this wasn't the same as meeting a stranger at a bar on a night out in Leeds. Even so, she appreciated Amanda's concern for her safety and said she wouldn't have needed to worry if Amanda had skipped school and come with her. Amanda had accused her of being a guilt-tripper and left an emoji of a ghost, a telephone and a grave.

Elinor left the house and walked to the bus stop. She had ample time because she hated being late for anything and struggled to be polite to those who rolled up at any time. Being late for no reason other than laziness was a crime. The number 36 was a posh bus, a Harrogate company, not First Bus. As she sat down, the calming tone of Harry Gration told her which stop would be next. Harry had been the anchor man of the local news programme Look North forever. When he died, the whole of the Yorkshire region mourned the loss of someone who was like an uncle to them, at six thirty p.m., every weekday evening after the main news. He would have been perfect narrating Bagpuss like Oliver Postgate. He had that safe and comforting voice. Then she realised it was as though Harry Gration was still speaking to her but from the other side. Was he trapped in limbo on the 36, doomed for all eternity to tell her that her next stop was the Lord Darcy pub or the Grammar School at Leeds? Before she knew it, Harry was telling her that this next stop was Harewood, so under her breath, she said, 'Cheers Harry.' And got off. She was also going to meet Harry. A spooky coincidence? She wasn't sure, but this whole situation kept on unnerving her. It was all about to get real.

As Elinor entered the cafe at the back of the village hall, she scanned everyone. No one was sat in a group of three. She must have got there first, so she ordered a tea and then took it outside to sit on one of the picnic tables. The local red kites weren't doing their usual Red Arrows display routine yet. There were about sixty breeding pairs in these woods and on the estate now. It was quite a common spectacle and whatever the equivalent was of a floorshow, this is what you got, but in the sky. She hoped they would come and perform later when that local lady brought the leftover butcher bones and threw them onto the garage roofs behind her. She DM'd Olivia to say where she was sitting, then shuffled herself to the other side of the picnic table so she could watch for arrivals. *Just arrived and waiting for them to show.* She texted Amanda. She knew she wouldn't get a reply in the middle of the day, but she promised to keep her friend posted with any news.

As Elinor looked towards the side of the cafe, a car pulled in. With the reflections from the sky on the windows, she couldn't see anyone's faces inside. What she did see were the dark clouds scrolling across the shiny surface of glass. Then the doors opened and Elinor knew this was them.

The younger woman who got out of the rear seat looked over and Elinor smiled, this had to be Olivia. Then that must be Edie getting out of the passenger seat and Harry came round from the driver's side. They looked like any of the other people who were already inside the cafe tucking into a bacon sandwich and a Yorkshire tea. They walked towards her and all smiled and Elinor felt the tightness in her shoulders and neck begin to relax. She hadn't even realised just how tense she had become, waiting.

Olivia called over as she got to the table. 'Elinor?'

Elinor smiled again. 'Yes, hi, you must be Olivia, so I'm guessing this is Edie and Harry, hello, it's lovely to meet you all.' There were pleasantries all round and handshakes. Harry asked what Edie and Olivia fancied and then disappeared inside.

Elinor had not lost her touch and went into "teacher trying to relax teenagers" mode. To begin with, she asked about where they lived. Weardley was literally just a row of houses on the other side of the Harewood estate. Elinor loved those houses and mentioned how she enjoyed walking past and looking at all the fantastic gardens. That went down well and Edie said they had moved there twenty years ago and no one has sold a house there since. When Elinor explained she lived not too far from Roundhay park, but nearer the M&S food hall really, everyone agreed that the park was gorgeous and Edie reminisced about taking toddler Olivia out onto the lake when they still had a jetty and lots of rowing boats. The conversation flowed easily and the mutual, shared memories helped to settle them all into a moment of trust. Harry appeared with the drinks and joined everyone by squashing onto the end of the bench on Elinor's side. He put down the cardboard cups with urgency. 'Bloody hell, they're hot.'

'So, have we started on the main topic yet then? Have I missed anything important?' said Harry as he tried to sip his nuclear hot tea, that he could barely hold. Edie explained about Roundhay park and Elinor walking past their house.

'Do you think it's important that we live close by?' questioned Harry. So many questions and coincidences were yet to be revealed.

'I just can't believe that you came across my tweet and took a punt on trying to connect with me,' pondered Elinor to everyone.

'What are the odds of you finding me in your timeline Olivia?' Harry took a deep breath. 'It wasn't that random. When we got the call and I spoke to Mam, she told us to find you, Elinor. She gave us your last name too. Coates. She even told us to find you on Twitter. She died before Twitter was invented.' *If this was an act, then Harry was brilliant at it,* she thought.

Elinor felt a cold line make its way up her spine. Not down it, but up. Harry had just said that someone who was dead, that she had never met, knew her name and told her son, to contact her. 'Well I don't know what's going on, but I'm buggered if any of this makes any sense on any level at all. My call was from my neighbour, Tom. He died over a year ago. He said he wanted me to do something, but the phone got so heavy with static I couldn't hear anything and he never replied and then it went dead.'

'Oh, we've had that static too, haven't we Harry? It was really loud and Gracie didn't stay on the line long enough to explain why before it went dead too.' There was a moment's pause from everyone. Then Olivia chipped in with a sensible suggestion. 'Right, well without any further instructions from wherever, from whoever, there's nothing anyone can do really is there?' They all nodded and mumbled in agreement.

'So, I suggest that we get each other's phone numbers, and if anything else happens and we get another call we can have another conflab and take it from there.' They all thought that was a very good idea and very sensible. They all liked sensible.

They were then completely distracted by a woman who purposefully walked past them towards the side of the garages edging the picnic area. She was carrying a plastic carrier bag of indescribable things. One hand was covered in a bright pink marigold washing-up glove. The show would be starting very soon. She shoved her covered hand into the bag, grasped at the contents and pulled out a handful of flesh-covered bones of various sizes. Covered in sinew, tendons, meat and skin, the bones were launched up onto the roof of the garages. Everyone sat outside and inside near the window, watching in anticipation. Normally, twitchers with ridiculous-sized zoom lenses on their cameras would have taken up position by now, but today they had the air show to themselves. The woman kept on throwing until her bag was empty and then walked off. Within minutes the red kites had come in closer and were circling and swooping. Elinor noticed that they seemed to scope out their prey first. Harry noted that some kept missing their target and Edie mentioned that they seemed to work as a team, allowing each one to take their turn. Olivia commented that this was something magical to experience a bit of majestic nature and said, she would bring the girls and hope they got to see the awe and wonder that might stay with them.

As the last of the big swoops ended and the remaining bones had been snatched, Harry looked at the time. Elinor said that she would continue to research everything about landlines and let everyone know if anyone else contacted her about anything. It might not just be Harry and Edie who had been told to contact Elinor Coates on Twitter. As a natural common courtesy, Edie invited Elinor round to their house at some point in the near future and Elinor agreed that she would love to get to see the house and garden from the inside. Then as quickly as they arrived, they piled back in the car, waved, smiled and headed off. Elinor spent her remaining time texting Amanda with the details from the meeting, then headed off herself, to the bus stop and her return journey with the ghost of Harry Gration.

Chapter Three – Connected

Ed and Pat had decided that they would wear no clues to this seance, so that meant no patterned clothes or jewellery, except their wedding rings, which they thought would be so obvious anyway. They wore dark colours and kept it simple. They had the address and Pat had used Google maps and street view to identify exactly which house it was. *Just an old terrace house, nothing fancy,* thought Pat. She had noted that it wasn't too far from Waitrose. The clairvoyant was called Karen Wilsden, which seemed like a perfectly normal name and at least it wasn't Mystic Meg. They were hoping it wouldn't be Crazy Karen, by the time they had ended the evening. Despite having eaten early and allowing their food time to settle and digest, both of them felt slightly uneasy, even a little queasy at the prospect of what they were going to do.

'Are we going to have a safe word?'

'That's a good idea Ed, what about, sod this for a game of soldiers?' They both laughed and began a series of ludicrous suggestions.

'How about, total bollocks? Crock of shit?'

'No, we need to stop, otherwise, I won't be able to control myself, either by laughing or evoking sweary Mary and feeling a terrible urge to say something outrageous.'

Eventually, they just decided on "we need to get home for the cat". Simple, believable even though they didn't have a cat. Then they had to decide what type of cat they had, how old it was, its fur type and colour, what it was called and it's gender. This level of secrecy was exhausting already.

To normalise what was potentially about to happen, they reminded themselves that people did go to tarot card readers at the fair, or Blackpool and Scarborough. Pat had remembered going to a big party at a friend's house where two readers played the cards and the guests for fools all night. They asked everyone for thirty pounds each, spent fifteen minutes with everyone individually and walked away from a few hours' work with four hundred and forty-five pounds cash in hand. Pat had been accused of being a "blocker" and not taking it seriously. How could she? She was four gin and tonics in by the time it was her turn and had listened to people recounting what had clearly been a mega scam. They were both adamant that they would not be hoodwinked.

When they pressed the bell, a dog barked and Pat gave Ed's hand a little squeeze just as the door opened. Karen was tall, but as she was up the steps, Pat couldn't make out exactly how tall. The light from the hallway behind her, made Karen appear more silhouetted and they were both pleased to be invited in and away from the evening chill. It was still too early in Spring for the daytime warmth to last into the evening. An unseen dog was ushered into the front room and the door closed. As soon as Pat saw Karen in the brighter light of the hall she seemed to relax and felt a sense of calm come over her; Karen looked perfectly normal. Ed felt the same and they smiled warmly.

In down-to-earth tones she welcomed them in. 'Hi come in, make yourselves at home. I'm Karen and you must be Pat and Ed. Lovely to meet you.' She shook their hands and it was just the right amount of strength and squeeze and duration. *Nothing worse than a horrible handshake, it can really put you off someone,* thought Ed. Karen was aware that they were scoping her out as much as she was doing the same. These two were going to make for an interesting evening, she just didn't realise quite how interesting it was going to get. Pat was second-guessing everything about Karen. She looked about the same age as her. She wasn't too tall now she was standing on the same level as her, but her presence still added to her stature somehow. Her medium-long hair was greying but it also had natural warmth in it, which gave off more gold tones under the hall ceiling light. Pat thought that Karen had an air of youthfulness about her, just like she thought of herself. Still in jeans and a big cardi.' Nothing old or mumsy. As Karen gestured them towards the back of the house, they both started to pay attention to the surrounding decorations.

'Let me take your coats.' Karen hung them up on the pegs in the narrow hall. There were coats and jackets of varying description already bursting into the space. She just managed to squeeze two more onto the hooks that were still visible. There was a definite age to the place and it wasn't just the colour scheme. Along the wall further down from the coats, near the staircase, was a small hall table, the like of which Pat hadn't seen for years. Ed nudged her and gestured towards it. There was an old phone and a vape on it. Karen ushered them into the back room which had a big table in the middle and four chairs. Pat gave herself a gold star for second-guessing some of the features, soft furnishings and colour schemes. The house seemed to have lots of old furniture, some antiques were nestled between some more familiar items, that Pat remembered from when she was small back in the late sixties and seventies. Karen spotted her looking at the decorations on display.

'I've lived here all my life. It was my mum's house and then when she passed away, I just decided to carry on living in it. It might seem old-fashioned to some who want everything modernised, but apart from updating the wiring and adding central heating, it's pretty much as it was. I've also saved a bloody fortune not having a mortgage and spending money on...' She gestured quotation marks in the air. '"Improvements", or moving house of course.'

Ed said that was a very smart move and commended her on getting the house rewired. He thought how amazing it must be to have never had a mortgage or have to pay rent, then remembered how lucky their inheritances had made them.

They sat down at the table and Karen offered them a cup of something, but they both declined as it was too late for caffeine and too cold for a soft drink. The curtains were drawn and only the side table lamps were on. This kind of light was fine when watching television, but a bit too gloomy for anything else, thought Pat. As if she had read her mind, Karen piped up, 'I have the lighting like this so nothing is too stark or distracting for you. The less you want to stare at what's on my walls or shelves, the easier it is to just focus on what's going on in the centre of the room you see. It's all about focussing the mind.' Ed decided that because Karen had a northern accent it helped her sound very, well, believable and matter-of-fact. She could have been describing how to build Ikea furniture.

'I don't do many seances, mainly because people don't ask for them. Most folks want their cards read and want to ask questions about their future. I can't read tea leaves or look into crystal balls and see anything other than tea leaves and balls.' That broke the ice and Pat and Ed chuckled and thought that was very funny.

'You can see that it's just a classic board.' She pointed into the centre of the table.

'And what you will need to do is tell me who you want to reach. There's none of this "is there anybody there" nonsense, when you know exactly who it is you're looking for. So, if you're ready?' Ed hoped they didn't have to hold hands; he could feel his palms starting to sweat.

'We're wanting to contact my dad, George, George Johnson.'

'OK,' said Karen calmly. 'Before we do, I just need to ask you to put your cash on the table for me too, please. There have been too many times when I've bloody forgotten to ask for it and realised too late that I've done it all for free. Sorry it seems so transactional, but that's how it is.'

Both of them agreed and Ed said that was very sensible and laid out two twenties and a five.

Then they were told to put their index fingers onto the small heart-shaped planchette; this was the device that was supposed to move around the board pointing at all the letters and numbers. The phone pinged in the hall and their fingers both twitched on the wood. 'Don't worry about that, it happens every now and again, I don't even use it. It's just there for emergencies,' said Karen and then began to ask her question. There was no melodramatic change in her voice, no theatrical extending of vowels, no Brian Blessed over pronunciation or volume, just Karen asking if George Johnson would like to come to the board and say hello to his son. 'If you can get closer George, your son Ed wants to ask you something.' Nothing. No matter how many versions of polite coercion, Karen tried, nothing happened.

'This is a bit awkward,' said Karen with clear embarrassment. She wondered if she was losing her touch.

Momentarily, the planchette seemed to judder, so Karen asked again. It faltered a little more and she was beginning to think that either Ed or Pat were trying to take control. But then underneath their fingers the planchette turned around, making a movement that could not have been forced by any finger and it pointed towards the hall.

Instantly the phone rang and broke the silence, harshly and the dog barked in the front room.

'I'm so sorry,' blurted out Karen. 'That never happens. No one ever rings my landline. I'll just get it and we'll try again.' She pushed back her chair and headed to the hall. Ed and Pat looked at each other. They had a very strong idea of who might be calling.

Karen lifted up the receiver and the static was loud. 'Hello? Who's this?'

'Hello Karen, it's George, can I speak to Ed please?'

Karen looked round at Ed and Pat in disbelief, eyebrows raised higher than an average surprise.

'What the actual?' She stopped herself from saying "fuck" out loud. 'It's for you Ed, he says it's, George.' Karen passed the phone to Ed and moved into the back room. These two must be the best scammers she had ever experienced. How on earth had they moved the planchette like that? And how had they got hold of her landline number? She only ever used her mobile for work. Obviously, she knew that the internet would deliver lots of personal details if you wanted it enough, so that's what these two must have done, but they were good. They had seemed so normal, friendly, trustworthy and sensible. She went over to the table and subtly put the money in her trouser pocket. Why would they be trying to con her though? Were they secretly recording her? Was it for a programme to hunt out fakers and fraudsters? Karen knew she had a bit of a gift and was good at not going overboard with the embellishments of facts. She was now very intrigued to see what these two would do next.

'Dad? It's Ed, where are you?' The crackling was still loud but he could hear his dad just enough. 'I'm at the exchange Ed, I can't explain everything, the connection doesn't last, the line's faulty. We have to try and stop the switch off Ed. Find the others, find Elinor Coates.'

'Dad, that's a lot to take in, who am I looking for again? Where are they? How do I find them? Dad, are you real?' The crackling was getting louder again and George's voice was fading.

'Yes, I'm bloody real, son. I'm dead but on hold Ed. I can't pass on until…' Excessive static blocked out the rest of the sentence. There was louder crackling now that even Pat and Karen could hear from the back room. Then just enough space between the disturbance to hear "find Elinor Coates". Then silence and Ed put down the receiver and turned to face the two women who were gawping at him.

Pat asked for a rundown of exactly what George had said. Karen was playing along pretending to believe, until Ed came out with the curve ball that knocked her over. 'He said we had to find Elinor Coates; didn't say where she was, who she was, or how we could find her.' Ed was exasperated. 'This is unbelievable. Not that it wasn't bloody unbelievable before, but now I am so confused.'

Pat went over to Ed and put her arm around him gently. They both looked at Karen who had gone quiet. 'Sorry, Karen I'm sure this isn't a regular part of your usual invocations.'

Karen spoke slowly and calmly and looked at them both very intensely. 'I've never had anything like that before.'

'Look, Karen, we are trying to cope with this after we got our first call from George when we were on holiday last week in Settle. It was from a bloody phone box.'

Karen shook her head in disbelief. 'No Pat, it's not that getting a phone call from the dead once or twice isn't weird enough for you, it's just that I know Elinor Coates, or at least I used to.'

Karen explained that if it was the same Elinor that she thought it was, then they had both gone to the same high school. They shared the same classes for Art and English in the 6th form, but Karen hadn't seen or heard from her or about her ever since. Now Karen was getting confused. She couldn't see what they would be trying to scam her out of now, it all started to seem, well, real.

They sat back down around the table and Karen packed up the ouija board into its box and put it back into the bottom of the sideboard. The discussion rambled, as the couple explained how, if truth be told, they really didn't believe in this kind of thing, but they couldn't think of any other option than trying out Karen's skills. George wanted Ed and Pat to do something important, or at least that's how they were interpreting it. If no one knew where Elinor was now, they were no further on and now had more questions and loose ends. 'What did he mean he was at the exchange, Ed? What others, besides this Elinor, and what did you have to try to stop being switched off?'

'I don't know love. God I'm not going to sleep well tonight, but I suppose we can knock ourselves out with a brandy or two when we get back, that's for sure.'

Karen looked at the clock on the mantelpiece and realised she was almost about to overlap with her next client. Thankfully that was just a card reading. She grabbed their coats, apologised for pushing them out and then set up the room with her cards ready to go, still distracted by the unusual context for such a complicated scam. How on earth would they know she knew Elinor Coates? After thirty-nine years of last speaking to her? Karen thought she would do her own tarot reading when the next client left. She would have a large nightcap too.

When Ed and Pat closed their front door behind them, they leant into each other for a massive embrace and Pat got one of Ed's best bear hugs ever. 'My mind is racing, don't know about you, Pat.' She was in the same state. They were exhausted and wired at the same time. They got themselves ready for bed and tottered back downstairs in their nightwear, dressing gowns and slippers. Ed poured two very large brandies and in the glow of the dimmed alcove lights, they cuddled up on the sofa and talked back through what happened that evening.

They had similar thoughts to Karen. Was she part of some elaborate plot? Pat wondered how perhaps choosing Karen hadn't been a random choice after all, somehow. Identity theft, monitoring calls and following their every move; were people on the dark web setting up the long game for a massive move to scam them out of all their savings? It was too much of a coincidence that Karen would know who this Elinor Coates was. It was too random to be really random.

Karen's last customer said thank you and left smiling. She had just followed the usual script, and enough bog standard statements had resonated with the woman for her to believe that future events would happen. Past events had been loosely connected and that was another forty-five pounds. Ninety pounds for an evening's work was not to be sniffed at and she hadn't even needed to put the kettle on. It was too late to bother reading her own cards and to ask tough questions about tonight, so she poured herself a large whiskey. Then she moved into the front sitting room and curled up on the sofa, moving a mountain of cushions until she was in a nest of plush and velvet and fake fur. The dog jumped up beside her and nestled down.

She couldn't remember much about Elinor Coates now. Imagining what she looked like back then was not easy, so imagining her today after a well-lived life was impossible. She could be anywhere in the world too. Who might know where she was or how to find her? Karen had been on Facebook quite a few years back but had lost interest in it a long time ago. There had been a school Facebook group though and she wondered if anyone would still be on it. *Nothing to lose*, she thought, *except her dignity.*

'Trying to contact Elinor Coates, class of '84, if anyone knows where she is, please?'

There were lots of "no" responses, after all, it wasn't just their school year that was on the group. Someone mentioned that they thought she had become a teacher, possibly at Grangeway Secondary. Well, that was a start at least. Karen googled the school and up came the website and details. She jotted down the phone number took another slurp of whiskey and smacked her lips. God, she loved a whiskey. After checking through her bookings for the remainder of the week, she could see that tomorrow morning was free and then she was busy until the weekend. Taking the last gulp and then putting the glass on the coffee table, Karen struggled to get purchase on anything that didn't give way and squash underneath her. Inelegantly she fumbled around, swamped by cushions until she finally managed to grab the sofa arm and coffee table, stand up and head to bed. The dog followed.

The next morning Karen sent a quick text to Pat.

'Hello Pat, Karen here, from last night. I may have found where Elinor is. She could be working at Grangeway Secondary. Here's the number. Good luck and let me know if you want me to do anything else. cheers.'

Pat's phone pinged and she read the text. Without even thinking about it, she clicked on the number highlighted and underlined in blue and the phone began to ring.

'Good morning, Grangeway Secondary,' said Amanda in her on-duty, as polite as she could, voice.

'Oh, good morning, sorry to bother you, this is a bit of a long shot. I'm trying to contact Elinor Coates and I don't know if she works there.'

'I'm ever so sorry, but she hasn't worked here for years.' Amanda knew that you never passed on staff details to anyone.

'Never mind,' said Pat downheartedly, 'it had been a long shot anyway. Thank you for your time, er have a good day.'

'You, too,' said Amanda and put down the phone. Then she stared out of the window as the cogs of her brain began to turn. Someone else, a total stranger, was trying to get in touch with Elinor. At least, they sounded alive. She pressed the "recent calls" button and the screen lit up with Pat's mobile number. Amanda wrote it down on a Post-it and put it in her pocket.

At break time, Amanda sent Elinor the number and the message.

'Hi, Chuck, some woman rang school today asking for you. She said she was trying to contact you. I said you don't work here anymore, but here's her number, your call. See you this evening? X.'

Elinor was heading out of the door when she checked the message. Once she was on the bus, she texted Edie and told her there may be another person out there having the same experience. Edie suggested sending a text and asking why this person wanted to contact her, so that's what she did. Then she went for a swim.

When she pushed herself off from the side of the pool, Elinor stretched as far as she could. For her, it was all about the rhythm of breathing and movement combining, so that she became a machine, keeping perfect time through the water. It wasn't about trying to be fast or splashing about like some of them seemed to do. Although Elinor was in the fast lane, she was there by default. In the slow lane were the people who swam and had a chat at the same time. There were the women using noodles, just holding onto the sides, bobbing up and down and those who tried to stroll through the water majestically, holding onto the swim weights or a float. She remembered the old bloke called Geoff, who was so slow, she could swim three lengths to his one. It was almost like he was just flotsam, being dragged along by the undercurrent that every other swimmer created. Elinor didn't want anything to break up her pace, but it was easier to deal with the Aqua Marina speed queens and the men from Atlantis, who were so fast she had to swim like crazy just to avoid total embarrassment.

This morning the pool was nearly empty and she had the whole of the fast lane to herself. The sound of bubbles rising up around her ears as she breathed out through her nose underwater, was loud and almost electronic. As she surfaced, the splashing sound of her and others' strokes was open and light, underwater it was surreal and hypnotic. Then as she submerged her head she suddenly heard music. From no particular direction, it was somehow small and subdued but still quite clear. She turned her head to the

68

left and took another breath in rotation with her crawl stroke. There was no music. As she went back under and breathed out, there it was again. Maintaining the stroke meant that she couldn't just stop to look around, but as she approached the end of a length, the music got louder and then Elinor spotted where it had come from. The man in the slow lane had bone-conducting headphones on. She had read about them. They don't transmit through the air, they transmit through solid matter, bone and obviously water too. This was fascinating. She would look up more about it later. Did the signal have to be physical electromagnetic pulses, like the phone? She knew she didn't have a clue, but she also remembered the amazing space in Kew Gardens, the Hive. She had experienced it herself. She put a wooden stick into her mouth and clenched it between her teeth. Then she placed the other end onto the metal structure. She had heard the buzzing of the bees directly in her head. Elinor knew she would be getting into some more research very soon. She checked her swim watch and had reached fifty lengths, then went for a very long shower, to ponder bone conductors and bees and water and ghosts.

Once she was dried and back in the changing room, Elinor checked her phone and there was a reply to her initial text. 'Hello, my name is Pat. This sounds mad I know. My husband and I received a phone call and we were told to find the others and Elinor Coates. It's a crazy story, but if this is who we hope you are, perhaps it makes more sense. Could you let me know if you want more details? Thank you.'

Elinor put her phone into her coat pocket and grabbed her bag. Well, that seemed like it came from the same bizarre starting point as her own phone call. She wondered if the others mentioned were Edie and Harry. Perhaps there would be some direction for this all to go in now? Unless any more people had received calls from the dead and been told to contact her of course. 'Why have they been told to contact me?' she said to herself under her breath in the changing room as she got ready to leave.

When Amanda knocked on the door it was nearly six p.m., and there was only freezer food on offer. She couldn't defrost more lasagne and didn't fancy anything else, but she could treat Amanda to a thali from Anand's and that would go down very well.

'I think you all need to get together now, don't you, El? It'll save endless texts and passing messages on and everyone can ask and answer questions all at the same time. No Chinese whispers or misinterpretations. You're going to have to get to the bottom of it one way or another. I'm still convinced you've been chosen for a big TV hoax show. In a few weeks, there's going to be a knock on your door and Davina will be there with a microphone up your nose, saying "Elinor Coates, you are live on Channel 4, please do not swear".'

'Well, if she does, I'm going to swear my head off and they'll have to have someone with a bleep button on over drive. For fuck's sake, Mand, it's crazy. One minute, I'm washing up, and the next minute, I'm hearing dead people.'

The delivery arrived and they both eagerly tucked into their food. Gesticulating with her fork, Elinor told Amanda about the bone-conducting headphones in the pool and how spooky it was. If the pool had been full, would everyone have heard it the same? Was it an amazing way for mass communication for humans as well as bees? She had researched about it that afternoon of course, and it was the same principle and naturally, the bees had harnessed it first. Amanda persuaded her to send out a single text to everyone and to invite them round the following weekend. Pat and Edie's phones both pinged at the same time.

Ed and Pat wondered if George would contact them anywhere else. It would be good to meet the others. It would be like a therapy session, said Pat. Ed thought it could end up more like when people say they were abducted by aliens. 'If we bang on about this to anyone else Pat, they could come and take us away. Onset dementia.' He pretended to be the voice of a neighbour.

'Yes, we thought there was something up when they started saying his dead dad was talking to him, giving him a mission, like God or something.'

'Oh don't Ed. It goes no further than these people unless absolutely necessary. And if we do tell anyone else, we have to vet them thoroughly first.'

Pat got onto Google Maps and Street View and found Elinor's house. 'Ooh very nice, look.' She held the laptop up to Ed. 'It's not the whole thing though, it's just a flat.'

Harry and Edie knew where they were going too. Olivia had no babysitter, so she would have to stay at home. Elinor didn't even suggest that she bring the twins with her. Her flat was not child-friendly and Elinor had chosen to teach Secondary school-aged young people and admitted that she was not child-friendly either. Thankfully, Amanda could make it and Elinor instantly felt more relaxed and in control of the situation. She would get some drinks in, but not much as she expected that drivers wouldn't be having anything and one or two drinks was enough. Amanda would be staying over so they could crack open another bottle when the visitors had gone and then they could relax properly.

Chapter Four – The Exchange

'Hi, come in, how you doing?' said Elinor through a broad grin and as chirpily as she could. She hoped it wasn't over-chirpy, she hated it when it was obvious that people were pretending to be friendly. Harry and Edie stepped inside. Just put your coats on the bannister there, that's fine. Come in, sit yourselves down and meet my friend Amanda.' The meeting and greeting finished and they sat down and began to discuss what Pat and Ed might be like, when there was a knock at the door and Elinor went to answer it. Ed squeezed Pat's hand just as the door opened.

'Hi Pat, hi Ed, I'm Elinor, come on in, how you both doing?' She hoped she had toned down the chirpiness just enough to sound sane and happy to see them. Edie explained that Olivia, couldn't be there because of the twins. She tried desperately not to go "off on one" describing how energetic and exhausting they both were, but Elinor nodded and said she completely understood. Dealing with the early years was like herding gerbils and she didn't know how anyone managed one, let alone two and a whole class full, was masochism, surely. That's why she could only ever teach the older ones.

Without needing to force the conversation, everyone seemed to naturally and lucidly explain a bit about themselves and how they had been contacted. They agreed and nodded respectfully with each explanation and they seemed to like each other well enough, especially for a first meeting. Elinor thought it felt like an AA meeting somehow, everyone was trying to be very attentive and understanding. Perhaps it was their shared disbelief in what they had experienced themselves and the need to be believed that drew them together quickly. There seemed to be no formality to their meeting and throughout their conversations, they joked about how this all sounded, how it would be perceived and about when the white van would turn up and cart them all off.

Although Amanda knew this was potentially some enormous hoax from either one of them or an external set-up, she could see the gelling together of the people sitting around her in Elinor's sitting room. Ed and Pat seemed to be the closest, physically as well as mentally. Amanda had watched how Ed put his chair closer to Pat's when they moved over to the dining table. Ed was good at balancing out Pat's bold statements with an opposing view or balanced reasoning. Edie seemed the happiest of all of them. There was a childlike eagerness to her discussing the supernatural context of all of this and she was very keen to learn more about the seance and what Karen was like. Although Harry looked tired after his long day sorting out someone's underfloor wiring, Amanda thought that he seemed very good at calming Edie's more fanciful ideas. When Amanda looked across to Elinor, she still saw the teacher, checking that everyone was getting their turn to speak and doing it all quite subliminally in her gestures and wordplay.

Elinor couldn' t help herself from going into teacher mode again. She folded back the cover and laid out an A1 newsprint pad onto the dining table. When she mapped out any research, she explained that she always started with a big piece of paper with the main focus written large right in the middle of it. She wrote the word "ghosts" and a big question mark in the centre in capitals, with her Sharpie. Then she wrote: *Want to connect with us, want to bring us together, have to stop something from being switched off.* Spreading outwards, she wrote the ghosts' names, then everyone else and how they were connected. She even wrote down Nel and Erin's names next to Olivia's. She remembered that it was one of the girls who picked up the phone and spoke to Gracie. Edie beamed that her granddaughters had also appeared on the page. A different coloured Sharpie was used to link people together. From there, she wrote down all the questions that were bubbling up from their conversation.

'I don't understand how your dad managed to call you at a phone box and then at someone else's house,' puzzled Harry to Ed.

'That seems extra random somehow.' Ed agreed but also reminded everyone that seeing as how they had all met because dead relatives and neighbours had contacted them, perhaps they should suspend their disbelief in anything that didn't make sense.

Everyone nodded and agreed that logic had flown right out of the window.

'We don't have a landline,' explained Pat to everyone. 'We got rid of it years ago when they actually put in the new system at Oakwood; but it kind of suggests, that we were being followed, doesn't it? George knew where we were and when.'

They hadn't thought about it like that and it added more questions to their list. 'I'm not sure why Tom wanted you to go round for a cuppa and a biscuit, Elinor. I mean, go round where?' Piped up, Ed.

'Me neither,' replied Elinor. 'But he was starting to lose his memory a bit towards the end. Sadly, I wonder if he took that behaviour with him. Why should we presume that the dead miraculously heal their bodies and minds when they die, or that they're in heaven? It sounds more like they're in a big waiting room of nothingness – with a really bad communication system,' They hadn't thought of that either and another problem went on the list.

Then Harry put two and two together and made a bold statement. Perhaps it was the connection that was going to be switched off. Why hadn't these ghosts rung them on their mobiles, or sent them all an email? Heck, why didn't George use the Ouija board? Why did they use the landline? Then the gears whirred inside Elinor's mind. 'They're turning off all the landline system by 2026. I read it online last week.'

'Well then, we've got loads of time,' said Ed.

'No, we haven't Ed,' replied Pat. 'Think about it. If we've already disconnected ourselves, we know that's happening everywhere. Fewer and fewer people have a landline. 2026 is almost irrelevant. There'll be no landlines left way before then.'

Elinor scribbled down this next revelation. They thought they were on a roll. If there were some landlines that were going to be kept in remote places, as Elinor had talked about the five thousand to be kept, that might be enough but they agreed that they couldn't all just turn up at strangers' houses or hunt down locations that still had a working phone box and be able to connect. For every suggestion, there seemed to be a but after it.

Amanda had taken a back seat in the evening's proceedings, just providing top-ups and more snacks, but she put her two penneth in at this point.

'Well, I suggest you get your spiritual switchboard operator to get back in touch with them. Then try and nail down the whole thing that they're trying to get you to do and you need to do it quickly. If they can barely get a sentence out before the static drowns them out or the signal gets too faint, you might have a lot less time than you think, Ed.'

That set them off again and the questions flew around the table. 'So, we should get Pat to get back in touch with this clairvoyant,'

'Karen,' butted in Edie politely.

'Karen, yes,' said Elinor correcting herself.

'We should ask to speak to Tom, George and Gracie, in turn, don't you think?'

'It's forty-five pounds a go,' said Ed. Under the circumstances, they agreed it was worth it and perhaps they could strike a deal with Karen.

'Mates rates,' suggested Edie, looking at Elinor. 'I don't really remember her, but we can try.' conceded Elinor.

They said they would all check what they had on in the evenings, but none of them had anything on in the evenings. They might occasionally go out for a meal, but the midweek evenings were all about being at home, indoors, watching something on telly. Without realising it there was a lot of hugging as each one left Elinor's hallway. 'Avengers assemble,' said Ed loudly as he put on his jacket and was the last to leave. The group all laughed.

'Oh Lord, that couldn't be further from who we are could it?' Laughed Harry. Elinor stood at the door and waved them off, smiling, then closed the door and went back inside to Amanda.

'Well, they all seem like a nice bunch El. I was expecting at least one of them to seem crazy, but they do seem normal.'

'I know thank God. We really do need normal right now, because nothing about this is normal at all,' replied Elinor thoughtfully.

'Edie's funny though isn't she Mand? It's like she can't wait to get stuck in. We'll have to remember that because if we need to send anyone in to go meet one of this lot, it might as well be someone who's keen. Like Richard Dreyfus in Close Encounters, when he goes off into the spaceship at the end, smiling as he's being lead off by small aliens holding his hands.'

'Mind you, you can't really hold hands with a ghost can you?' asked Amanda. Elinor agreed and leaned over with a bottle and filled Amanda's glass.

She raised her own glass towards her friend. 'Here's to interesting times ahead and answers,' declared Elinor.

'Avengers Assemble,' shouted Amanda and they both laughed loudly.

'What the hell am I doing?' shouted Elinor at the ceiling and took another big gulp. The friends continued to analyse their visitors, with increasing stupidity as the alcohol flowed into the small hours.

Pat was going to text Karen but then decided to call instead. It seemed to make it more friendly and perhaps it would be easier to negotiate that mates rates reduction price. She just needed to make sure she didn't push her luck too far, or Karen might just refuse to do anything else, then they'd have to start again and Pat really didn't have the energy to meet anyone else new. Four new people were enough and she hadn't met Olivia yet. She was also hoping that she would never have to meet the twins, they sounded extra tiring.

The phone was answered. 'Hi Karen, it's Pat from the other night, thanks for sending me that phone number.' *Always start with a thank you before asking for something else,* thought Pat.

'That's OK, was it any use?'

'Yes thanks, very useful, we found her and we met up with the others too and now we need your help again please.' Karen was intrigued. Pat was clearly very sneaky, what a dark horse, pretending to be so normal, when she could be hiding her true reasons for this scam, very cleverly.

'So, what do you want Pat?'

'Well, we need to arrange another seance please Karen.' Karen heard forty-five pounds whispering in her ear and was happy to oblige.

'Thing is Karen, we actually need more than one seance.' Karen was smiling into the phone; ninety pounds now, this was getting better.

'OK, two seances, one after the other, that would work. I can fit you in on Tuesday or Thursday next week if you still want an evening.' Pat went for it and crossed her fingers that it wasn't being too cheeky.

'Could we be cheeky and get three in for ninety pounds Karen, but still in the two hours? I won't blame you if not.' Karen thought Pat was showing just what a hustler she really could be. However, another ninety pounds for two hours of work, cash in hand was a done deal.

Karen got her calendar up on screen and Pat jotted down the date and time ready to send to the others. 'How many of you will be coming altogether Pat? I need to make sure I've got enough chairs.'

'Five including me. We can bring spare chairs if you need us to, no bother honest.' It wouldn't need to come to that said Karen as she could just borrow a couple from next door.

Pat made a group text. She hated WhatsApp as sometimes not everybody wanted to be part of the conversation, so this way it was easier to group and separate.

'Hi, everyone. All booked in with Karen for Tuesday, 16th at seven thirty p.m. Here's the address. See you all next week,' Elinor responded with a copy of all the questions they wanted to ask each of their contacts if they got through.

Tom: What little job do you want me to do? Do you still want me to come round? If so, where and what for? Is Lynne with you?

George: What is being switched off? Why are we stopping it? How do we stop it?

Gracie: What does Harry have to do with this? How can he help?

For the next few days, life pottered on as normal for everyone and yet they all felt a little off-kilter knowing that something strange was happening and it was going to get more bizarre on Tuesday evening. Pat had talked about Karen in more detail, at Edie's request. She hoped that everyone agreed with her description when they finally met. Amanda and Olivia were going to be on call for the evening if necessary. The twins would hopefully be in bed and fast asleep so that Olivia could be ready at the other end of the line. Amanda had already promised she would wait up for the post seance de-brief from Elinor, if she wanted to talk straight after.

Chapter Five – Assemble

On Tuesday morning, Pat was visiting staff, patients and carers at the local hospice to talk to them and offer some encouraging advice from her experiences. When she was retired, she was in a senior role and was greatly missed. For someone who hadn't had children, Pat more than made up her nurturing skills with her later life caring abilities. Her visits happened about once a month, when sadly each time she visited, the patients and carers would be different people. She wandered into a small ward of just three patients and said hello and smiled at some family members holding the hands of their relative at the nearest bed. At the farthest end of the room, near the window, was a man obviously very close to his end-of-life care. Sallow, ghostlike, sunken cheeks, painfully thin arms and alone. Pat was not afraid of death. As a specialist care worker, she had been surrounded by it for decades. This stage was limbo, it was the fading and crossing over. It was like watching the point in Star Trek when people were beamed up. You saw them dissipate, but still hold their form for a while. You saw them continue to fade and separate into shadows, before they disappeared completely. Now Pat wondered where they might be re-materialising and how.

She had always considered death as finite, now she wasn't quite so sure.

Pat looked at the patient chart at the end of the bed and introduced herself.

'Hello, Samuel,' said Pat gently. 'I'm Pat, I hope you're getting treated very well in here and everyone is looking after you properly?'

'Oh yes,' replied the weak voice from the pillow. 'Call me Sam.'

'Will do. I hear you're a Rhinos fan Sam.' She had asked the nurses in reception who to visit and had asked for some information to help a conversation.

'Wise choice supporting rugby rather than United eh?' Sam made an attempt to smile and raised his arm towards her. The paper bracelet that had his name and patient number on it, slid down to almost his elbow. She moved in closer and gently held his hand.

'Hate football, always have. I used to play rugby you know.' Pat imagined him as a young man with broad shoulders and thick muscular arms.

'Aye, I bet nobody messed with you Sam, did they?' He tried to smile again. They chatted about nothing, for as long as Sam seemed engaged, then she felt his hand grip a little stronger.

'I'm ready now,' he said with more clarity in his voice. Even though there was no explanation, Pat knew what he meant.

'Listen, Sam, I'm going to tell you something before you go, OK? I think you will be absolutely fine and well looked after, but if you do need to tell anyone anything, let me know now and I'll pass it on. It'll save you having to wait around.'

'Oh, I've nothing left to do here, lass,' replied Sam. The day was quite bright and the clouds were light. A red kite flew high and Pat spotted it out of the window. She doubted that Sam's eyesight would focus enough to see it. The sound of a trolley and rattling crockery broke the peace.

'I shall leave you to your tea break now Sam, it's been lovely to meet you.' Pat squeezed his hand gently.

'Bye, love,' said Sam, as he watched her become a blur by the end of the bed. The familial friendly use of "love" for a stranger, stayed with her for the rest of the day.

Elinor was in the study on Tuesday morning, preparing. It had taken her years to call it the study, instead of just the spare room. It would always be the entrance hall and never the vestibule, for example. She couldn't bring herself to use certain terms, even if they were accurate, but finally, the study had become more acceptable. This was mainly due to her using it as a study too. Not always, the laptop on the knee on the sofa was still the most common, studious place she worked. Although she knew she would regret the Blu-Tack marks later, she had hung up the big sheet of newsprint from the first gathering last week. Around the edges were A4 sheets added on. These had bullet points of questions, but also her discoveries. There was a page of details about the landline switch-off. She had found a list of those places likely to keep the connections.

As she had tastefully been told by Amanda, they were in the arse end of anywhere and the back of beyond. Elinor had made an attempt to plot them on a map of the UK and then given up, when she realised she had gone too far and couldn't be bothered.

There was another sheet that had a handful of Twitter names on it from people who had replied to her #HauntedLandline tweet, but none of them had been as keen as Olivia in responding.

She fixed her gaze in the centre of all the notes, "ghosts?" When she wasn't paying attention to this very word, it was all rather fun, adventurous and an opportunity to carry on learning things. She wasn't bothered about making any more friends at this time in her life and yet the people who entered her home last week were lovely and they seemed like the sort who she could share nice days out with, go for afternoon tea and walk with. What they didn't seem like was a crack team of MI6 agents ready to blow this whole thing open and save the world.

The final A4 sheet was thumbed into place on the wall. This listed all the communication methods she could think of through the ages. Drawing, drums, smoke, whistles, beacons, semaphore, letters, morse code, telegraph, radio, telephone, TV, fax, 2G, 3G, 4G, cable, internet, 5G and then some question marks for whatever gets invented next. Then she went back in with her Sharpie and between beacons and semaphore, squeezed in tarot cards and Ouija board.

With a final mighty shove, Harry pulled himself out from under the floorboards. He had finally finished rewiring a very tricky sitting room. He was covered head to foot in rubble dust from the crawl space. He switched his little headlamp off. 'That should be it,' he said proudly. He knew he still had it, he was a bloody top-drawer electrician.

'Marvellous,' said his customer. 'Can I help you up?' Harry was now just about on his knees and ready to attempt to stand, but everything stiffened up so quickly these days.

'Thank you, I won't say no to a lift.' The lady was four foot nothing and couldn't have lifted his arm if it was a dead weight, but Harry knew it made her feel useful and it could mean another cuppa and some more Jaffa cakes, so he played along and did his best not to groan too much at his rigid back.

'You really have been so neat.' He had avoided ripping out the plaster from the walls and been very careful to pull the wires from underneath. It meant that she didn't need a decorator afterwards.

'Oh, thank you, I still like to do my best.'

'You still get a buzz from it then?'

'Not if I can help it.' Smiled Harry. Then the lady realised what she said and blurted out laughing.

'Would you like another cuppa before you go, Harry? I think I've still got some Jaffa cakes too.'

'Er, let me see the time, oh aye, go on then, just a quick one.'

As he drove home, he was thinking about getting into a hot shower and washing off all this dust and grime. He was convinced there would be spiders and woodlice in his hair and pockets. He was imagining being completely clean and fresh and in crisp clothes. Then his thoughts turned to the evening ahead. What would it be like if they did manage to get his mam back on the phone? Was Dad with her, or was it just her? She had been dead for over ten years and Dad even longer, but had she been trapped all that time unable to rest and alone? That thought made him suddenly overwhelmed with sadness for her. Surely after such a good life, there should be a good death and then a peaceful nothingness after it? He realised that he had somewhere along the line, allowed this to be real. He had stopped thinking it was a hoax or a scam. Was that when he met the others and they normalised it all together? Harry wasn't sure what part he had to play in all of this. They had managed to find Elinor, then Pat and Ed. This had to be premeditated in some way. Accidents, flukes, randomness, none of this was a coincidence at all. It was too easy to discover everyone and it was their proximity to each other that was also clearly by design. Perhaps there was another question to ask. Were Tom, Gracie and George planning how to connect everyone for quite some time? Perhaps they had been working together to come up with a plan from their end, or side or wherever it was? How had they found each other in the nothingness? How long had they been watching the living world, especially if Mam knew what Twitter was?

He was ready for that shower to wash away the dust and hoped it might also clear his mind from all these swirling crazy thoughts.

Karen had suddenly been overwhelmed with anticipation about the evening's group seance. She never felt like this. Fair enough, nothing like this had happened before and she never really liked more than one person turning up anyway, two max, so this was unusual. She did, however, feel like she was going to be outnumbered and scrutinised. There was an overriding sense of regret that she had let herself see the pound signs in front of her eyes, before thinking things through. There was still a chance that this was going to be her downfall. What if these others were the police? What if it was the inland revenue, seeing how much she was pocketing cash in hand and not declaring? Had Elinor harboured some kind of resentment from school and been planning revenge for all these years? What on earth had she just let herself in for? It would make for a good TV detective storyline; she had to admit that.

Karen wanted everything to be perfect though. When she did her regular tarot readings, the house was always clean and tidy. Being slovenly was an easy way to lose repeat customers. Keep it inviting, warm and clean, that helped. She knew she had too many things on the coat rack in the hall, but everywhere else was just right. The creative way that every group of pictures, objects and colours worked together, was all part of the aesthetic of someone who was an artist, as well as a clairvoyant. She never resorted to tacky kit and stereotypical appropriated nicknacks. There was no obvious paraphernalia on the shelves. She just collected beautiful things and knew where they looked best. The back dining room had framed photographs that she had taken herself. Some were abstract, some landscapes, but all were serene and intriguing. No people, no faces or eyes. That was important. She had learnt from her past. One woman had caught a glimpse of a portrait, only catching sight of the eyes in the low light and had freaked out and screamed the house down. The neighbours had banged on the door thinking it was Karen who was being attacked. It was very embarrassing and even harder to explain.

Karen went back into the hall and worked her arms around a mass of coats nearest the door. She felt like she was giving them a massive hug. Working a lift upwards she eventually managed to wrestle them loose from the hooks, then very tentatively climbed the stairs, one at a time and made for the box room at the end of the landing. As she threw them onto the bed, she remembered all the family parties where it was her job to take all the coats and put them onto the same bed. As everybody left, it was also her job to ask what coat belonged to each person and bring them down to the correct owner. The house was full of memories. The happy family gatherings every Sunday evening watching That's Life and Sunday night at the London Palladium.

It was probably time to take some of these to the charity shop, especially as she had just discovered a coat she hadn't worn for a least five years. Back in the hall, she redistributed the remaining items and it all looked so much better. It was so easy to lose sight of the best things when you piled too much other stuff on top and never organised things properly.

Reception school finished at three p.m. Olivia walked to meet her girls. As they appeared from the school doors, they spotted her and ran towards her. She held their hands all the way as they walked home until they got to the front door.

Nel and Erin raced inside the house, dropped their bags at the door and somehow managed to take off their coats in full flight, throwing them away, anywhere and headed straight into the kitchen. Their mum always let them have a snack after school. Today it was a bowl each of blueberries and redcurrants. They were also given a cocktail stick and had to eat one berry at a time. They were allowed to read their favourite books too. Their mum didn't seem to mind when they got things squished between the pages or reddy purple fingerprints on them either.

Mum asked them what they had learnt today at school and neither of them could remember a single thing. But Daniel had trumped when they were sat in the carpeted area at story time and they had all laughed and Mr Wilton had told them off so he could carry on with the story. It was pink custard day and they had it with a sponge, but they couldn't remember what was the main course because it was disgusting.

Then Erin said she did a million skips at playtime and Nel said she was fibbing, but then said she did a million and one skips. Their mum looked at them both, as they grinned at her from over the table top. She smiled at them and said that she thought they might be the best at skipping in the whole world, but they would have to practise a lot. That would mean that after they had finished their fruit, they should go outside into the yard and practise their skipping. They had a rope each and just enough space. Mum made them stand to attention as she wiped down their faces and hands. Then they ran into the backyard with their skipping ropes and energetically thrashed around managing only a few skips at a time before entangling their feet and legs in the rope.

A million times, eh? thought Olivia to herself as she stared out of the back door at the pair of them. She wondered what Nel thought had happened when the landline phone rang and Gracie had spoken to her. Hopefully she actually thought nothing of it. As long as she never asked about it again, she would probably forget it happened and if she did remember it, then she wouldn't have a clue that it was the voice of her dead great-grandmother. Olivia emptied the two small school bags. There was a letter from school about a trip, a couple of books, their pencil cases and a sock with an apple core stuck to it. The two small Tupperware boxes that contained their playtime snacks, now had some grass, a few twigs and some stones in place of grapes and sultanas. She wouldn't throw the contents out just yet, in case it was something they had been told to collect on purpose. Olivia was grateful that there was nothing alive in there. Then she double-checked their bags and coat pockets.

Pat had suggested that everyone should meet just down the road from Karen's house. Then they could check how they were all doing, have a bit of a plan of action and be able to start straight away once they were inside. That was a very sensible suggestion and everyone agreed that safety in numbers was best. 'I wonder what Karen will make of us all rolling up at once,' asked Edie. 'We might look like a right mob.'

'Us?' laughed Harry.

Pat and Ed said they would pick Elinor up on the way and drop her off afterwards, even though she said she was more than happy to walk down and catch a taxi back. Elinor was very pleased that they wouldn't hear of it and took the offer up graciously.

It was 7.20 p.m., and both cars parked close to each other down the side street. They laughed when Ed said it was like a stakeout. Elinor had the list of questions; they would ask for Tom first, then Gracie and then George last, seeing as how they had already spoken to him once. 'Are we all ready then?' asked Harry. They all nodded and with Ed and Pat leading the way, the other three walked behind. Elinor heard the intro tune to Reservoir Dogs in her head as she looked at everyone. Five people with a combined age of over two hundred and eighty years. It couldn't be more dissimilar, but she grinned as she imagined them all in black suits. She didn't need to imagine it in slow motion, they really were walking at an amble. Then they arrived at Karen's front door and Pat knocked. A dog barked and a few moments later Karen opened the door.

Chapter Six – Party Line

Karen welcomed them all into her home. Pat introduced them one by one and Edie was excited and shook Karen's hand very enthusiastically, as if she had been introduced to a celebrity. The dog barked from the front room. 'Don't worry about her,' said Karen. 'She'll lick you to death, not tear you to shreds. She'll also want to be the centre of attention, so she's best where she is and she knows she'll get an evening walk after.'

Karen looked at Elinor intensely but struggled to recognise her. Elinor did the same. 'Is it wrong that I really can't remember you that well?' she asked, embarrassed that thirty-eight years had caused her to lose a photographic memory she never had in the first place.

'Oh God no, me neither.' Sighed Karen, relieved that it wasn't just her. 'We can discuss who we can remember after, I haven't forgotten Mr Scott though.'

'He was a class act for sure,' remembered Elinor. 'But you're right; this isn't what we came for.' Karen wondered what they had really come for. Ed led the way into the back room and gestured at the coat rack to Pat.

'Yes, I've had a bit of a clear out, just pop your coats here,' said Karen, who was pleased she had made room, but was a bit gutted that the difference had been spotted.

The six chairs were squashed around the small table and as they sat down and looked around the room, Karen was very grateful that everyone declined a drink. 'Right then, let's do this shall we?' There was a boldness to the way she spoke, as if she knew it was going to be arduous, or difficult in some way.

'Well, it's what we've come for, now where do we start?' asked Edie with relish in her voice.

'Well if you don't mind, could you put your money on the table first please?' Harry laid it out in one pile, there were five crisp twenties.

'We didn't want to be too cheeky asking for three seances in two hours and it was easier to divide the hundred between five since we've been using less cash and coins.' Karen smiled.

'Well that's very nice, thank you.' She was warming to them even more and then she remembered that they were all out to bring her down, probably, possibly. Well, an extra tenner was still a nice touch from these wily characters. She put the money straight into her pocket.

'Who are we starting with then? Who's going first and who are we trying to contact? Six fingers on the planchette are too much, I recommend a maximum of four, but two will do.'

'I'll go first, please,' said Elinor, realising that her voice had weakened somewhat. She wasn't expecting that. So she cleared her throat and continued, 'I'm trying to contact Tom, my neighbour.'

'What's his full name?'

'Keswick, Tom Keswick. He died when he was eighty-three, just over a year ago.'

The corner lamps were off and Karen had dimmed the "big light" above the table. Pat thought the scene looked like Van Gogh's The Potato Eaters, but without the hunger and potatoes and it was far more middle class. Then Elinor stood up and apologised. 'I'm really sorry, but I really should just nip to the loo, before we start. Then I can concentrate.'

'That's a good idea,' said Edie.

'OK, how about you all go and then no one will ask to stop mid-way through? This is as bad as a school coach trip,' said Karen in a friendly tutting way.

'I know,' replied Elinor slightly embarrassed. 'But let's face it, we're all of an age and we don't want to get too spooked and have an accident. God, an unexpected sneeze is worry enough these days.' There was laughter and understanding mixed in with acknowledging that age could be a bugger sometimes.

'Don't you two sit there all smug.' Smirked Pat at Ed and Harry.

'It happens to you too, but you just won't talk about it.' The men went a little sheepish and both of them followed the trip upstairs after the women. Edie said it was less hassle getting the twins to go before every car journey, no matter how short the trip.

When everyone was settled, Karen asked whether they still wanted to use the board, after all, it had been almost totally unnecessary last time. Edie said it needed to be used for those who hadn't been contacted before, but perhaps it wasn't needed for George this time. Everyone knew that this was a bucket list moment for Edie, so they agreed to her suggestion. After changing seats, Elinor settled on being sat opposite to Karen. It also looked more balanced and symmetrical, which wasn't important but seemed to be at the time. She placed her forefinger very lightly on the planchette opposite Karen's. Edie grinned in expectation and imagined herself surrounded by Vincent Price and Peter Cushing. Ed and Harry looked nothing like them, but the dim lighting helped her imagination.

'Tom Keswick, Elinor Coates is here and would like to speak to you. Tom, can you let us know if you can hear us? Elinor wants to help you, and the others are here too, Tom.' It was difficult not blurting out something stupid and Ed was doing his best to only look at the planchette and not catch anyone else's eye. He could feel himself wanting to break the silence with a daft one-liner, but he held it together. It seemed interminable as they listened to Karen calmly ask for Tom to make contact, over and over again. Then the planchette faltered under the women's fingers. They lifted their hands slightly to take off any weight, so only the gentlest touch remained. Was it just their own inability to keep completely still that caused the first twitch? The mantel clock chimed, the planchette moved and in the hall, the phone rang and the dog barked. 'Shit!' said Elinor involuntarily.

'Answer it.' They all seemed to say at the same time. Elinor got up and went into the hall and picked up the receiver. It crackled and then she heard him.

'Elinor, it's Tom, can you hear me OK?'

'Yes, just enough Tom, are you OK?' *What a stupid question*, she thought instantly, *he's dead.*

'Look we have so many questions.' Then Elinor gestured back into the room and mouthed that she needed her notepad with the questions in it and a pen. She was normally so organised and this was a rookie error. Harry brought her the pad and pen quickly.

'We're losing our ability to communicate with you Elinor, we need a boost.'

'How Tom? Where are you?'

'I can't describe it, it's like I've just been woken up and I'm sensing things.'

'Have you met up with the others?' asked Elinor, hastily, knowing the connection probably wouldn't last.

'Yes, they found me, eventually.'

'How can we help you, Tom?'

'You need to find our exchange Elinor, but you need help.' She was scribbling down everything as quickly as possible. The others were listening intently, but with only half the conversation, they were clueless and on the edge of their seats. Karen was sucked in and then shook herself out of the excited performance and looked at them all.

'Just keep sight of the scam Karen, don't let them suck you in. Keep a grip lass,' she repeated this over and over again in her head as Elinor spoke on the phone.

The static was getting stronger and Elinor asked Tom one more question. 'Tom, are you with Lynne?' His voice was fading.

'No Elinor, Lynne went all the way, I have to stay to help you sort things.' And then the line went completely silent and the ticking of the mantel clock seemed to be as loud as everyone's heartbeats.

'Jesus, that was weird,' exclaimed Elinor to everyone as she sat down at the table. Everyone clambered to ask her what Tom had said. She relayed his words as accurately as she could reading from her notes.

'They're losing their ability to communicate with us and they need a boost and I need to find, our exchange.' She corrected herself. 'I'm still clueless even though I've got more information.' It was baffling them all and Karen watched the floorshow as they played out a perfect performance of seriousness, nervousness, practical suggestions and then laughter. What on earth were they up to? 'So, shall we continue?' she butted in. 'If you swap places with Elinor now and then you're both sort of still opposite me and we can take it from there.' A brief palaver of chair swapping ensued and Elinor went and put her notepad on the table in the hall, with her pen and opened it to the correct page for Harry's note-taking. Edie suddenly came over very flustered. This was it, what she thought she wanted, ever since she was a TV watching kid. She was about to be part of an exchange between the living and the dead and now all of a sudden, she was frightened. So, she made Harry swap his planchette hand over so that she could hold it under the table.

'Right, who are we after now?'

'Gracie, Gracie Blackmoor, please. She's Harry's mum. She's been dead over ten years now,' offered Edie.

'We did what she asked first and found Elinor, so we don't know if that's all there is to do, but now we've found her and we're here, there has to be more to tell us.'

Karen asked Edie and Harry to place their forefingers onto the planchette as lightly as possible so that they could barely feel it with their fingertips and then she asked for Gracie to make herself known. With every passing second, Edie looked at their fingers and looked up at Karen and back again, repeatedly. Harry just stared at the board. 'Come on, Gracie love, do your best. Harry wants to help you as best he can.' The mantel clock ticked and chimed for eight thirty p.m., and they all jumped.

'Christ on a bike,' blurted Pat. Ed sniggered quietly, his sweary wife was obviously fully focused.

'So sorry,' said Pat. 'The whole thing has made me more jumpy these days.'

Karen asked again and it seemed like there could only be one communication per session. Why would they give her so much money if it wouldn't happen again? But then the three of them felt more of a current run through their fingertips and the hall phone rang once more. 'Get it, Harry, quick,' said Edie forcefully. 'It's her.'

Harry had seized up again, sat on the chair for so long. 'I'm going, I'm going love, OK.' Edie was nudging Harry towards the door.

'Mam? It's Harry.' The poor connection was causing a constant faltering of the signal, like the strange sound that used to happen when someone accidentally called a fax number by mistake.

'Harry, can you hear me?'

'Yes, Mam, just speak as clear as you can though.'

'They need your skills, Harry, you've got what they need. You need to make it, somehow.'

'Make what, Mam?'

'The connection, the booster, love.'

'For what though? What am I connecting exactly? Where am I putting it?' Gracie managed one more sentence before being lost in the chaotic signal. 'For the exchange and when you've done it, I can rest.' Those last words hit him hard in the chest and he took a deep breath and went to sit down.

'Oh lord, sorry, Elinor, I haven't written a thing down.'

'Not to worry, Harry, it's more than overwhelming isn't it?' she said kindly. 'Just try and tell us everything you can remember and I'll jot things down.'

Harry did his best to explain that he had to make something that was a connection, a booster for a signal at the exchange and if he didn't do it then his mam couldn't rest and he couldn't live with that guilt. Everyone was very supportive and agreed that they all felt the same. Elinor just wanted Tom to be at peace and preferably with Lynne. Ed and Pat wanted George to be back with Ed's mum too. If they didn't manage to sort this, it was not their fault. They were clutching at straws, and all agreed that they still didn't know if this was real or not. Karen was starting to feel like this lot might not be the undercover gang she initially thought. But if they were genuine then this was the biggest thing that she had ever been a part of and she wanted to be involved even more.

Everyone had become quite tired from the proceedings and knew they would all just like to be at home with a drink, right now. But there was still one more connection to try and make. Deciding whether or not to use the board was a short-lived decision. They would keep the board out and if there was no connection, they would use it. After the repeat musical chairs, Ed and Pat had now taken up their positions opposite Karen and even though they did not use the board, they found themselves staring at it. Pat held Ed's hand on his lap. Once again, Karen asked if George would come to speak to his son. The response time was far quicker than any of them expected, but instead of the phone ringing normally, it pinged erratically, glitching as though it was being electrocuted. Ed wasn't too sure he wanted to pick it up, but he did. The distortion was too much and he couldn't hear anything coherent at all, so he just spoke and hoped George could hear him.

'I hope you can hear me, Dad. We'll do our best, I love you.' Harry regretted not saying that to his mum too.

They agreed that they had probably pushed their luck anyway and that it had been diminishing returns on the quality of that signal. Karen looked at the clock. 'Well you've paid for two hours and there's still quite a bit of time left if you want to thrash things out a bit more.' There was no way she wanted to hand back any of the money, but knew it would be the most honest thing to do. Her moral compass kicked in. 'Or I can give you twenty quid back, for the reduced time?'

'Oh, don't worry about that Karen,' said Edie politely. 'It's still worked well I suppose.'

Karen was pleased she had said the right thing and offered everyone a cuppa or a nightcap. The offer was declined but they sat there for another fifteen minutes or so deciding what their next move should be. Elinor texted Amanda, *loads to tell you about, but shattered now, I'll call you tomorrow.*

And Edie texted Olivia, *Hi Liv, did the girls go to sleep quickly? What a night. I'll call you when we get back, in about half an hour or so.*

They agreed to let the events of the evening soak in and to get back together at the weekend. As they left Karen's house shouting their thank yous, they heard the sound of the dog barking and Karen's voice calling. 'Come on then, let's get your legs stretched and then you can have some supper before I have a huge whiskey.'

Elinor got into the back seat of Ed and Pat's car and they waved at Harry and Edie as they drove off. 'Well, I'm bloody shattered, Elinor, don't know about you?' said Ed looking at her through the rearview mirror.

'Totally, Ed. I'll try and find out what exchange Tom might be on about and hopefully Harry can see what sort of booster he might be able to make.' And then she said what they were both thinking. 'Is this genuine, or do you think we really are being taken for some massive ride and we're just a bunch of ageing folk who have nothing better to do and we're just easy targets?'

'I hear you, Elinor,' said Pat. 'One minute I'm caught up in it all and the next I feel like an absolute fool, but I can't believe anyone would go to this length as a scam.'

'That's the whole point though isn't it love? Make it as unbelievable as possible. Anyway, I'm pouring a very nice brandy when I get back in, what will you be having Elinor?'

'A gin and tonic, unmeasured.'

'Good call,' said Pat.

As Karen walked her dog back from the nearest patch of grass, she asked herself the same question over again. Were these five innocuous-looking people, just how they seemed or were they the best confidence trick in history?

Ed and Pat huddled together on the sofa with a glass of brandy each. Pat wouldn't normally have had a brandy, but she didn't fancy the fizz of tonic now, it wasn't serious enough. The warmth worked its way down her throat. 'Actually, I think I do quite like brandy,' she said. They talked through the evening and between their serious concerns about what was happening they laughed about how they thought Karen was also a magician.

'Did you see how quickly that money disappeared when we put it on the table?' They laughed at themselves, having to go to the loo, like old people. And they laughed at how nice and sensible everyone was, despite the absolutely ridiculous situation that had unfolded around them.

Harry went into the kitchen to make a "snoozy" tea for himself and Edie, whilst she phoned Olivia and asked how her evening had been first. The twins had actually been quite good, comparatively speaking. It had been bath night, so Olivia had planned the wind down as meticulously as possible. Tea time, followed by sedentary colouring, then bath time, then a story, then lights out. There wasn't too much felt tip to clean off afterwards and not that much water on the bathroom floor either. It was a bit of a coup. Edie then described the evening in detail. Harry butted in occasionally next to her, when he thought Edie had slightly over-exaggerated a moment in the proceeding.

At home, Elinor checked her phone and Amanda replied.

'Not sure I can wait till tomorrow for you to tell me all about it; call me when you get in; doesn't matter what time.'

Elinor got herself ready for bed and curled up on the sofa, but with a hot chocolate, not a gin. She selected Amanda's number and before she knew it, an hour of talking had passed. As Elinor offloaded the evening's happenings, she explained that Tom had said to meet him at the exchange, but even said "our" exchange. Throughout the conversation, Amanda logged onto her laptop and opened Google Maps. Then she typed into the search bar,

"telephone exchanges near Moortown" and pressed return.
'Aw, no way, El. This is bloody ridiculous.'

'What? What Mand?' She had heard the tapping of keys as they spoke.

'No wonder he contacted you, of course he did.'

'What, Mand? What?'

'There's that bloody BT exchange behind the Sainsbury's near you. Where all those Open Reach vans are always coming and going.'

Chapter Seven – Maintenance

On Wednesday morning, everyone went about their usual routines, but just a little bit removed from the tasks at hand. If they had all been teenagers, it would have seemed perfectly normal. Pat poured her hot water into her bran flakes and because he was distracted, Ed's tea trailed across the kitchen floor, then onto his feet. Elinor sliced right through her marigolds with a kitchen knife and narrowly missed her thumb. Harry picked up the wrong screwdriver and gave himself a thankfully small electric shock and Edie forgot to switch the oven off and narrowly avoided the smoke alarm kicking in. All of them were being distracted by the voices from the past and trying to work out what to do next. It was becoming all-consuming.

Olivia, however, was working like a finely tuned machine. Even the twins were surprised that their mum had everything ready to go in the morning. She walked them to school, waved them off and headed into town to enquire about a job. The divorce had been mercifully quick. The twins had been priority number one throughout, so Olivia managed to keep a roof over their heads, even if it was rented and small. The maintenance and child tax credit had kept her ticking over whilst she looked after them full-time. Now, as they entered their school years, Olivia needed that extra money even more and wanted adult company and conversation, or the other way round, she wanted money and needed adult conversation? It was both and she knew it. The twins were rubbish at discussing the news. This was time to test the waters and was something with shorter daytime hours that would work around the school drop-off and pick-up times. It was worth a shot. Initially, this was just going for an informal chat about working with a cleaning company. Olivia was not proud when it came to work, regardless of her excellent qualifications. A job was a job and she wanted, needed that pocket money and focus to get her back into the routine of work. It would also mean time out of the house and not using electricity and water for a few hours a day and that was a bonus. She'd be active, warm and in the company of adults. All she had to do was actually get a job. Olivia had not told her parents. She wanted no conversation about the position until she could actually say she had it.

The cleaning company office was behind a nondescript door with a sign next to Waterstones and she rang the bell. The buzzer on the door unlocked it and she climbed the narrow stairs. After reminding the lady on reception who she was and why she was there, Olivia knew she had nothing to lose and made a good impression on the woman sitting in the office. The supervisor reminded Olivia of her own mother and so she played the role of obedient daughter very well. The company managed many sites around the city. Their main warehouse was just on the outskirts and this is where supplies, vans and deliveries were sorted for distribution. Olivia, if she got the job, would work within a radius of locations, turn up every morning to meet the head supervisor and be given the tasks and worksheet on site. At the end of a shift, she would hand over her materials and walk away. It was someone else's job to collect and return everything to the warehouse. The sites differed as did the number of staff on each job, according to scale, complexity and hours. Olivia nodded at everything and said she could work well in a team and independently. She said she could think on her feet, troubleshoot and follow instructions. She also said she looked forward to working through all level assessments and tests concerning health and safety and risk assessments regarding equipment and hazardous materials. And she was very much looking forward to basic first aid training too. It had been a very positive and amicable meeting; they had her number and would call in a day or two. Olivia could do no more and at the end of the meeting, she went back downstairs and nipped into Waterstone's for a mooch.

There was nothing she was looking for in particular, but she found herself picking out *The History of the Telephone* by Herbert Newton Casson and sat herself down to scan through it.

After lunch, which included some slightly overdone – well burnt round the edges, but not going to waste, biscuits that Edie had made that morning, Harry went to check on the treehouse. Regular maintenance was vital to avoid splinters and worse. He couldn't get right inside it, but he

110

could open the top door and let the light in, remove all the soft furnishings, give it a good hoover and spruce up. There had been a family of mice in there last Autumn. Harry joked that they were treating themselves to the five-star accommodation and facilities of the Ritz for mice. Then Edie had mentioned Ritz crackers and their conversation meandered. He had been out and bought a solar-powered light source that when fully charged, would rotate and cast stars and shapes around the walls. It was very cute and he knew the girls would love the surprise. The angle was perfect and the small solar panel faced south, so it could pick up maximum rays, when it was actually clear enough. Measuring twice above the door, and the exit for the slide, he drilled some pilot holes and screwed in the two new features that he had spent some time carving and varnishing. "Nel and Erin's place" read one sign and "Erin and Nel's place" read the other. There would have been no end of arguments otherwise and there still might be anyway. The final addition was placing a shiny new tin can and newly stretched string phone across from the treehouse to the patio. Harry smiled and gave the string a very satisfying twang.

Edie had gone up into the loft and hadn't come down yet. 'Love? Are you all right up there?' He called through the hole in the ceiling. The sturdy fold-down attic ladder he had installed did have a handrail and was quite steep, but the light he had fitted up there was bright.

'Yes thanks, I'm coming down now anyway, could you grab this for me please?' Edie's hand appeared, well

111

lit, from the hole and it seemed to be holding a weighty tome.

'Crikey, what's this you've found?' He caught a glimpse of the front cover. It was the catalogue of electrical equipment, that he remembered from the counter of Edmunson's when he had gone in for his cables and fittings and to smile at Edie.

'I have no idea why I remembered that I'd kept this, but I thought it might be useful for when you build your booster,' said Edie proudly. 'Love I'm an electrician, not an electronics engineer. It's like saying that because I walk everywhere and I've got feet, I can be a podiatrist. Plus I have never built a booster of any kind, let alone a supernatural one.' Edie did understand, but as she explained, very calmly, he was the best and nearest skilled person out of all of them. Then he reminded her, that she had looked inside the contents of that catalogue far more than him and she could probably do it better.

'Oh, bloody hell.' She laughed. 'If it's down to me, we've got no chance have we?'

Pat and Ed had decided to have a nice drive out. They just wanted to drive, as far as they could, so they chose Helmswell and the huge antiques centre on the old RAF base. It would keep them occupied for hours and it did. They found some nice old pots and carvings for the garden. Pat didn't know what she would do with them just yet, but that didn't matter, they were a bargain. One dealer sold old domestic ware. There was a huge kitchen table that groaned under the weight of bundled bone-handled cutlery, old mince meat machines and weighing scales. There were old kitchen cabinets that they both remembered their grandparents having. A table slid out from the middle between the bottom and top cupboards and legs moved out from the sides to support it. This was like a museum, not a shop. Then in the next space, it was all things for the living room and hallways, dining rooms and bedrooms. So many tasselled standard lamps, footstools, fire iron sets and countless piles of cheap dinner services. They remembered those smokey brown glass tea cups too. Ed looked into a dark corner lit by an old Anglepoise lamp, sat on top of a doily on a table, was an old rotary Bakelite-looking telephone. Next to it was an ivory plastic rotary telephone and next to that was an avocado green Trimphone. 'Look, it's a sign, Pat.' He pointed.

'A sign for what, Ed?' replied Pat.

'That we need to buy them and then Harry can take them to pieces and use them, possibly, hopefully, could he?' As he spoke, his own enthusiasm waned as the complexity of the task seemed impossible.

Pat climbed carefully past old vacuum cleaners and folding chairs, went over to the phones and took one look at the price tags. 'Not a chance in hell,' she said in disgust. The Bakelite one was a hundred pounds. The ivory one was more like it, at thirty and the Trimphone was more niche at forty.

'Haggle,' offered Ed. 'You know you're good at it, you love a good haggle on holiday and you always get the deal.'

'Yes, but that's playing with small money, Ed, this is a lot.'

'OK, Ed, listen, I'll haggle if you cough up.' She was good at this. Trying to find a stallholder or salesperson in this cavernous place took a while. Mistaking other visitors for staff was easily done, but eventually, they found a man about their own age, wearing a badge, and took a chance. There was the usual routine of only accepting the ticket price. Then offering all of them for a group reduction, but Pat needed to wade in with a massive reduction. She made her pitch and explained why she should get a much better deal than the ticket prices. For a start, all three phones were at the back of the display, well out of reach and were covered in dust. Pat had nearly given herself an injury trying to look at them. She explained that they had clearly been there for a very long time and that surely a sale would leave more space for better higher-priced lots. *God she's good,* thought Ed. When the man finally asked her what she was willing to pay she said her final offer was seventy pounds in total. Three useless phones were surely only worth that. The man went off to phone the owner of the stall and although they couldn't hear the call they could see his hand gestures and expressions. When he came back, he said it was eighty or no sale. Pat shook his hand and Ed went and grabbed the phones and then remembered that he was paying.

Elinor typed *inside a BT telephone exchange* in the search bar and images that looked like walls of filing cabinets and shelves of lever arch files appeared. It was like the most boring supermarket stock imaginable. 'So, Tom, you think I'm going to be able to find you here somewhere, do you?' she said it out loud. It was common for Elinor to mutter to herself and now she felt like she did actually have someone to talk to, or at least a reason to say things out loud so that Tom might hear them. This was the point at which she fell down the research rabbit hole. She read about what was happening on all these MDFs, which she now knew stood for Main Distribution Frames and not just medium-density fibreboard. There was the physical linking up of all the cables across the country and that giant one she saw that went from the telegraph museum at Porthcurno in Cornwall, all the way under the ocean floor to America. It reminded her of the documentary film she had seen about mushrooms and the mycelium networks. Nature has made a communication system underground as old as time. Then she also remembered that trees communicated with each other; their roots touch each other, they shared water and looked after each other when there was potential life-threatening danger. Her mind went back and forth between the inadequate, forever-changing human invention and nature's creation that was perfect from the start. The sheets of paper full of ideas, doodles and bullet points were becoming more complex. She knew there was a potential connection here and that its value could be substantial, but this wasn't her field of expertise and she knew it wasn't Harry's either. Who would relish this challenge and not ask questions? The first thing anyone would ask, is why did she want them to do this for her?

The Open Reach vans had been out trying to install fibre broadband to everyone's home. These still seemed to come from the telephone poles and she wasn't sure if the other side of life, where Tom, Gracie and George were, would be able to upgrade somehow. Did their communication evolve over the years too? She looked back at her list of communication tools through time once more. Firstly, people had to just make noises at each other, but then they drew and made marks so that they could leave messages. Then they used sounds and smoke for distant communication. 'OK, this might be going somewhere.' Elinor carried on working and then realised the daylight had gone from around her and she was starving. She popped one of her homemade batch-cooked frozen lasagnas in the microwave and when the oven pinged, she took it back to the sofa on a tray and ate it straight from the container. Then she cracked on, thinking and thinking.

The plan was to all go round to Harry and Edie's on Sunday at three p.m. Edie wanted to provide afternoon tea and no one refused. Harry ignored those burnt biscuits from the other day, as Edie was normally a supreme baker, though he preferred cooking the main meals because it was more "cheffy".

Pat explained that she and Ed were taking part in a midnight walk for charity to support the hospice she volunteered at, so if they looked a bit shattered on Sunday, that would be the reason. Everyone offered to chip in a tenner in sponsorship, and she was very grateful.

Chapter Eight – The Connection

The sponsored midnight walk for Gemmafield's Hospice was always well attended. Not only did the carers of those who were being looked after, take part, but also those who had lost their family members and continued to support the care home. The local schools often joined in too. This year the trail was from the Stray in Harrogate, through and around the outskirts of Harewood and would end at the Hospice. Meandering through the smaller villages, woods and field footpaths to avoid any traffic, the twelve miles should be interesting and enjoyable. There would be pit stops and kind volunteers offering snacks and drinks along the way, as well as those strategically placed people directing the walkers. The speedy ramblers could probably manage it in four hours and the slower end would make it in six.

Pat and Ed would be walking almost past the end of Harry and Edie's and had already discussed ducking out for a cheat, or at least a loo stop, but they knew they would just carry on to the bitter end. They had parked their car at the hospice ready for the drive home and used the minibus facility to take them into Harrogate. At the starting tent, hordes of people chatted and organised themselves. There were school groups and scout groups, individuals and

118

couples just like them. There was a great number of reflective jackets and hi-vis, as well as torches and flashing LEDs

Carol and Nigel were corralling a small bunch of enthusiastic sixth-formers. They were using it as part of their Duke of Edinburgh Platinum training and walking in the dark was going to be educational and fun, as well as a fundraising sponsored walk. Carol had been a teacher for years but had left and started on a different path as a total life change. She had bought a wreck of a barn and done it up slowly over a number of years. The land it sat on was perfect to let the D of E groups stay on it for a small fee. The money was pretty constant throughout the year and helped with odds and ends for the build. Carol was fully qualified to keep working with the groups and she loved inviting them to her campsite and being part of that crowd. The bigger group had been divided up and she and Nigel had been given this Magnificent Seven. The students hadn't heard of the Magnificent Seven.

Carol was keen to get this bunch accustomed to the differences between night walking and not being able to rely on landmarks. No mobile phones were allowed. They were equipped with reflectors, attached to their rucksacks and coats, front and rear and all manner of first aid equipment. It was the clearest night and the stars were leading their way. The light pollution was still an issue, but nothing like the major cities. Nigel had given them a short session on identifying the night sky, the North Star and other astronomical features. Knowing what would be visible at this time of year. The students knew they had been let in on a secret that would last them a lifetime. The four girls and three boys, had their head torches firmly placed over their hats and well-stocked rucksacks of every snack known to man. The thing that would really keep them going, of course, was their ability to chat nonstop for as many hours as you gave them.

As part of the event organisation, each named team or walker was given a departure time and number, safety was paramount. Everyone set off at a staggered time, to lengthen out the hundred or so people who had signed up. They would be ticked off and ticked back in. No one ever wanted another incident.

Headlights and torches lit up the trees, hedgerows and shrubs. Looking across fields and into gardens and woods, creatures' eyes flashed and rustles, yelps and howls added to the excitement. People called back to each other to listen out for the owl, and watch out for the mud and slippery rocks and tree branches at eye height across pathways. The walkers were experiencing the added jeopardy of poor vision and Carol told the sixth formers to imagine what it would be like to be blind or partially sighted and have to deal with this level of unknown obstacles all day. Was it always nighttime for the blind? And did finding their way eventually give them a greater sense of awareness when they remembered where they were, or knew distances with highly tuned muscle memory? The students mulled it over and realised how lucky they were. The conversations were varied and broad, serious and fun. Carol enjoyed their positive approach to life as well as their company and they thought miss was all right too. Nigel led from the front and Carol brought up the rear. She had lost count of how many walks and hills they had climbed over the years. Group after group, the same complaints and ailments, injuries and occasional sunburn. Watching them get lost and struggle with tents, was all part of the fun. Watching them smile with satisfaction when they completed their missions was joyous. She knew they were getting skills and memories for life. This was her happy place.

As the group walked down a narrow lane, their head torches caused the shadows to play and dart across the road. Ghosts of trees lengthened and shrank as they moved their heads in conversation. They caught the stares and silhouettes of deer in the fields and a badger shuffled into the undergrowth not too far ahead. Nature comes into its own at night, Carol told them. She wondered if she should tell them the urban myth of the "don't look back" tale, which seemed to have been the scary story everyone told everyone when she was at school. Then thought better of it, under the circumstances. That could wait for a night at the campsite when they were completing the award, officially. On they strolled until one of them spotted a dull light up ahead on the verge and into a hedge. As they got closer, they saw that it was an old red telephone box, its internal bulb was just emitting enough light to highlight the old black phone and the shelf. Many of the rectangles of glass were broken, the door was ajar and the whole booth leaned back towards the hedge at an unnerving angle. Inside, the ivy had taken hold and the cobwebs covered everything.

Their mobile phones were deep in their rucksacks as required, to avoid the temptations that they could bring. 'I really want to get inside and take a picture,' said Ryan. 'It would have cost you 2p for five minutes, back in the day,' said Nigel.

'You could reverse charges too, but you had to call the operator, give them the number you wanted, then they rang it and asked if reverse charging was OK. If the person you were calling refused, they just put the phone down on you' he added knowingly.

'Yeah, that's like ghosting in the past, isn't it?' replied Keisha wisely.

They joked and laughed and carried on walking and just as Carol walked past at the back of the group, the phone rang. Everyone turned round and looked at the phone and Carol. 'You gonna answer it, miss?' It took a few seconds for her to make a judgment call. If someone had rung the wrong number, they might carry on trying to call the same one, not realising and wondering why no one picks up. If it was important, then she would feel guilty. So, she squeezed through the door and got inside. She found herself leaning at a strange kilter and having to support herself against the shelf. When she lifted the receiver, the static was strong, but she spoke up as clearly as she could.

'Hi, I think you've got the wrong number,' said Carol politely. 'This is a phone box.'

'No, I haven't Carol, it's you I want to talk to.' It was Tom. Carol's eyes widened more than the startled deer's, they had just passed.

'What the fuck?' she whispered very quietly.

'My name is Tom and this is really important Carol. You need to find Ed and Pat, they are on the walk, not too far behind you. Please wait for them. They will know what to do when...' The voice faded into the static and the phone went dead. Carol stood for a moment, put the phone back on the hook and carefully manoeuvred herself back into the upright position.

'Who was it, miss, what did they say?' There was no point in attempting to explain this. 'Yeah it's OK, wrong number and they said thanks for letting them know.' As the group continued on their way, Carol turned back to look at the phone. She watched as the internal light switched off and the box was plunged into darkness. Carol was pleased that she was at the back of the group, so she could mull things over. What on earth was that? As far as she could tell, the only logical explanation was that she was being followed, it was a wind up and when she got to the end, all would be revealed. Of course, Carol didn't have a clue that Tom was dead. Carol didn't have a clue what was coming. The sixth formers continued to chatter about anything and everything and Carol slowly got back into the groove of chipping in with one-liners, in response to some of their conversations as they approached the finishing line, she was thinking about what and who would be waiting for her.

Parents were coming to pick up their children, and Carol had her car on the road by the hospice. The decision was whether or not she should wait or ignore the whole thing. If these two people weren't that far behind them, then perhaps the wait wouldn't be too long. But how would she spot strangers – in the dark? She certainly wasn't going to ask every person their name. She waited with Nigel and the students until the last one had been picked up and then Nigel headed off too. Carol went back to the "sign-in" tent and walked up to the chap at the table. 'Excuse me, could you tell me if there are any groups of people called Ed and Pat on the walk?'

'What's their surname, love?'

'I'm really sorry, I don't know. I've just been told to wait for them.' The man presumed that Carol had been asked to meet them for a lift and as there wasn't much else to do, he was happy to sift through the remaining people, still not crossed out on his sheet. As he scanned the sheets, flipping the pages forwards and backwards, Carol tried not to get irritated by his lack of methodical approach. She knew she was tired and should be grateful that he was helping, *but for heaven's man*, she thought. Carol's planning was meticulous and anything less was unacceptable, especially when it came to organising groups and events. No one had the experience she did though and this man was probably just a volunteer, so she calmed herself down and remembered that she wasn't in a rush. Eventually, he rested his highlighter over Pat & Ed

Johnson. 'This might be them. Their start time was ten minutes behind you, so they must be relatively close now.'

'Thank you. Will you make sure you call me over when they sign in, if I just go and grab a cuppa from the refreshment tent, please?' The man promised and Carol went and sat down with a warm drink in her hands, thinking about what she would say to these strangers. At least she might be able to find out what the wind-up was all about.

As she sipped her tea, which was at least warm, even though it tasted like a tea bag had been merely wafted over the top of it, Carol checked her phone for messages. There was the sound of footsteps coming towards her and she looked up. 'Hello.' Smiled Pat. 'The gentlemen said you were asking for us. I'm Pat and this is Ed.' Ed smiled and waved.

'What can we do for you?'

Carol stood up. 'Oh, hi, er I'm Carol.' She was thinking rapidly about how to say what had happened, they genuinely looked like they were not in on a ruse. It was clear that her name meant nothing to them.

'Right well, look, I don't mean to be funny, but something really weird happened on the walk and, well, er, sorry I'm rambling verbally now not just physically.' Something stirred in both Pat and Ed's minds, but they didn't say anything just yet.

'Take your time love, it's OK,' offered Ed, kindly.

'Well, I was with my group and we were on that last bit of the road near Huby. There was an old telephone box by the verge.' Pat and Ed felt their stomachs churn, their separate hunches were right. Even though they didn't know the exact details, they knew what she was about to say. It was still a surprise though. 'Well it rang and because I thought it would be a wrong number, I went to answer it and tell the person on the other end, but then the man knew my name and said I had to wait for Pat and Ed, but he couldn't tell me why because the line went down. I'm not being funny honest.'

They knew Carol wasn't being funny. They knew exactly what had happened. 'Did he say who he was Carol?' asked Pat.

'Yes, Tom.' Ed and Pat looked at each other and then back at Carol. Carol didn't like that look, it unsettled her.

'Carol? Erm, do you want us to tell you what's going on now, or would you like to go home and sleep and I can call you tomorrow sometime to explain?' Carol had no idea what she was about to be told, but she was intrigued enough to not want to wait until tomorrow.

'Well after waiting around, I'd like to know now please.'

'OK,' said Ed. 'But let's just sit back down and you can absorb what we are about to tell you.'

They joined her on the wall and Carol felt very nervous, but at the same time, she was baffled. These two people who didn't seem that much older than herself, began to tell her what they had been experiencing over the past few weeks. It was the middle of the night, in a car park and Carol wasn't sure if she was now actually at home in bed and this was a highly lucid dream. Ed and Pat talked about Elinor as the ringmaster, Harry as the maker, Edie and Olivia and of course Karen. They were so serious and convincing. 'I'm in a kind of state of shock really, but you are having a laugh aren't you?' There were so many alarm bells going off in Carol's brain.

'We're really not, Carol. Look, tomorrow afternoon, we're all meeting up to discuss what we do next because we really haven't got a clue and we're clutching at straws here. How about we just have your number and then we can call you if we have any brainwaves or ideas about why Tom wants you to join us?'

There was the phrase that made Carol recoil, 'Join them.' *No way*, thought Carol. This was the hook into the cult, the weird hidden underground arm of the Women's Institute or that U3a, University of the third-age thing, she'd been hearing about.

'Look I'm really not sure, sorry.'

'Please Carol, we can meet on your terms, anywhere you like so you feel totally in control. We've all had exactly the same thoughts as you promise.' Pat was good at using her bedside manner to reassure Carol as best she could.

'The only thing I might be able to help you with.' Carol couldn't believe she was actually saying this, but Ed and Pat seemed so nice and normal. '…is that I did teach electronics, so I know my way round a circuit board.' Carol had trained in Design Technology and taught electronics for decades. It was all CNC machines, laser cutters and 3D printers now. It was coding and everything

127

else that took away the nimble requirements of manual dexterity, so she made for the school gates and never looked back.

'Perfect,' said Ed smiling warmly.

Pat took Carol's number, Carol took Pat and Ed's. Pat said she would text her tomorrow just to check in. They thanked her profusely for listening to them and offering help and said she would love the others. That made Carol think of a cult again. She said goodbye and Pat turned back to her. 'Oh, just one more thing please Carol, no one will believe a word we say, we don't believe it ourselves, so could you keep it to you yourself too for now? See what you think, but if it can stay between us, that would be very much appreciated.' Carol promised and then drove off home. Now she was even more awake and with a head swimming in bizarre tales of Ouija boards, ghosts, telephones and so many questions. Carol laughed out loud in the car. 'What the hell was that?' At least she could have lie in, but she wouldn't, she would be up at the crack of dawn completing chores, with her head buzzing.

Pat couldn't wait to tell the others about Carol and how she had been contacted by Tom. As they drove home Ed asked the question. 'So, do we think that's it now? Will there be any more people Tom wants to introduce us to, do you think?'

'Oh, I hope not, Ed. I know I'm tired from the walk, but this is exhausting me mentally too. Heaven knows what's on the cards for whatever happens now.'

'Should we see if Karen can read the tarot to predict what's going to happen next then Pat?'

'I don't know if I can cope with any more witchery in this at the moment.'

'What bit of this isn't witchery love?'

Chapter Nine – The Plan, Part 1

Edie had laid the table with all manner of afternoon tea treats. There were finger sandwiches, small slices of pork pie and a selection of crudités for the dips. There was also a chocolate cake and pile of scones with Rodda's clotted cream and some strawberry jam that she had picked up from the Allotment Spring Show the day before. Over on the sideboard, Harry had been quite reserved and there were only four bowls of little eats, but he had selected his top four.

They had warned everyone that the twins would be there too because Olivia wanted to be in on proceedings, but the girls would be off in the garden and had been told that they were going to have to occupy themselves. Olivia had loaded up some cartoons and Finding Nemo, on the iPad. If they were all fed and watered after playing out, perhaps they would be able to just surround themselves with the cushions and sit still. It was a long shot but worth trying.

Elinor arrived first. She had taken the opportunity to enjoy a longer walk round the back of the Estate up to Weardley, as it took in the whole valley and the deer and Almscliffe Crag always looked impressive. Her backpack was full of all the lists and notes she had made and more spare paper for more lists and new notes. Her pencil case was full of the best selection of pens and highlighters and she even had a block of Post-its, just in case things got really serious. Harry Gration had woken her up from her daydreaming and reminded her to get off the bus at the right stop, again. She explained that Amanda had a busy Sunday but hoped to join them by four.

Then Pat and Ed arrived, both walking slightly more slowly than usual and Ed was carrying a medium-sized cardboard box, which intrigued Edie, as she saw them walk up the path. 'Hi, come on in, what have you got there Ed?' said Harry as he greeted them at the door.

'It's a gift for you Harry, might be useful. It was an impulse buy, but we didn't want to regret not getting them.' Ed popped the box on a chair. He had clocked the feast on the table, out of the corner of his eye. He opened the top flaps and Harry leaned in to look.

'Whoah these are older than ours. Where did you get them?'

'Out at the antiques place in Helmswell.' Pat haggled. He didn't say how much they had cost him, but he said they were a bargain and Pat had got them for less than half price. 'We thought they might be useful to pull to pieces and see how they worked. Perhaps some of the innards might look familiar.' Harry looked bemused.

'That's a great idea,' said Edie, as she appeared from the kitchen. 'Now, more importantly, tea or coffee or anything else?'

131

Edie and Harry's guests were trying to steal themselves for the arrival of Olivia and her two daughters. When the doorbell went on and on, there was a palpable intake of breath and Harry opened the door. 'Gramps!' Came the double shout from the hallway and Harry appeared with a granddaughter on each arm, holding them firmly and grinning broadly as they kissed his face and played with his hair. *Clever move* thought Elinor. Nel and Erin were introduced to everybody. Their shyness would not last long. The patio door was opened and Harry released them both back into the wild and they shot off towards the treehouse. Then he closed the patio door, which three feet from the base, now had a sticker with a silhouette of a bird on it, just in case. Edie asked Pat and Ed how their midnight walk had gone.

It had taken Pat every morsel of reserve to wait until now to tell everyone about their meeting with Carol and how it came about. 'Well,' said Pat. 'I think we should sit down and Elinor, I think we will need that notepad.'

As Pat and Ed relayed the events from the small hours of the morning, their yawning occasionally got the better of them and they apologised throughout. Elinor wrote it all down and added questions as they popped into her head. Edie wanted to know what Carol looked like and Harry wanted to know if the poor woman had run off screaming, having been bamboozled by Ed and Pat appearing out of the darkness and telling her a crazy story. They settled themselves down sensibly and tried to unravel what they knew so far.

'So, it seems clear that Tom and probably George and Gracie can predict our whereabouts, when we get near a phone, at least. And they are hunting down useful people to help us. They're trying to get us to work together to try and sort this connection. But Why? Why us and why now and what's so important?'

'Well because of the dying signal, if they end up trapped and can't properly pass on, or over or exit stage left or whatever,' suggested Edie. 'That's so true Edie, when I was researching it became really obvious that for as long as the dead have been trying to contact the living, which I presume has been forever, their communication systems have come and gone too and so they have developed ways to keep in touch with the living. Somehow they have adapted at their side.' Everyone nodded with the logic of Elinor's research.

'There's nothing to say that this same kind of thing hasn't happened each time the technology has evolved though is there?' responded Edie and everyone agreed that was a very sensible suggestion. 'That perhaps in the past, for example, other people were contacted by the dead and asked to try and develop a better connection because, say, the telegraph was no longer being used.' They agreed that was a very good comeback from Edie.

'So perhaps this is really the first mass communication with individuals in their own homes because we all had phones wired and connected to a big mainframe,' added Elinor. 'Now they can't communicate to mobile phones, and their system is becoming obsolete as fewer and fewer people use it and there's not enough supply to keep it all going.'

'So, do we think that the ghosts we hear about, who are on our side are those who have been trapped forever?' Edie continued. 'Because we don't hear about our relatives haunting us, do we? It's only ever historical characters like Roman centurions in York or the blue lady at Temple Newsam. Perhaps some of the really weird things that happen like cats and dogs staring at nothing down a corridor, are just them seeing and hearing the ghosts that we miss?' Edie was on a roll. 'I think we need to go back to Karen.' Edie was not scared anymore, she was like a dog with a bone.

'Let's focus on one thing at a time as a group, or decide if we should try to follow two lines of enquiry and work in two teams,' suggested Elinor. Both suggestions were considered very sensible indeed, but no one wanted the added responsibility of being a team leader and really wanted Elinor to be the coordinator, if she was OK with that and didn't mind they would completely understand if she didn't want to do it. She did, after all, write the best notes and had the Sharpies and the Post-its. As they agreed to work on just sorting out the connection issue, Amanda knocked on the door, and had less than a minute before the saga of Carol and the next steps were being discussed. Thankfully, plates and napkins were distributed and everyone tucked into Edie's spread.

Olivia divvied up a selection of sandwiches and little eats into two Tupperware bowls. She filled two plastic drink containers, with fitted straws, and then headed out to the treehouse. "Brring, bring" went the tin can telephone. 'Hello Gramps,' Came the duet reply. 'Luncheon will be served in your cabin today; your butler service is delivering it to you now. Expect a knock at your door.' The giggles were turning into squeals. Olivia called when she was by the treehouse door. It opened and two faces popped out smiling.

'Deliveroo for two, that's you, will it do?' The girls thought that was hilarious and giggled even more as Olivia passed them their bowls and asked them what they would like to watch on the iPad. After much deliberating, Olivia chose for them but made it seem like they had both made the best choice. She retrieved the iPad from her bag and set it up inside the small room. Olivia couldn't fit herself into the space completely, so her back end just hung out of the treehouse door like it was eating her. She stretched and twisted until the iPad sat very securely on the shelf in the corner and the girls looked comfy in and amongst the cushions. She made a mental note to tell her mum and dad to take out all the cushions and vacuum them down, along with the wooden floor afterwards, or the mice would be back at the Ritz. Then she pressed play and hoped that they loved Finding Nemo.

Everyone made a point of telling Edie how gorgeous the food was, and no one refused seconds. Amanda headed up the next phase of the proceedings and tried desperately to talk and eat at the same time, with an air of decorum. Those sandwiches just hit the spot and that pork pie was gorgeous. 'So down the road from Elinor is a parade of shops, we're talking less than a quarter of a mile away, and behind them is a telephone exchange, which has been in use for decades. It looks like one of those old 1940s, 50s square, red brick ones with no details. It's now regularly got about five Open Reach vans parked out back and is surrounded by a big metal fence. I did a recce on it this morning and there is one security camera outside, looking at the gate.'

'Could we look into finding legal ways to do things before we think of breaking and entering please?' asked Ed. 'I'm all for an adventure, but, you know, explaining this one in a court of law, would have us all sectioned, wouldn't it?'

Amanda recognised the issue, but everyone was still very grateful that she had paid attention and it meant they knew more facts, which should never be underestimated. 'Won't they need a booster on their side though? I mean, we have all the different communication methods here, but they don't. They're stuck with less,' suggested Harry.

'How do we pass them something, that they can install?'

'Oh heck, I'm finding this all very wearing, is anybody else? asked Pat. Everyone sighed. Olivia chipped in.

'Look, none of this makes sense, does it?' They all nodded and muttered in agreement. They also realised that as Olivia was talking, they could grab more sandwiches or make a start on the cake and scones.

'What I mean is, it's all so preposterous and stupid, that none of it makes any sense, so don't even try to work it out or explain it. Don't even think about asking how things work. We should just try any ideas. I'm guessing that none of us have any experience of making things for the dead, so let's just have a go, suspend our disbelief and take a punt on anything.'

That was so sensible and it made them all relax a bit more. No one would have a scientific brainwave, because there couldn't possibly be one. 'Somewhere along the line,' said Edie. 'We have to accept that this is just magic and it is supernatural and we are literally mere mortals, trying to help out. I think we have already experienced something so precious, that we can't share with anyone else, but that doesn't matter does it?' Referring to communicating with the dead, Edie continued. 'I think we want to help because we hate the idea of the people; we love being trapped somewhere horrible for eternity and we also know that we could end up in the same predicament when it's our turn. I don't like the thought of me trying to contact Nel and Erin to ask for their help.'

'Well not right now, that's for sure,' chipped in Harry and everyone laughed at the thought of two five-year-olds working it all out better than they were doing right now.

'They probably would too,' said Olivia. 'Because they wouldn't have disbelief. Right now they will believe that fish can talk.'

'Brace yourselves, I've got an idea,' declared Harry and they all leaned in close. Elinor took a massive bite of her scone, cream and jam. Amanda tucked into another sandwich. Edie crunched on her crudités, Pat slurped her second cup of tea and Olivia just leaned back to check out of the patio door, all seemed quiet out there.

'We have a signal booster for our internet because it doesn't have good coverage at the back of the house, so if their system is the same, we can add boosters anywhere, depending on where we think the signal is better at being picked up. If we can't get to one exchange then we try and find another. There must be manuals about making systems to boost all kinds of signals, especially speaker systems and radio waves, it's why every house needed its own aerial for the TV, isn't it?' They all nodded, not wanting to speak with their mouths full.

'So, let's make a Frankenstein thing that seems to cover the lot.' They looked at him in awe.

'Don't look at me like that, I don't know how to build it and we don't know where to put it or what to connect it to, but at least it's a start.'

'That's brilliant,' said Elinor. 'I think that deserves another bite.' And she began to slather Rodda's over the other half of her scone.

'We need Carol, don't we?' asked Amanda to Pat. 'Can you text her now and see if we get an interest or at least a reply? As long as the comeback isn't "leave me alone I'm calling the police" we should be OK.' She crossed her fingers and spotted some egg and cress on her index finger and licked it off. Just as Pat texted Carol, Amanda dealt a blow.

'Mind you, don't forget that this won't be worth diddly squat after 2026 though, will it?' The mood changed.

'Well, it'll have to do for now, won't it?' replied Harry. Everyone agreed that it was the best they could hope for right now.

'Hi, Carol, this is Pat from the walk. Hope you got a good night's sleep. Sorry, it was a bit mad. Could we meet up, please? If so when is good for you? Would you like to meet all of us or just me and Ed again, up to you no pressure, but you really need to meet Harry. Thank you.'

Carol was up in the dales. The derelict building she had bought many years ago, was now a beautiful little two-bedroom converted home called Barn End. Its thick stone walls and Yorkshire stone roof made it a rock in the worst that a North Yorkshire winter could throw at it. When she first bought the place, there was no phone signal at all, but Carol researched where the nearest outpost was and contacted BT to see about extending the connection. It had taken months before anyone even bothered to visit and then they sucked the air in through their teeth and told her it was impossible. Carol would not give up so easily. She had calculated and planned, then she had mentioned that this was a campsite for schools completing their Duke of Edinburgh awards and in the event of emergencies, getting an ambulance could be critical. She laid it on thick, she laid on her best homemade Victoria sponge and convinced them that it would be a promotional coup to support this location getting a mast. Within a year, she had a telephone mast just behind the barn. While they were constructing and connecting it, Carol had lost count of the biscuits, cakes and cups of tea and coffee she had made the workers, but it had all been worthwhile.

She was at the kitchen window looking down the road, keeping an eye out for the next school group who would be staying over that evening at the campsite. She had an acre of land that she converted to the most appropriate site possible. Over time she had added a composting toilet block with two separate loos and sinks, an external cold tap, strong brushes on chains for boot cleaning and three bins. There was one for food waste, one for recycling and one for general and there was a separate container for glass. There was a solar-panelled roof, which generated just enough electricity to illuminate the inside. Carol had fitted that herself and was very proud when she switched on the light. The area was marked out with enough spaces for twenty tents around the perimeter and a larger mess tent or two in the middle. Over the last Summer, she had cut in and created three stone fire pits. She was in the process of finding enough tree stumps to use as seating around them. There was a three-sided and roofed shed for storing things out of the rain, two old portable barbecues on wheels and that was more than enough. She had placed an old table on the shed's decked base and was getting a selection of drinks and snacks ready to greet the tired and hopefully happy walkers. Then she caught sight of them in the distance. She calculated about fifteen more minutes before they were at the gate. Then her phone buzzed.

'Oh lord, it really wasn't a dream was it Dorothy?' she said to herself. Carol preferred a phone call to play text ping pong with conversations and called Pat straight away.

'Oh wow, Carol, thank you for getting back straight away, I wasn't expecting such a quick response. How are you?'

'It's OK, Pat, I'm fine thank you. How can I help?' She wasn't sure if she wanted to help, but that's what Carol did.

'I'm very busy until Thursday afternoon, but I can call round then if that's any good?' The others had gone quiet but could hear Carol's voice clearly as Pat held out her phone like young people do, not against her ear, like "normal" people. They all nodded at Pat. 'Yes, Thursday is great Carol. It's best if we meet at Harry and Edie's is that OK? Weardley, just near Harewood,' Carol said that would be fine. She would come that way and kill two birds with one stone and do a big shop to take back with her. Pat said she would forward the address and they agreed that two p.m., was a good time. As Carol said goodbye, everyone else said goodbye too and Carol realised that they had all been listening. She was extra pleased that she had been nice. Then she walked down to the shed and set out the portable urns of hot water, the mugs, tea, coffee, milk, sugar, a big jug of juice and a selection of nice biscuits. Carol loved her new life. What was coming next would make for a great tale sat around the campfire soon enough.

Olivia said she would go and check on the girls, the film would have finished by now, so it was a good opportunity to call it a day and head for home and then she remembered. 'Oh, bloody hell, I forgot to say, what with all this nonsense going on, Mum, Dad, I got myself a little job.' She received a call back later that same day she had visited. 'It really is just to keep me ticking over, though, it's just a cleaning job.' Olivia wasn't sure how they might react as they had said they didn't want to see her waste all that Higher education, especially as it was such an expensive waste otherwise. But Edie was still happy. If Edie had done as she was told, she wouldn't have gone for a Saturday job in a shop, she wouldn't have stayed there all those years, and she wouldn't have met Harry, had Olivia or the twins. No, as far as Edie was concerned, life is what you make it and a job's a job, regrets are pointless.

'Oh well done, Liv, when do you start and where will you be?'

'Well, the city is divided up into sections and I've opted for North Leeds, so that's anywhere in LS7, 8 and 17, which is still massive. I'll start on Wednesday, but they'll call me tomorrow to talk about a rota and shifts, as well as locations.'

'That's great love. But let us know if you need anything doing, you'll be absolutely knackered, I bet,' said Harry supportively.

Olivia was pleased and went out to the treehouse. Edie looked at the dining table, there was virtually nothing left and she smiled. She cut a couple of slices of chocolate cake, from the remaining piece, for the girls and wrapped them up in a couple of paper napkins. Elinor got her bag together and said she would get to Edie and Harry's at two p.m., on Thursday. Pat offered to pick her up and she accepted thankfully. Ed wouldn't be able to come because he was having another meeting with Joel and now felt obliged, in his role as Joel's Council guru. Amanda would be at work and was seriously contemplating "knocking off", but decided that she would be the one to be caught on CCTV out and about, so wouldn't risk it. And Olivia would now be at work. They agreed that at least it wouldn't be too outfacing for Carol if there were only four of them.

Olivia peered into the little arched treehouse window and couldn't believe what she saw. Both the girls had fallen asleep, slumped in the cushions. The iPad was asleep too. She turned away silently and went back inside. Pat, Ed, Elinor and Amanda had left and the house seemed calm. 'You have to see this,' said Olivia to her parents and stealthily they made their way to the treehouse. They took it in turns to peer at their sleeping grandchildren. Olivia was now worried that they would be grumpy if she woke them up and tried to get them organised.

'You get everything you need together and I'll sort the girls and get the iPad,' offered Harry. 'I have a little surprise up my sleeve.' On the outside of the treehouse, there was a small weatherproof plastic box. He lifted the cover and inside was the switch to the moving star lantern he had fitted the other day. He turned it on. The bulb came on straight away and shone the shapes across the walls and the girls' sleeping faces. Then the motor kicked in and the scene moved around the space, lighting up the objects and distorting the stars as they glided silently over every

143

undulation. Then he gently called their names and his two sleeping beauties woke up and stared around them in amazement. Harry beamed more than the lamp itself.

The girls slid more sedately down the slide and Harry picked them up after he had retrieved the iPad from the shelf, it had been some squeeze and stretch but it was doable. Olivia and Edie watched him carry them towards the house and they beamed too. Everyone agreed that they loved each other and said their goodbyes and the girls avoided any over-tired tantrums, at least until they were safely tucked into their car seats and half a mile down the road. It was progress.

Edie set about cleaning up the dining table and restoring order and Harry went to remove the cushions from the treehouse and tidy up. It's a good job he did. And it was a good job that the cushion covers were removable and washable.

Elinor invited Amanda in for a quick de-brief and cuppa. Amanda declined the tea and asked for one glass of wine or Prosecco or anything stronger. 'I am sloshing about with tea El and I ate too many pieces of pork pie, but God it was lush.' The rooms were dark in late afternoon and out of the corner of her eye, Amanda saw a flashing light in the study. It was the answering machine. 'El! El! You've got a message.' Amanda was overly excited. This could also be the residual sugar rush from too much cake.

'Hold your horses, it could just be the telesales buggers.' But it wasn't. Elinor pressed the button underneath the red LED showing a number one.

The signal was faint, but it was there and they could rewind it as many times as they needed to make sure they heard things correctly. 'You have a new message, message,'-click- 'Hello Elinor it's Tom. You have Carol now, that's good. You're all in it together. We're counting on you. Tell Pat that Sam was here. He said to thank her. He's not stayed though, he's passed on. Keep up the...'

The line couldn't hold the signal for long, but the answering machine had done its bit.

Chapter Ten – The Plan, Part 2

Elinor went out to meet Pat and walked towards the car. The sun was starting to have some real warmth in it now, especially in the middle of the day. She waved and smiled and got in the passenger side, suddenly feeling apprehensive. She was about to tell Pat about Tom's message and she wasn't sure who Sam was. 'Hi Elinor, ready for our next exciting instalment? Ready to meet Carol?'

'Hi, Pat, I reckon so.' Then she decided to just let Pat know straight away. She explained that Tom had left a message on the machine. 'Then he told me to tell you that he had met someone called Sam, who wanted to say thank you to you, and that he didn't stay because he had passed on. Does any of that make sense?'

Pat looked at Elinor. 'Oh, bless him.' Her eyebrows raised in sadness, but her mouth seemed to smile warmly. Elinor hadn't really understood the depth of Pat's role as a volunteer until now, or her career. As Pat told of her visit and meeting Sam at the very end of his life, the sun broke out through the clouds and the shadows receded. There and then it cemented their belief, that this was absolutely real. Davina would not knock on Elinor's door and ask her not to swear in front of a live audience. As she explained further, it reaffirmed Pat's understanding that she should carry on just helping the most needy at their most vulnerable time, offering the comfort of the next phase. Potentially, she could stop whoever it was, from being "on hold", if they could get things off their chest beforehand. 'Do you think it's a bit like asking to have a priest or a vicar?' asked Elinor. 'To atone for your sins and things?'

Pat still didn't believe in a God of any sort. 'I don't know about that, but if someone just wants to let someone know they left the washing in the machine, or to apologise for pulling up the flowers instead of the weeds, that might be more than enough. It doesn't need to be righteous, just courteous and caring, I think. If you could tell someone that it's all OK and not to fret anymore and to get on with life, you'd want to do it wouldn't you?' Elinor agreed completely and gently squeezed Pat's arm, and then they drove off to Edie and Harry's, arriving before the others.

Carol had done her big shop and placed all her freezer goods into the large cooler box she had in the back of the LandRover, she then covered it in the ice packs she had brought with her. She parked close to Edie and Harry's, but it wasn't quite two, so she waited and checked through emails and messages on her phone. She also took a good look at the row of houses and admired their incredibly well-structured gardens. Greenhouses and vegetable patches were beginning to burst with the start of this year's produce. There were small orchards and climbing frames of beans. The lawns were immaculate and the Spring flowers were beginning to really show off. There was no garden at Barn End, yet. What survived up there would have to be very hardy indeed. Although she knew she still had plans. She checked the time went to the back of the car and took out a bag and a toolbox. Harry peered out and saw her and the toolbox. He knew it was her and he couldn't wait to find out more. He called to the others that she was here.

Both Edie and Pat went to greet her. One familiar face at least. 'Hi, Carol,' called Pat, opening the front door before Carol was even close to it.

'Hi, Pat, well this is rather gorgeous isn't it?' she replied, looking round at the well-kept garden. Edie smiled proudly.

'Well, I'm only the visitor; this is all Edie and Harry's hard work.'

Edie stepped forward. 'Hi, Carol, thank you so much for giving us your time. Believe us, we wouldn't hold it against you if you ran a mile.' Carol wondered if she could run a hundred yards back to the car, that would be enough.

'It's OK, let's see what craziness this is all about eh?'

Carol was welcomed in and introduced to Harry and Elinor. There was a brief description of Amanda and Olivia too. Edie also explained that Olivia would be arriving at about four with the twins to drop them off. They would be staying overnight, so Olivia could catch up on herself and have one quiet night. Edie would be the chaperone on their trip the following day, to the Disco. Edie explained that neither of the girls had been able say "discovery" correctly, so it had been shortened and now stuck.

Then Pat asked Carol if she had any questions. 'Apart from, who are you all, really? What's this actually all about and just what shenanigans are really going on here? Apart from that, no I'm good.' They all burst out laughing and Elinor said that it was reassuring that Carol was as sceptical as they all were. They sat round the dining table, each hugging a mug of coffee or tea, and Elinor carefully moved the plate of homemade biscuits off to one side, so she could lay out her updated A1 sheet of brainstorming notes.

'Oh, now I love a good diagram,' said Carol perking up. 'It's so much easier to see the connections, like this. It really is just a visual circuit board.' They agreed that it was a very good analogy.

Elinor talked through the events so far and Carol could tell she had also been a teacher. She was a natural storyteller and highly believable. As they chipped in and added their specific contributions, Carol was being sucked in. She knew it too. They were so down to earth about it all. 'I'm not being funny, but you are asking me to believe in the darn right ridiculous aren't you?'

'Yes,' they said in unison.

'Carol, you could have just thought that phone call from Tom was a scam, right there. You could have put down that phone, walked away and never waited to see who would appear, let alone, come and find you. For whatever reason, you waited. Your curiosity got the better of you and now here you are,' said Harry, rather sagely.

'You also chose to come here today and you know you can just get up and go, but we really hope that you don't. We really want your help and we can't prove to you a single thing that makes this believable.'

'Bloody hell, this is nuts, isn't it? But in for a penny in for a pound, *eh?*' There was a look of relief on all their faces.

Harry explained that they wanted to make a booster of some sort that would help them get a better signal for the phone lines. They knew it wouldn't last, but something to concentrate more electricity would be a start. Carol opened her bag and took out a manual, so Edie went over to the sideboard and pulled out Edmunson's catalogue that she'd brought down from the loft. Carol took one look at it and her eyes lit up. 'Oh, now you're talking, this is a relic and a half, where did you get this?' How Edie and Harry met, was one of the loveliest stories that Pat, Elinor and Carol had heard and Harry squeezed Edie's waist and smiled at her. 'This will be really useful,' said Carol getting back on track. 'Sometimes when you repair something that's old, you have to find the right bits from the right age. You can't stick in a modern version. All the amperage and wattage are different.' Harry knew what she meant, the others just nodded. Carol flicked from her manual and cross-referenced to the Edmunson's catalogue, then drew the most amazing diagram of a potential circuit board with arrows and names and even started highlighting key aspects. Elinor praised the clarity of drawing as well as layout for understanding. She guessed that Carol had also been a teacher. They were getting an excellent class lesson in electronics.

Between more drinks and demolishing the biscuits, the group realised they were planning to make something that had never really existed and they didn't really have a clue where they needed to put it. Carol had explained how complicated it had been to get the signal up at Barn End. They hoped it wouldn't take quite so long. She had rummaged through the toolbox and selected all the items that would be useful. 'I need to get hold of all of these bits, sooner rather than later really,' said Carol, pointing to the very long list she had written down. 'I'm going away in two weeks to France.'

'We'd best get a move on then,' said Harry looking at the sheet. Then he disappeared off to the shed where he kept all his work equipment and came back with some more pieces of the jigsaw. 'We could also do with one of these beauties.' Carol pointed to a strange looking object in the catalogue called a Fleming insulator. 'Rare as hen's teeth, these are, but if we can't find one, then we have to try another route even more Heath Robinson than this already is.' There were lots of interestingly shaped insulators on the page, but Carol thought that only a possible two would work. These ones were small and had an electromagnet inside. This was the safety valve so that all the power created by the copper wire and magnets, wouldn't just overheat and catch fire. None of them wanted that on their conscience. She drew a big arrow on a Post-it note and stuck it facing the right object. It looked like a twister lollipop and was about the same size, but made of ceramic with a brown glaze and two metal connectors at either end. 'I am, of course, clutching at straws here and I think I'm just making it all up as I go along. It could be total bollocks,' she said honestly, looking at them all and Harry in particular. They burst out laughing.

'There's a logic to it though, Carol,' Harry said supportively and he knew he couldn't have suggested any better. The others agreed wholeheartedly, that Carol was their best shot.

The doorbell rang for far too long and Edie said out loud, 'Brace positions, everyone.' Then into the room ran Nel and Erin beaming and excited. After a big hug from their Gran and Gramps, they saw Carol at the table and her toolbox on the floor and were instantly interested. Carol was introduced to Olivia and then the girls. 'What's in the box?' asked Nel.

'All my fun things,' replied Carol. 'Would you like to see what's in here?'

'Yes please,' they both blurted out quickly. Carol moved over to the space on the floor near the patio doors. And got out a large plastic pot full of resistors and capacitors, transformers and other small items. The colours and stripes made them seem like sweets or coloured beads and the girls' eyes lit up. Olivia hugged her mum and dad, got the girls' drinks from her bag and took them over.

'Keep them occupied for as long as you can,' begged Olivia, only half joking.

'Right, girls. In this pot, we need to find four of these, and she held up a resistor, they have to be the same colour and have the same stripes, so this is a matching game.' Everything was the perfect size for small fingers. 'If you find them, put them in this pot please.' She poured out the contents of the pot into the lid of the opened toolbox and watched the twins wade in. They were engrossed in their hunt. Little fingers picking through the little jewels.

'Lock the door, Edie, we're keeping Carol,' called Harry beaming. Carol laughed too and then hoped it was just a joke, after all, she was outnumbered. Then she laughed again. 'Oh, I've been practising with my nieces and nephews for years.' Olivia talked about the cocktail stick and berries trick, to slow them down and everyone remembered being given half a pomegranate and a pin to eat the seeds with. Olivia took two plastic plates of snacks over to the girls, and then told Carol that she may find snacks in her toolbox later.

The discussion continued at the table. Perhaps they could position the booster somewhere close, perhaps one of those green boxes on the ends of streets, that have all the wires in them. There were hundreds of those to choose from, and they seemed to be everywhere. They knew that they were jumping the gun a little, but that forward planning would help to avoid delays. The meeting was

153

rounding up and Elinor and Pat asked Olivia about how she had found her first two days in her new job. It had been more tiring than expected, but Olivia had been surprised by how much more technical and efficient it had been. She had done two shifts at the same offices so the second day was easier when she knew how long things would take. Carol asked what the company was called. 'CCC, Commercial Cleaning Company, they just do business premises and council work, nothing domestic.' Carol thought she remembered seeing the vans out and about. Then Elinor asked the obvious question. 'Do you think they might clean the BT exchange?'

'I'll have a look on the sheet next week,' said Olivia and everyone thought that was a good idea, but no one should jeopardise their jobs doing anything illegal, especially when they had only just started.

Ed and Amanda would need updating on today's proceedings and Pat and Elinor said they would talk through everything as soon as possible, this evening. The plan was for Harry to get back to Carol as soon as he had got hold of as many parts as he could locate. Then Carol would come back around and they would build it together here. Edie made a point of saying it would happen in the shed, not on her dining table. They probably couldn't get the elusive Fleming insulator, so if they had to cobble something together, it could get very difficult. As everything was difficult, they agreed to take it one step at a time. Carol gave them the dates for when she was away and also her commitment to the campsite bookings, then went back to the girls and her toolbox. 'Oh, my goodness, you legends!' exclaimed Carol, over effusively. 'You two are incredible, you are proper explorers and discoverers.' The girls squealed in delight. They had found six of the resistors and Carol had only asked for four. 'I bet you two could find a needle in a haystack, couldn't you?' They both yelled back, "yeah", without a clue what that meant. Then Carol spotted the snacks, on every shelf of the toolbox. She would need to clean that out sharpish, so the metals didn't rust and oxidise.

Olivia was the last to leave. She brought out the girls' overnight bag with their clothes for tomorrow as well as their pyjamas and teddies. Then she gave them both a massive hug and lots of kisses. There were two more very grateful hugs for her mum and dad and she headed off home for a quiet night to actually relax and hope for a good night's sleep too.

Harry settled the girls down at the dining table and Nel asked what the big book was. Harry tried to explain, but it was the most boring book ever. Erin and Nel looked at the black-and-white photographs and illustrations. Nel looked at the big arrow on the -Post-it note and where it was pointing. 'What's this, gramps?'

'That is a very very special thing, Nel.'

'Why?'

'Well, it is so important that it could be magic.' Harry felt there was no need to try and explain the intricacies of a Fleming insulator or what it did.'

'It's swirly,' she replied and traced her fingers over the shape and looked at it intensely. It reminded her of a lollipop she liked. Erin leaned in to see what the fuss was about.

She gave a little sigh that intimated it was very boring. 'What's for tea?'

After eating, the girls were allowed half an hour in the treehouse with the magic star lamp on, then it was time for a bath, then a bedtime story, and then lights out. Every stage was like trying to catch wriggling eels. Edie and Harry played dutiful grandparents and looked forward to tomorrow afternoon when Olivia would be coming to pick them back up. They knew their time together was precious though and allowed themselves to play and be silly too, but they were exhausted.

Chapter Eleven – The Surprise

Edie was up earlier than usual. She had laid out the twins' clothes for the day and made them their packed lunches and snacks. There was an iced bun for each of them with a smiley face on. One said Erin and the other said Nel. It would make the girls very happy when they opened their lunch boxes and would make their classmates very envious. She packed the boxes into their little backpacks. One had Nemo on it and the other had Dory. She had been down the middle aisle at Lidl and couldn't resist, not for that price. Getting them both up, cleaned, dressed and fed, took both of their efforts. Harry was more than happy to give them a massive hug and squeeze and wave them off from the gate. Edie was going to be with them all day on their trip along with twenty others. She readied herself for the task ahead and reminded herself that she did offer to be the parental support.

Edie looked on in awe at the staff working their magic with what looked like a sea of squirming gerbils in the playground. There were umpteen backpacks all with the same designs of Thomas, Paw Patrol, Spiderman, Lego and far too many pink unicorns and rainbows. She hoped that everyone's names were written inside. Making sure that every one of them had been to the loo reminded her of that night at Karen's. The twenty-minute coach journey would seem interminable. Regulation mini hi-vis vests were placed over every child and adult versions were placed over every accompanying member of staff. Off they went and Edie watched her granddaughters interact with the other children and the teachers. They were bold and eager and keen to talk. They looked happy and full of life and Edie was very proud.

Edie watched as the adults took control of the group. She wanted, and needed, pointers and would watch the tips and tricks for dealing with her easily distracted, overly jiggly, bundles of love. The way the teachers and staff spoke to the children was metered, calm, authoritative, but also kind. They repeated everything they said, at least twice. They spotted the distracted and reined them back in. They were worth their weight in gold. The children were lined up in pairs and Edie was intrigued to see that the twins had selected their other friends to partner up with and then saw them wave at each other, cheekily. They were marched inside and into the education room, where they jettisoned all their backpacks into a mountain of bright-coloured fabrics and plastics. The very nice members of staff at the Discovery Centre also spoke with experience. They knew this was a tough crowd and that the children's attention span would only give them so long to tell them some facts. Firstly, don't touch anything. Although they would be allowed to touch certain things later. That would confuse the majority. Secondly, absolutely no running, at all, anywhere and thirdly, don't go wandering off. Stay together and make sure you can see an adult at all times. That seemed to be the holy trinity of rules for any trip. They weren't crossing any roads, so at least that was one hazard they didn't have to remember.

The children were told that they were going on an adventure and had to look out for certain things around the centre. It was all about observation and paying attention, and behaviour and damage limitation as far as the accompanying staff were concerned. Erin and Nel had been before of course, so they were on the lookout for all their favourites, the big bear and the old-fashioned toys. The place was vast. Huge shelving that went up into the rafters, created steep-sided corridors like canyons, especially from the eye level of these five and six-year-olds. It was more like a huge shop than a museum. Taxidermied faces looked out through glass eyes on the lower shelving and a couple of children screamed and cried and had to be taken to one side and told that they wouldn't be eaten. Various hands came out from sleeves and stealthily tried to touch objects and boxes down the rows. Erin pointed to the old telephone and Edie smiled as one of the others batted her hand away. Here, there were Trimphones and wall phones, telegraph machines and an original Apple Mackintosh. On the lower shelf was a box of computer mice and keyboards, the very first electric typewriters and a Petite typewriter that came in its own carry case. Edie had one of those as a child. There were boxes of electronic items too. It was an abattoir of telephones and the innards looked like guts and offal of wires and cables and batteries and transistors.

The children however had turned away from the lower items. Behind the teachers was a huge elephant skull and a stuffed bear. The member staff from the centre asked them all to sit down so he could tell them a story. After the usual kerfuffle, legs were crossed and arms were folded. The teachers demonstrated fingers on lips, and they gradually went quiet. He weaved them a tale of travel and adventure and discovery and they hung off his every word. As he told the story, his colleague passed him objects and items to bring his tale to life and all the children stared, bewitched. They "oohed" in all the right places and they "aahed" in all the right places. They giggled and clapped on cue. The group sat on the floor in the biggest space available, just away from shelving and boxes of sundries, tucked underneath on the floor. Even this was planned so that at this location there was nothing of value anywhere close. The storyteller had the children and the adults, in the palm of his hand and they all watched him and the parade of objects. Nel was sat at the very back, nearest the huge corner of one aisle. She looked up and the metal post seemed to go on forever up into the roof, she looked around intently, peering into boxes just behind her and through the shelving across to other aisles. *So many things to see,* she thought to herself. So many things she wanted to touch. Sat on the floor, she felt very small indeed.

No trip for this age group would last more than a morning, because as much as they couldn't concentrate for longer, the adults also needed a break, so the final part was to just enjoy their lunch in the education room and play with some of the objects that had been brought out especially for them to handle. The big old black telephone that Erin and Nel had played with before, was one of the items, along with spinning tops and pull-along wooden toys, but nothing too noisy.

The table tops became awash with plastic tuck boxes, cling film, foil and drink bottles. Erin ran up to her grandmother. 'Thank you for my face bun, it was yummy.' Erin rubbed her belly and licked her lips. Then a huge bin liner appeared and was wafted over the table. The adults made sure that the museum items, tuck boxes and drinking bottles didn't end up in there along with the rubbish and leftovers. Then they swept the floors and retrieved various shoes and one pair of trousers. Although it was easy knowing who they belonged to.

After the children had all said thank you to their hosts, very loudly, they were herded out and back onto the coach. Edie sat at the back with two other parents, who looked just as frazzled as she felt.

Harry had been preparing dinner all day. First, he had selected a recipe from the Good Food Guide, then gone to buy the ingredients that were not in the cupboards or fridge at home. Olivia would be staying for tea too and the twins needed to be able to eat the same food. He was not having them being picky. It was a Cumberland sausage shepherd's pie and he was proud of it. The whole house smelt warm and tasty, as it bubbled away in the oven, waiting for the family to arrive.

He heard the key in the door and then the clattering footsteps, so he knelt down ready, open-armed. 'Gramps!' they shouted, as he squeezed them together. He asked them about their day as Edie offloaded their backpacks onto the kitchen table. 'Did you have fun at the Disco today?' The experience that Edie had seen unfold throughout the morning, seemed to not be the same as the twins. They described Gran's face buns, some of the objects, the big bear and Nerin, taking off his trousers at dinner time. They did remember story time though and tried to retell it to their Granddad. It was very much lost in translation but he listened and he "oohed" in all the right places and "aahed" in all the right places.

There was enough time for them to go and play in the treehouse and off they shot.

Edie relayed the adult version of events. Nerin had indeed taken off his trousers, and luckily, he had been spotted in the nick of time and whisked off to the toilet. That could have been horrendous. She began to empty the girls' backpacks of their packed lunch boxes, and colouring sheets and then she felt something in Nel's bag. Nel had opted for Dory. She wasn't sure what on earth it was. About the size of the head of a round brush, cold and hard and quite weighty, she pulled it out in front of Harry. 'Holy fuck! I mean shit, er sorry. Harry.' She held it out to him. The catalogue was still on the table open on the page with the Post-it note stuck to it. Edie rolled the Fleming insulator from the palm of her hand over onto the catalogue and it rolled to a stop in between the pages. 'Oh Nel, you observant little thief.'

'Eagle-eye Nellie, eh? Bloody hell she's clever'

'Yes, but, Harry? How do we tell her off for this?' worried Edie.

'Let's wait til Liv comes and we'll ask her what to do. She is Mum, after all.'

Nel had paid attention, very close attention. This object looked like a twister lollipop. The picture in the catalogue was clear and distinctive and she had looked at its unusual shape and listened to her grandfather describe it. Gramps said it was special and magic and they said they needed one. As the group listened to their story, Nel looked around her. Inside a box not too far away, she spotted a similar object to the thing she had seen in the book. She squeezed her arm into the box and felt around until her fingers agreed with her mind's eye that they had landed on the right object. She did not ask if she could have it because she knew she would not have been allowed. They had been told not to touch anything. She knew what she was doing was wrong, but she took it from that box of bits, put it in her pocket and was careful to do it when everyone was looking the other way. When she got back to the education room, she put it in the bottom of her backpack when she grabbed her lunch and totally forgot about it. She was then distracted by face buns and Nerin's trousers.

Olivia was mortified. 'She's never done anything like this before, ever.'

'Then she may never do anything like this again,' offered Edie.

'I'm going to take the blame for this,' said Harry. 'She thought she was helping her Gramps. I said we needed one and she found the magic piece we were after and she took it. She did it because she thought making us happy was more important than stealing. That's the mind of a five-year-old, well she's nearly six, but you know what I mean. We can't second guess everything they interpret and, well, I only think she should be told off lightly.'

'I agree,' added Edie. 'Can't we just say, that she must never ever steal again, even if one of us really wants something?'

'Yes, of course, we can, Mum, but what if she tells someone that she took something, and we've turned a blind eye?'

'I'm not sure Liv, it's your call, we both feel guilty enough as it is.' Olivia was in a dilemma. 'What has this weirdness done to us? We've contemplated breaking into a building and now one of my five-year-old daughters is stealing to order.'

And then she burst out laughing. 'Holy crap, am I raising the Kray twins or something? What's Erin's next move? To outdo her sister by hot wiring a car and using it as a getaway vehicle for Nel's next bank heist?' Edie and Harry both cracked and the three of them laughed loud and long. The girls came back inside and wanted some cake and saw their grown-ups laughing hysterically. They both grinned and ran to their mum to ask for their promised treat.

'Right listen up you two, I need to tell you something.' Olivia took the girls into the sitting room. She played it calm and she made sure that Erin knew she was not in trouble at all. She made it clear that Nel wasn't in trouble either, but that they were old enough to know what was right and wrong. 'You will both be six very soon and that means that if you want anything, even if you think it will be a nice surprise for someone, you always have to come and ask either me, Gramps, or Gran. Do you both understand?' Erin didn't have a clue where this had all come from but just said yes quickly because she wanted cake. Nel looked at her mum a bit longer, and her bottom lip started to tremble.

'Yes, Mum,' she said quietly. 'Good that's all sorted then, now let's go and see if Gran will give us some cake to take home too. I would like a massive piece.' Nel hugged her mum and Erin was already out of the door heading for the cake.

Harry took a photo of the Fleming insulator and texted it to Carol. Underneath it, he wrote, *'Happy Christmas!'* It didn't take long for Carol to reply.

'Where the hell did you get that?' Harry replied. *'I'm afraid I can't tell you that Carol, but let's just say, I know people.'*

Chapter Twelve – The Boost

Harry had edited down the list of remaining parts needed and Elinor had copied it and forwarded it to Amanda. *'Any chance you can see if there's any old electronics equipment down in DT?'* It was a long shot. When Carol had left her school, they threw out everything. So much valuable and useful equipment. It was no one's job to try and sell anything on eBay or see if another school or college could use the resources. So a board member of staff just threw it all in the skip. All her organised trays and boxes. All her neat wires and alphabetised pieces of circuitry were dumped.

Amanda hadn't been down to the DT department for the best part of ten years. The school was old and had only been updated in certain areas, DT was not one of them. New equipment had come and gone, depending on the government's latest directive. The old electronics kit had been mothballed along with the collection of wood saws, planes and hand drills. Amanda didn't know if there was anything left, but she would go and ask, so she headed down the corridor and hunted out the technician's office, looking for Russell. Russell had worked as a technician there for a few years, but she had hardly ever seen him. The DT lot had their own kettle and rarely came up to the staff room for breaks. She was ready for the charm offensive.

Russell was trying to fix something that was wedged firmly in a vice. 'Hi, Russell.'

'Hello, Amanda,' he said puzzled. He hardly ever got visitors.

'What can I do for you?' Any visitors always wanted something.

'Well I have a request that you can say no to straight away, because you might not have any, but if you do, could I have some and if so, I'm willing to pay for them.'

'Er, well that's an interesting way to start,' he said chuckling.

'I've got a list of some old electronics stuff that I need for someone.' She handed over a piece of paper and he scanned down.

'Crikey now you're asking. Who's it for? Father Time?'

'Ha yes, er no. They're trying to fix something, I haven't got a clue, but it's old so they need old kit you see.' That made sense to Russell and he gestured Amanda to the corner of the workshop.

'Follow me. Let's open the vaults, shall we?' They headed over to a stock cupboard and Russell sighed when he switched on the light. Behind the cobwebbed tenon saws and long panel saws, was a wall unit of small drawers. Each drawer was named with its contents and his eyes moved from the piece of paper and back again. 'Let's see. Could you pass me that empty glass jar there please?'

Amanda grabbed the old Rose's lime marmalade jar and Russell started to add things to it. As he looked inside boxes and pulled things out from the back of shelves, they talked of how sad it was to see the loss of making and sawing, hammering and drilling. Everything was at the press of a button now, the fun was gone. Everything was too crisp, there was no need for rasps and files and sandpaper. They laughed about the lack of accidents, cuts, burns and bruises.

'That's progress for you,' tutted Russell as he rolled his eyes, jokingly.

'Well I think that's as much as I have, Amanda, hope that'll do for your friend.' She was incredibly grateful and as they turned, Russell slipped on something and fell back on some packaging, crumpling himself into a corner. She grabbed his hand for a lift back up.

'You really should get out of here more you know.'

'Aye, that much I know.'

'Thanks again, Russ,' she called back smiling as she went.

'No problem, don't leave it so long next time,' he replied smiling, then started to sort through the things he had knocked over.

Amanda had taken the pieces and the list back to Elinor and Pat had come to collect the box of bits and then drove it to Harry. Carol had been called and Harry had cleared the work bench in the shed ready. Carol's drawing was pinned up on the wall and all the pieces were laid out and labelled where necessary. There was wire cabling, various screws, a board for putting everything on, his favourite soldering iron and the Fleming insulator was sat right in the middle. There was spare paper, his draughting pencil and a rubber.

Edie was organising food in the kitchen and the clouds had turned quite heavy and sinister, like there was an imminent downpour coming. There was that unusual light where the sky blackened but the foreground was still highlighted by the strong daylight. Then the sun disappeared and the heavens opened. When Carol arrived, she ran for the door and noted that yes, if needs be, she could run a hundred yards to escape something. Edie quickly showed her to the shed and said she would be over with sandwiches and drinks very soon. Harry made room for her at the bench and Edie said she would leave them to it.

Harry never really got to talk shop at home, Edie's interest had been work-related and not all-consuming like for Harry. Chatting with other electricians and discussing complicated jobs had always been enjoyable. Stopping potential fire hazards and electrocutions from shoddy bodge-it-and-scarper fly-by-nights, had always made him feel like a superhero; flying in and saving the day. In his own simple way of course and his superhero outfit was his Dickies overalls with external pockets, knee pads and his electronic screwdriver. Now he was sat next to Carol who knew her electronic onions and more besides. They talked through all the potential options and issues. They drew more diagrams and made copious notes. They laid out all the pieces onto paper and drew round them and then used different coloured pens to rethink the wiring. Harry was in his element. Once the kettle had boiled, Edie made up their drinks, organised the sandwiches and biscuits onto a tray and headed out. 'Knock, knock, 'she called loudly, having no spare hand to open the door. Carol opened it quickly and took the tray.

'Oh wow, look at this spread. Thank you, Edie. I'm normally the one doing the baking, so I'm just being spoiled rotten here and I do need to ask you for some recipes, if you'd care to share?' Edie said of course and asked which ones in particular. Carol had been keeping a list and surprised Edie when she rattled off her favourite top three. Edie smiled proudly and headed back to the kitchen to write them up.

There was a distant rumble of thunder and Edie stared out into the garden towards the shed. The rain was still coming down and the dark and gloomy sky seemed even heavier. She wondered if that's why they called it a leaden sky. The shed window was the brightest element in her view and she saw Harry and Carol deep in their work. It was like watching Dr Frankenstein and Igor building their machinery to wake the monster. She snorted out loud, having just imagined Harry as Igor, lisping "Yeth mathster" to Carol's Doctor. Then she felt a tad guilty, but not that much.

However, the actual goings-on inside the shed were completely different. Because of the tight space, Carol had splashed coffee and there had been a frantic mopping up.

Bits of sandwich filling had got lodged between the first bit of soldering work and suddenly egg and cress seemed evil. Then Harry had to get the dust buster from its wall-mounted charging station and vacuum up all the biscuit crumbs that seemed to be in everything. The well-oiled machine was a tad squeaky in these conditions, but slowly and surely things were being screwed, glued and soldered in place. The Fleming insulator had to be raised off the board and clipped into place. It became the hardest part of the process, along with fitting the two giant crocodile clips at either end, so they could connect it to – well whatever seemed like the most appropriate thing, when it was time to do so.

On the bench in front of them was now an A4-sized electronic circuit board. Currently, it didn't do anything. Carol wanted to make it smaller, but Harry said they needed old kit. Old capacitors were huge. The transistors were the most important components, and again, the older the bigger and they had six of those. They had checked that a charge could work through it and that was as much as they could do. Perhaps it would never work, but for now, Carol and Harry had made a thing and they were very proud of it. They were as proud as Erin and Nel when they made something extra big out of their mum's old Stickle bricks. Harry hoped that it was more useful than a Stickle brick sculpture, no matter how beautiful it looked. The rain had subsided and they tidied up the small pieces of wire and metal and broken mishaps. The bench was neat and tidy and the tools were all back where they came from.

Harry took a punt that wasn't too big to bring inside the house. The boy in him wanted Edie to be proud and say well done for what they had both made. So they carried it in. Edie saw it coming and put an old towel down first. She did not want anything to scratch the woodwork. She never did manage to get those deep fork marks out from one of Erin's tantrums at the dinner table. As much as they tried to explain to her, what they had made, no one would really know if it worked, until they tried it out.

'Well it looks impressive,' said Edie positively. 'Now we need to decide where to put it, hope we can put it somewhere without being arrested and then we need to let Gracie, George and Tom know we're ready.'

'Yeah, no worries eh?' Laughed Carol. They both looked at her. 'That look says I have to help you fit it Harry, doesn't it?'

'Well if you don't mind Carol?'

Harry and Edie said goodbye to Carol then Edie reminded her to let her know if the cranberry biscuits were a success. Carol promised and said she would be in touch. They both sat down at the table and stared at the strange booster mother board that was in front of them. It was quiet now. The stormy weather had passed and the late afternoon sun was cutting through low on the horizon, casting long shadows across the back garden. The stillness was calming and a blackbird chirped its dusk-time tune. Harry lowered his head to look at the circuit board from a more horizontal angle and in his mind's eye, it became a city of buildings and streets criss crossing each other. *Would it work?* He thought to himself. The phone on the sideboard suddenly rang. 'Jesus H Christ!' yelled Edie. Harry leant over and opened the bottom cupboard door as quickly as he could, only just managing to steady himself on the chair. The ringing was even louder until he lifted the receiver. The static was now extreme. Amongst the white noise, he heard Gracie.

'Well done, Harry love, thank you.'

'Mam, Mam, I love you.' He wasn't going to forget to say it this time.

'I love you too. Get it connected Harry, as soon as you can, we haven't got long.'

'I know, Mam, I will. Where do we put it?' There was silence once more. Edie came round to his side of the table.

'Oh love, you've done your best.' Then she kissed his head and rubbed his back. Harry put the receiver back on the hook and closed the cupboard door. He groaned with sadness.

'This is so hard Edie. One minute I'm enjoying making something and the next I'm remembering what it's for and it's all a bit overwhelming.'

'I understand love, but I wonder how many people get to tell their mums that they love them, one more time, when they thought it was too late, eh?'

The news had been spread that the "thing" had been built and was ready. Explaining how they had managed to find the Fleming insulator had caused lots of laughter and even Olivia had lightened up about it. Everyone agreed that in her misguided way, Nel had shown an incredible level of cognitive development, which would serve her very well as she grew up. Her nimble fingers and art of misdirection skills could lead to a career as a magician too. Elinor needed to co-ordinate some kind of plan to get this thing attached to something useful, and quickly. So she decided to go for a walk and she tried not to look suspicious.

As she closed her front door, Elinor looked at her clipboard. On it was an A4 print out of the local area, taken from Google maps. Just opposite was the first green metal junction box. She put a cross on the map. She worked out a route and went for a walk. They were everywhere. As she got closer to the BT exchange, she decided to take a walk around the back of the shops to where the entrance gate was. If anyone asked what she was doing, she was going to have to think on her feet. The entrances to the flats that were above the shops were here too. Story number one could be deciding if she could live somewhere like this. If she was peering through the high metal gates, then she would just say she was a nosy woman, who had always been intrigued by the building. She was fifty-seven after all, who wouldn't believe her just having a poke about? Story number two hadn't come to her yet, but if she sounded a little mad, perhaps people would leave her alone. Then she realised that all she would need to do was tell the truth. Everyone would just think she was mad. She chuckled to herself and carried on. There was no way possible to get in without being invited. Elinor strolled past the exchange. By the time she had crossed every street on the map, she had twelve of the boxes marked. She lifted the strong clip, put the top sheet at the bottom and looked at the next map. This one included the entrance to the local woods on the other side of the exchange. It was a steepish drop, but there was a very narrow path.

On she went, and then there it was. Covered in graffiti, overgrown with bracken and nettles, was a very old concrete junction box, bigger than the newer green ones. It looked like it hadn't been touched for a very long time. She was not dressed for off-roading of any kind but decided to take a closer look. Even the graffiti was old, although she completely agreed with the sentiments about Thatcher. Elinor could see the two front panel doors, with a big metal plate across them and a rusted padlocked chain that looked like it hadn't been opened in at least twenty years. Elinor drew a big "X" on the map. The ivy, weeds and ferns looked like they were holding it upright, to stop it from sliding down the wooded slope. Squashed at the back were bracken and blackberry branches. She wrote it all down, took photos and crossed her fingers that this might do. Then she decided to do one more thing. She leant across the nettles and thorns and put her hand onto the surface. Elinor could feel the "hum". She was a bee, back at Kew Gardens. The noise and machinery vibrated the concrete casing and Elinor could feel it in her finger tips. There was the faintest sound and she felt she was back in the pool, feeling the bone conducting noises.

Back in her kitchen, Elinor scrolled through the pictures she had taken and then texted everyone.

'I think this one might work. It's right behind the exchange. A bit out of the way, not recently listed and it could be done at night. What do we think? Harry? Carol?'

Then she added the photos and a picture of the map with the big X on it and the exchange highlighted too. The replies came in quickly and everyone agreed that even though this was a shot in the dark they should go for it. Harry would liaise with Carol. Ed said they should wear black from head to toe. Pat said she would knit them balaclavas. Then Ed texted they could just wear tights over their heads. Harry replied that his eyesight was bad enough in daylight. Carol chipped in, *'Thunderbirds are go.'*

And Ed replied, *'More like Saga Ninjas.'*

Chapter Thirteen – Best Laid Plan

Carol and Harry made a plan. They had studied Elinor's photos and discussed all the equipment they needed to have with them. Harry loved the idea of "tooling up". Carol loved the idea of seeing Harry, tooled up. She knew that she looked ridiculous and he would too. The pair of them were going to look like a comedy double act. Harry's Dickies overalls were grey and black so that was good enough. He had a black fleece, gloves and hat. Carol had a selection of black clothes to choose from and was good to go. Her past life as a Goth hadn't quite left her wardrobe. Into Harry's tool bag went the big pair of bolt cutters. If these didn't work, the game was over. Then he added a crowbar because the doors were very likely to be seized shut. He had his head torch, a myriad of wrenches, electrical mains testing screwdrivers – he was not going to electrocute himself ever again – and lots of electric tape and duct tape. Carol also had her head torch, snips, pliers, spare wires and adhesive copper tape. As Elinor only lived round the corner, they made that base camp. Edie said that was good as they could use the loo before and after. Carol was going to be driving all the way back to Barn End, so she was very pleased with the suggestion.

Edie gave Harry a massive hug. 'Just do your best Harry and don't get caught. God knows what I'll say to the police. Yes, it's OK, I know my husband is playing ninja dress up in the woods with another woman.' Harry laughed.

'Oh God, I've tried not to think about that.' Olivia had texted too and Pat and Ed had told Elinor to wish them both good luck. It wasn't a bank heist, but it might as well have been.

'Right well we can't let this night go unrecorded, so stand there.' Edie directed Harry to hold the motherboard, facing outward, so she could see all the bits. He had his tool bag down by his feet and he was as proud as punch, as if he was holding another grandchild.

'Say Wensleydale.' Harry beamed and Edie took the photo on her phone. She kissed him one more time and sent him on his way.

There was no moon and heavy cloud, so even though the evening light seemed to linger, it was dark in the woods by nine. They convened at Elinor's and prepared for their nighttime manoeuvres. Carol placed their homemade motherboard into her holdall and Elinor tried to nonchalantly walk with them to the site, before leaving them to get on with it. 'Don't forget to keep letting us know what's happening, especially if you need anything. And text me when you're on your way back, OK?' They promised they would and disappeared into the undergrowth.

Where the very narrow path had been previously disturbed by Elinor, it was clear not much else came this way. They knew they had to keep low and quiet, even if that seemed like a difficult task at first. 'I've got the theme tune for Mission Impossible going round my head now,' said Harry.

'Don't! If we start laughing we're bound to be heard. Or I'll throw my head back laughing and the beam from my head light will arouse suspicion, like a search light beaming up from the woods.' As they moved closer, Carol got herself caught up in the large thorns of the closest branch.

'Bloody hell, I'm already snagged.' Harry tried to grab her arm and lift up the branch, but slipped forwards and his face went straight into his tool bag. Carol snorted too loudly.

'*Shhh* – fuck's sake, sorry.' They held it together, just, trying desperately to avoid a fit of the giggles.

'Breathe man, breathe.'

'Christ, now all I can hear in the theme from Laurel and Hardy.'

'Stop it!'

Their head torches scanned the front of the big old concrete slab junction box. Firstly they knew they had to get to the chains. 'I suppose we just go for it, what do you reckon Carol?' pondered Harry surveying the rusty padlock.

'Nothing else we can do Harry, but let's see if we can pull back all this bracken and ivy. It would be good if we could put it back over when we're done, so it doesn't look too obvious that we've been here.' They went for the middle and tried to yank everything over to the left so that Harry was in the best position for using the cutters. Carol got caught again but decided she might as well stay where she was and be a form of Velcro until Harry had cut through. He positioned the cutters across the chain first. They had a good ratchet system and the blades went through easily. Mostly due to rusty and weakened metal. Now he just had to get through the padlock. Trying to get a purchase was the hardest part, so eventually he leant into the long handles, putting his body weight against it. Carol offered as much encouragement as she could, whilst at the same time, knowing it really was just down to Harry's brute strength. Eventually with much subdued huffing and grunting, the blades went through and the padlock fell.

We have cut through the chains and padlock, texted Carol to Elinor. A thumbs-up emoji appeared almost instantly. Carol scraped at the ground below the doors to try and remove the soil and debris that would wedge the wood from opening. Harry got the crowbar and now things moved quicker. 'Nice work Stan,' said Carol.

'Right back at you, Oli,' replied Harry. They grabbed a door each and pulled. It may as well have been the crown jewels they saw.

'Holy moly, look at this thing!' beamed Harry with a sense of awe. 'This won't have been seen since the day it was padlocked and I wonder how long that is?'

'Well it's quite something isn't it Harry? Look at the size of all the capacitors!' Harry and Carol were in nerdy electrical heaven. They pointed and questioned and admired and wondered.

'I suppose we should look at where our mother should go now then *eh?*' suggested Carol. The options were limited. Their A4 board could only fit in two spots if they wanted the doors to close. As they turned it every which way, they scraped their knuckles trying to figure out the best angles and where support and crocodile clips could be fixed. They fumbled around and bruised their arms and knees, yelping every now and again. They tried to add support braces from the small quantity of bits of metal and wood that Harry had in his bag. Carol had fitted LEDs to all the main elements on the board. This was so they could see which pieces had a current running through them. She found one of the main supply wires and carefully added a connector to the board. The crocodile clips worked a treat. When the final connection was made and the board was secured, they held their breaths. 'Let's see if this is a damp squib or if it lights up like a Christmas tree?' And then Harry flicked the switch on the side.

'Oh, you beauty!' yelled Carol. And suddenly, she put her hand across her mouth and whispered, 'sorry, too excited.' The LEDs glowed like a string of lights at a fairground. Carol gave Harry a celebratory punch on the arm. 'Nice one, Stanley,' she said. Harry gave Carol a too heavy-handed, punch on the arm and as he was about to say the same to his pal Oli, Carol was knocked over sideways into the bracken and got snagged again.

'Ooh sorry, Carol, I thought you were secured.' He leaned over and pulled her up. Carol pushed him with her fingers. She shook her head and in an American movie accent declared

'Why I oughta.' Then shook her fist at him. They both sniggered like naughty school children and tried to stand.

Harry's knees had seized but he managed to hoist himself up. 'Let's take a photo of this as proof that we've done it and not just been to the pub,' suggested Carol. The brief camera flash from her phone pulsated light in the space around them. They stared at their handy work one more time.

'Well there's a good chance I'll never see that again,' said Harry, as they pushed the doors back in tight, catching the last glimpse of the LEDs against the blackness. They did their best to pull all the vegetation back over the front and carefully backed out from the undergrowth at the edge of the wood.

We think we've done it. Heading back to Elinor's now. Carol texted everyone at once and added the photo of the fitted motherboard after it, with four thumbs up, a grinning face and a fingers crossed emoji. Various clapping hands, thumbs ups and grinning faces responded. The two ninjas headed back to Elinor's and were greeted with big hugs and thanks. After a quick debrief and one more trip to the loo, everyone said their goodbyes. Carol would be heading to France in a few days but still wanted to be kept informed. They wished her bon voyage and she headed off on her long night journey back up to the Dales. She was grateful for the lack of traffic and the flask of strong coffee that Elinor made up for her.

'Do you think they'll know we've done it?' asked Harry by the door.

'I'm not sure, but they seem to know our whereabouts, so we have to presume they're watching us somehow,' suggested Elinor. She gave Harry a kiss on the cheek and wished him good night, thanked him again and asked him to send her love to Edie. He promised he would.

As Harry drove home, he reflected on the adventure he had just experienced with Carol. He thought that those kinds of things were well and truly in his past and he couldn't wait to tell Edie all about it. It had been serious, childish, fun and dangerous. When he walked through the door it was gone eleven. Edie was waiting for him with a big hug and let him tell her all about it. He was far too wired and excited by the events. Even though he was tired on the outside, he reminded Edie of Nel and Erin; giddy and rambling, over-tired.

The next morning, Elinor had a busy day ahead and wouldn't be home until late. She was going to gather some research for an artist project and then she was heading to Amanda's for dinner and a wind down. She was about to leave the flat when she had a brainwave. She turned around and went back into the study and over to the answering machine and pressed "record message". When the light came on, she spoke as clearly as she could. 'Hi, this is

Elinor; if this is Tom, can you let us know if our booster has worked? Get one of you to contact us, please. Thank you.' It was worth a try at least.

Everyone was having a busy day. Carol had packed and was driving to stay with her friend before their trip to France. Edie was out visiting friends and Olivia was at work. Pat was attending the hospice, Ed was out meeting Joel and another new Councillor and Amanda was firefighting as usual, in the school office.

Karen had just hung her coat up in the hall. She was thoughtfully patting herself on the back for removing half of the coats and managing to sell quite a few on eBay. The dog had wandered off into the kitchen and she was just hanging up the dog lead when the telephone rang. Karen hadn't heard from anyone since the second seance. She thought they had come and gone and she was trying to forget about them. There had been no interim phone calls. She looked at it for a moment, took a deep breath, braced herself and then lifted the receiver. The line crackled and almost fizzed. 'Hello?' Karen never gave out her number.

'Oh hello,' said a meek male voice. 'Is that Karen?'

Suspiciously Karen replied, 'Who's this please?'

'Oh sorry, how rude of me yes, of course. I'm Tom.' Karen thought he sounded like J.R. Hartley and wondered if he was going to ask if she had a book called Fly Fishing.

'No one seems to be near their phones today. Could you let them know that we can see their new booster, but we still need something more on our side. We need...' Tom was gone.

Karen stared at the wall for a moment. What had he said again? She rang Pat's mobile number and it went straight to voice mail. 'Hi Pat it's Karen. Er, I've just had a phone call from your Tom. He said something about them seeing your booster, but they still need something at their side. That's all there was and it cut off. I hope that means something to you. Anyway, er bye.' There was nothing else Karen could do. She walked into the kitchen, put on the kettle and gave the dog some fresh water.

Ed was home first and was thinking about dinner, but not seriously enough. He was actually thinking about Joel and his new Councillor friend, Heena. These were the new guard and he knew it. They had the fight in them, but their enemy seemed to be their own Council members. The fusty dusty crusties, he had decided to call them. Heena was clever and had her finger on the pulse. Both of them could connect far better with the younger voting citizens than the old farts who saw change as a threat. They wanted Ed's help in finding a way in, a way to get them on side. So Ed had promised to think long and hard about his own generation and older, to find out what could be done to change their mindsets. Joel and Heena were going to have to go on a massive charm offensive. They were going to have to let the miserable gits think that every good idea was their own and they were going to have to let them take the glory, for now. Ed reminded them that most of them would be dead soon, due to their dripping bread sandwiches and copious amounts of butter in their diets. 'When you hear them complaining, it's actually just their arteries, screaming for help,' he said. They were a perfect pairing and he told them that he could see them running the Council better than it had ever seemed possible and that one day, he'd like to see either of them as PM. Heena and Joel thought Ed was amazing.

When Pat came in, she was pleased to see him in the kitchen pottering. 'Hi love,' called Pat from the hall.

'Hi Pet, how was your day?' Ed gave her a big kiss and carried on chopping.

'Well, I said hello and goodbye to someone today in less than half an hour of meeting them.'

'Oh, love I'm sorry. That must have been tough?'

'It was, but they were ninety-four and I reckon that was a very good innings.'

'What about you?' Ed told her about Joel and Heena and he swore when talking about the old fuddy duddies who wouldn't let go. Pat understood and agreed with him and then checked her phone and saw the voice mail and listened. 'Ed, Karen got a call from Tom! They can see the booster but apparently, they still need something else on their side.'

'Oh, crikey. Well on one level it's great that they can see it, God knows how, but then we still might be no further forwards and so now what?'

Pat texted the others to let them know, then put down her phone. She looked over at the cooker. 'That smells nice love, what is it?'

'Sausage surprise,' replied Ed. This was an old joke. 'There's still no bloody sausages in it, is there?'

'Nope, but one day I will surprise you, and there will be.' Pat was not so sure. It would be a vegetarian bolognese with whichever pasta was closest to the front of the cupboard door. Pat didn't mind though. She hadn't had to cook and it was perfectly acceptable. Over dinner, they discussed having to have another meeting to decide what to do next. Pat and Ed felt guilty that they had not invited anyone round to their home yet, but were also aware that Edie might feel put out, as she seemed to enjoy being the hostess with the mostest, as Ed called her. Pat and Ed were both decent cooks but hated the thought of some kind of out-doing contest. Also, neither of them wanted to compete with Edie's baking.

'How about we invite everyone round for the evening, after dinner, then we only have to have drinks and nibbles?'

'That's a good idea, Ed. I can do some seriously good finger food, well, I can buy some seriously good finger food.' They both knew a trip to Waitrose would be in order.

'We can find some of the nicest non-alcoholic drinks too, for those who won't be on the tipple.'

As Pat's text was being read by everyone, there was a sense of melancholy that seemed to hit them all, in their own ways, they each felt deflated. Had they really expected the booster to just work and that be the end of it? In their heart of hearts, they knew they were facing the inevitable. They couldn't stop the landline switch off, how could they? The fantastic booster that Harry and Carol had made was amazing, but it was never going to be enough, or last. Harry worried about Gracie and couldn't stand the thought of his mam being nowhere and yet being somewhere she shouldn't be. It was confusing and sad and he felt completely helpless. The replies came back to Pat, and she suggested the get-together, for the last push and everyone agreed. Carol was in France, so they would try to let her know their next move, but wouldn't disturb her holiday.

Elinor had a wonderful day. She had needed the misdirection and the need to focus on something else. She had been to the central library and found the most beautiful natural history books, full of incredible illustrations. Then she had set off on a walk from Shadwell, up to Wike. It was there that red kites seemed to follow her and buzzards joined in, even higher on the thermals. The swifts had begun to return and darted in the fields around her. The breaths she took were deep and long and she felt reinvigorated. Her internal battery charge indicator was filling back up again. She knew she needed more of this and wondered what it was like to be Carol, staring out at her view of the moors, every day. But Elinor liked a big city too and knew that she just wanted the best of both worlds. Today, she had it in spades. Along the paths, she collected flowers and leaves and placed them in her little portable flower press. A simple device with elastic bands holding it together. She photographed moss and lichen on stones and bark. This is what Elinor liked to do best; to be in nature, observing it closely. It made her feel small and insignificant, but in the best way possible. She knew that one day, she would just be earth and that didn't feel sad at all.

As Elinor reached the top of the hill, before turning back towards her home, she gazed north. The sun was behind her and the view was clear. She could even see the white smudge on the distant hill that was the white horse at Kilburn. When she was overburdened with life and issues, it was a long view and a big sky that helped her rebalance and think straight. The top of a hill or staring out to sea were the same shot in the arm she needed.

Tomorrow evening they would all convene at Ed and Pat's house. This would be interesting, taking a look around their home. Elinor had tried to imagine it, but couldn't place their characters with any kind of furnishings. She knew Edie would want a guided tour, but so did she, so that would be OK.

As the door closed behind her, recent events came back into her mind even more. What next? Elinor placed her bag, twigs, stones, leaves and flower press on the kitchen table and put the kettle on. Her overnight bag was already packed for her evening at Amanda's and she just had to remember the bottle in the fridge door. Cup in hand, she headed into the study and stared at the newsprint and sheets Blu-Tacked to the wall. Half of it was already out of date. The phone exchange booster could not last, she was sure of that. It was there just to help them stay in touch with Tom, George and Gracie for a little bit longer until a better solution was available. She was convinced of that.

She looked at her list of communication through time. The telephone had survived the longest, but now things had changed and the use of the landline and physical connecting had been replaced with emitters, masts and satellites. If air-borne communication had been possible, then why had their otherworldly friends not communicated via radio waves and DAB? It was surely something to do with the physical touch, the line from one thing to another. Pulsing through an object, like the landline and even the bone conducting headphones in the water. There was so much to think about, but Elinor felt she was just missing a link, something to take this on and get things moving again. Then her mobile pinged and Amanda was on her way to pick her up.

Halfway down the second bottle of Prosecco, Amanda was regaling Elinor with another anecdote about today's weird happening at school. 'So, the blighters had been selling the phones behind the shops, right next to school. We could see them on the CCTV. I mean, they must have been making quite a bit of dosh before they screwed up with moving their shop there.' Amanda was indignant about their audacity.

'Of course, our lot were so daft, they went over wearing their school uniforms straight after the end of the day. Not only could we see they were ours, we could see exactly who they were, when the daft sods, came back inside the school building straight after. I mean if you're going to take stolen goods have a bit of nouse eh?' Elinor laughed. 'Nel, would be a better fence than those twerps!'

She was thankful it wasn't her trying to talk to parents and police anymore, but also, she was laughing at the actual stupidity of some kids today. Then realised what she and this bunch of fifty-somethings were actually doing. The teenagers had a lack of experience on their side, she and her friends did not. Amanda saw her friend starting to glaze over, a combination of Prosecco and boredom and the fresh air and walk of the day, so changed the subject to more pressing matters.

'Where are we at then, El? Any more brain waves and ideas of what our next move is?' Elinor sighed.

'Oh, I don't know, Mand, I've got a half-baked notion and an undercooked idea or two, but nothing's coming together.' Then there was a text from Olivia to everyone.

'Hi, all, just got the girls to bed, forgot to say, I've got a shift at the big exchange and the postal sorting office on Harrogate Road on Monday. I've had a talk through the job. There's no way to really know what's what, but I hope I can get one or two photos if that's any good?'

The comebacks were positive and thankful. *'Any port in a storm,'* replied Pat. Harry wondered if he could fit Olivia with a Go-Pro camera; he was now convinced that he was Tom Cruise.

Elinor said she needed to think things through and do a bit more research. She hoped that she would be able to make better suggestions at Ed and Pat's. Amanda said she could go and ask Russell for more electronic bits and bobs if they were needed. They carried on drinking and talking about what they thought Ed and Pat's house would be like.

'Chintzy or IKEA, or complete William Morris?' Posed Elinor.

'Ooh, now you're talking El.' They were both three sheets to the wind.

'Right, place your bets, avocado bath suite or nice white porcelain and old taps?'

'Guess the fixtures and fittings,' took them into the small hours with lots of laughs at their outrageous suggestions.

'Crocheted lady toilet roll cover, or clown leaning against a wonky lamp post, made of glass?' They howled.

'How are we going to hold it together if we see any of these?' squealed Amanda, now horizontal on the sofa.

The next morning, they wished they had remembered to drink that pint of water and knew they would be on the non-alcoholic stuff later. Amanda dropped Elinor back at home just after lunch. There was no way she was going to drive anywhere early doors and without a couple of strong coffees down her. 'See you later, I'll pick you up about seven,' called Amanda as she drove off. Elinor headed straight to the kitchen. *Kettle on and a big glass of water,* she thought to herself. Then she went back into the hall and saw the answer phone flashing.

'What have you got to tell me today, Tom, *eh?*' She smiled as she pressed the "play message" button.

'You have one new message, new message, click-
"Hello, Elinor, it's Tom. Thank you so much for all your*

hard work. I know it's not over, but this little boost helps us talk a bit longer. We still need a new improvement on this side and I'm sure you will sort it. I'm just letting you know that I am passing on now, Elinor. Give my regards and thanks to everyone. I should be with Lynne hopefully quite soon. Goodbye, dear, thank you." End of message, you have no more messages.'

Elinor sat down and felt the tears welling up in her eyes. 'Oh, you lovely, lovely man, Tom. Bless you!' She sat on the chair by the computer, feeling the tears slowly roll down her cheek until she could taste the salt on her lips. Then she stared at the answering machine. Elinor never cried, so this was somehow unexpected. He was already dead, she hadn't even cried at his funeral, she just kept a solemn countenance throughout things like that. But here, in this post-death unbelievable situation, this lovely man, who she had drunk countless cups of tea with, refused countless biscuits from, meant the world and he was finally gone. She wanted to play the message again but was also apprehensive about actually hearing that departing voice one more time. Although she was trembling a little, she opened a text message to everyone and recorded Tom's final message, so they could all hear it. Then she pressed send. Elinor looked up at the ceiling and took some deep breaths. She needed another walk. Within half an hour, she was at the park, just sat on a bench looking at the clouds rolling by.

Chapter Fourteen – Upgrade

Everyone was saddened, upon hearing Tom's message. Ed wanted his dad, George to be back with his mum. Harry wanted his mam to be back with his dad too. Neither of them thought that losing them again would be this painful. Elinor wasn't even related to Tom, they were just neighbours, but they understood the loss and tried to steal themselves for when it was their turn. It would mean they had done their job and they should be happy with that, but that's not how it felt at all.

Ed and Pat had just loaded up a small shop of nibbles and were still sat in the Waitrose car park when they got Elinor's text. 'I think we should talk about Tom as soon as everyone has arrived,' suggested Pat.

'He deserves a eulogy of sorts and Elinor may like to chat about him if she wants. We should celebrate his life and now his afterlife too. What do you reckon Ed?'

'I think that's a wonderful idea Pat,' replied Ed. 'Let's just hope that we can all focus on being proactive and positive after such a blow. If we want to make sure Dad and Gracie can pass on properly too, we mustn't lose sight of that, must we?' It all began to seem more important to Ed now. He couldn't let his dad down and he knew Harry wouldn't rest until Gracie was safe too, even though they didn't know what that was.

Elinor looked back at her wall of paper notes in the study. The questions and indecisions all seemed somewhat pathetic right now, but then she picked herself up. This mass of words had helped them make a thing that helped Tom speak to her more clearly. No matter how exhausting this all was, it was worth it to know Tom had passed on all the information he could muster, by getting people together and now his job was done. Tom could rest and it was time for Gracie and George to get to their final calm place. Her bag was now full of paper peeled from the wall, Post-it notes, her pencil case and a new big sheet that she had been working on to show everyone. She hoped it would help to explain her thoughts.

As everyone arrived at Ed and Pat's, it was obvious that the greeting hugs were stronger. They had experienced the passing of Tom and it had felt significant. 'If you want to tell us a bit more about him Elinor, I'd love to know what he was like,' suggested Pat. This is what Pat could do so well. She made a space for someone to feel they could speak, safely and in a friendly comforting environment. Elinor told them of his past. She had always enjoyed asking Tom about his youth. As a young lad, his family had gone on camping holidays and they even took their cat. He said, she just followed them all on their walks. He had painted pictures of a happy, loving childhood and Elinor passed this on to everyone listening. She showed them a picture of when he was a young man, that she had seen at his funeral. He was debonair, to say the least. His cravat stuck out through his open-necked shirt. She talked of his love for Lynne and how he had nursed her in her final years and she told them of his final months and how they had last spoken together before he died. This was what Elinor was good at. Telling stories and being able to carry an audience with her. To instil empathy in those who listened. She painted her picture of a gentleman. A slightly spendthrift Yorkshireman, with a heart of gold.

'Here's to Tom and his final resting place with Lynne,' said Ed softly, holding up his glass.

'To Tom,' they replied almost simultaneously.

Elinor and Amanda hadn't really thought about what Ed and Pat's house and decor looked like. More important and serious events had taken over. Edie hadn't asked to have a look around either. She knew that was for another time and instead, she helped move everything forward. 'So what should we be hoping to do next do you think?' Olivia discussed getting her chance to look round the exchange on Monday, but recognised that could be quite limited and no one could break and enter. Photographs could still be very useful, so Olivia promised to do her best. She would feign interest and hope someone would want to show her more of the premises than usual. They didn't know if George and Gracie could offer them any more advice at this time. Elinor said she would keep her answerphone plugged in for a while, in case either of them could send a message that way. As Tom had managed to call Karen and Carol, they wondered if that had been his role. George was more unusual as he had managed two completely different phone venues and didn't have a "home" phone at Ed and Pat's, so keeping Elinor's machine on was a good suggestion. Everyone knew that Gracie's role was to make sure Harry was on call to use his electrical skills and make them a physical connecting thing.

They were ready for the nibbles and Pat brought them out and admitted that it was all shop-bought. 'There is no way I am competing with Edie's baking and amazing spreads, so this is just to fill some holes and I hope you enjoy them.' Edie bristled with pride and everyone tucked in.

'Right, Elinor, as chief of Ops, have you been thinking about plan B?' asked Harry.

'Well I have actually,' she replied and they all sighed in relief. She put her large sheet of paper out onto the floor in front of her and everyone peered at it, expectantly.

'However, I think we will always have issues and I have never had to second guess so much in all my life. I like facts and logic when it comes to planning and this is more like creating an abstract painting on a whim. Even if it looks good in the end, I'm not too sure where I'm going with it and it might not make sense.'

'Even so,' chipped in Edie. 'Your suggestions have been amazing, so let's hear it.'

They all agreed and Elinor took a bite of food, chewed and coughed .'Oh, that went down the wrong way.' And then began with her theories.

'OK, stay with me, people,' Elinor explained that as far as she could tell, the next thing in the line of communication was not going to be purely the mobile phone. After explaining that the others hadn't communicated via radio, she explained that it was because it was untrustworthy and those on the other side, couldn't call a transistor radio. It had a mechanism to receive information "live", but if the radio wasn't switched on, there was no answerphone facility. Also, finding an empty channel that had a frequency was just an added hassle. The others weren't going to try and communicate over the top of Radio four's Today programme. As the radio signal went through the air, this also seemed to be another failure of that system. Everyone was paying attention. Elinor was in teacher mode. She was trying to explain a difficult concept and her audience was an unknown quantity of understanding, or lack of it. They were all clever in their own ways, but she spoke as if she had a mixed-ability bunch of friends.

She ploughed on. 'That's why I don't think we will just hear our mobile phones ringing either and certainly not when we are out and about. I'm sure it's something to do with transmitting through solid cabling and down wires.'

When Elinor talked about the bees at the Hive in Kew Gardens and the bone-conducting headphones at the swimming pool, she could see that the penny was beginning to drop. 'I also did some research and they're going to switch off 2G in two years anyway, so it's obviously going to be 3G, 4G and 5G soon enough after that because they'll come up with something else.'

'Well now this seems bloody impossible then,' said Harry feeling all deflated and lost again.

'I know it does Harry, but this is where I think we may have another path to try,' Elinor told them about a film she had seen about mushrooms.

'Honestly, it was one of the most beautiful films of nature I have ever seen. The important part comes when they talk about mycelium.'

'My what?' asked Ed. 'Are you sure you hadn't eaten mushrooms, Elinor?' That broke the bubble of worry and they all chuckled. Pat nudged Ed and smiled at him, and then leant into his chest. He put his arm around her and Elinor continued.

'Mycelium. It's an organic network that grows underground and connects things. It can appear on the surface and that's where the mushrooms grow. It also grows in and around the roots of trees. There can be eight miles of mycelium in one inch of ground, in places, it's ludicrous. Humans also get covered in spores all the time.' There was a distinct recoil of disgust at that from everyone.

'But here's the next best bit.' They all moved and shuffled forward. 'Trees communicate to each other through their roots too. They can even share water and warning signals, how bloody cool is that? Mycelium and trees are our next communication possibility. We need to find a way to connect either with them both or like them both. Hell, think about all the people who are having woodland burials. They're being buried under trees. The trees are growing over them. The roots are getting nourished by the bodies of our dead. Everyone has this great green vision of returning to nature. What if that's it? What if a woodland burial ground is the new exchange? What if every tree would be our own home number because it would be in direct contact?'

'Fucking hell! sorry' exclaimed Pat.

'Fuck yeah!' added Olivia.

'Mind blown. What does your brain work on?' asked Ed.

Elinor rambled, 'I just don't know how we connect to it though. It's the biggest stumbling block. I'm not sure how we get to tap into the roots and mycelium and send and receive the communication. This is the bit that just won't come to me. With the last booster that Harry made, it was electric to electric. How do we go from human or electric to nature? But I'm convinced it can be the longest-lasting network, if we get it right.'

'Elinor, don't forget that all of this is just magic,' piped up Edie.

'Tell me that talking into a block of metal and glass and it being received by another block of metal and glass, a thousand miles away, and all making sense and it happening instantaneously, isn't magic? Don't get me started on how sending a photograph works. We have to suspend our disbelief again don't we?'

Elinor looked at Edie and nodded gratefully, then she looked at Olivia. 'I think that when the twins are grown up, it may be their turn, or not, it depends. But if we can leave a lot of notes and suggestions, perhaps they can be in a better starting position than we were. Even if it's not them. Perhaps we can leave something as a much better clue or manual?'

That prompted Olivia to check her phone. It was time to release the babysitter and hope she had survived the evening. She knew she would be thinking about her daughters' futures slightly differently from now on. She hugged everyone and saved an extra big hug and kiss for her mum and dad and off she went, wondering what would be waiting for her at home.

'I have to say Elinor, you make a powerful case with your art of persuasion, you really do,' stated Ed, just as a lightbulb went on in his head. 'Actually, come to think of it, I would really like to pick your brains about a council matter. I have two young councillors who would benefit greatly from your ability to hold an audience in the palm of your hand.'

'You're not a tough crowd though, Ed,' replied Elinor. 'No, but your kids at school will have been and I bet you had them eating out of the palm of your hand didn't you?' Sometimes she did, it was an art, not a science and no one should ever underestimate the group dynamic or Kyle. However, she offered graciously, and Ed was very pleased. Edie looked around the room.

'Pat, I would love a tour of your home, it looks wonderful.'

'Ooh me too,' added Amanda and Elinor tagged along. Pat walked them away from the men and began her tour.

Ed and Harry looked at each other. 'Well big fella, I think we are going to have to dig in and make the best of this don't you?' Harry agreed. 'Every now and again I still think this is all just a dream, but if it is, it's going on for a very long time. I'm absolutely knackered, Ed. How's it affecting you?'

'When we got our first call at the phone box in Settle, I couldn't believe it, Harry. I was spooked but still didn't believe in ghosts. And now here we are and I'm still at a loss. I know it's made me want to tie up all my loose ends while I still can. I don't want to be like my dad. Yet, if I go before Pat and I don't get to say goodbye properly, then perhaps I might like to be able to get in touch with her and tell her one more time, you know?' Ed's voice cracked and faltered. He was going to say that he wanted one more chance to tell her he loved her, but he couldn't say it out loud to Harry. But Harry knew exactly what he meant. 'I hear you, pal, I really do.' There was laughter from upstairs.

When the women had returned downstairs, Edie, Elinor and Amanda all praised Ed on a lovely house. 'What were you laughing about?' he asked.

'They saw the box of misguided gifts in the spare room Ed and your mother's knitted toilet roll cover.' The women burst out laughing again.

'Well on that laughter, let's get you home Edie,' offered Harry. Ed would contact Elinor to arrange a meeting with Joel and Heena and everyone was to keep on thinking and researching and hoped that Olivia might turn up another clue. Right now all they had was each other and hope.

This was Olivia's earliest shift. Because the sorting offices were round-the-clock distribution centres, there wasn't really a downtime. However, shortly after all the bags were ready for the post workers, Olivia had to be ready too. She had to drop the girls off with her mum and dad at seven thirty a.m. By the time she arrived at her shift, she was already shattered. The twins had been placed in the car, still in their pyjamas. They would have breakfast with Edie, who would dress them and take them to school. Their Finding Nemo bags were already packed with their lunch boxes.

The shift began at the sorting office and then moved over to the exchange. The back car park was empty of the post office vans, as they were all out on deliveries, but the Open Reach vans hadn't started their day work yet. Olivia was working in a group of four and all she had to do was sweep the small offices, the corridors between, the kitchen and the toilets. She could see in through the big double doors, to the cavernous mainframe room. There was a constant hum and the floor was vibrating slightly when she stood closest to it. 'Don't worry, Liv,' said her co-worker, Mike. 'We don't have to go near that lot. It's got a massive ventilation system to keep the heat and the dust down.'

'Best not go in there with me feather duster then eh?' Replied Olivia, and they both chuckled.

'It's still fascinating though isn't it, Mike? I'd love a nosy around that. It looks like the engine room on Star Trek.'

'Ha, you're not wrong there. Ask the bloke at reception, perhaps someone can show you round?' Olivia said thank you for the tip and continued down the corridor with the giant dust mop, weaving under and between the furniture and cupboards.

As they reached the front reception area and Mike was plugging in the vacuum, he did Olivia's work for her. 'See this crazy lady here, she wants to look inside the "big room", She's got a thing for motherboards, cos she's a bored mother.' Elinor wasn't too sure about the humour in that sentence, but she smiled and said it just looked fascinating.

'There's someone in there today, so feel free to see if they'll let you in. If you don't ask you never know, but they might turn you away at the door,' Olivia said that was perfectly understandable and then looked at Mike. 'Go on then, there's only ten minutes left. Just remember you owe me ten minutes for another time.'

'Will do Mike, cheers.'

'Can't believe you're that excited about looking in a room. Hey ho, each to their own I suppose.'

Olivia said thank you to both of them again and went back down the corridor to the main room. She opened the door and called loudly, 'Hi, anyone around?'

There was a quick response and Olivia walked over to a man playing with some wires in his hand, whilst staring at a board.

'How can I help you?' He smiled with an interested air that suggested no one other than him ever came in here.

'Hi, I'm Olivia, I'm just cleaning here today. I asked the guy on reception if I could have a look in here. It just seems mind-boggling and I can't figure out how it all works, so I was wondering if you could show me a bit. I totally understand if you have to crack on, but you know, if you don't ask, you never know.' The man could see an opportunity to let forth his intense knowledge of the main distribution frame and relished the chance to talk to someone for a change. Olivia was going to regret this, she could feel it, but if she got an ounce of useful information, then it had to be worth it in the end.

She tried desperately to pick out some facts that could be worth passing on to Harry and Carol. Occasionally she managed to ask a question, but he was no Elinor when it came to explaining the complexities of how this all worked. As she felt her eyes begin to glaze over, something on the far side caught her attention. 'What on earth is that?' she asked with renewed enthusiasm. Over on the far wall was a series of huge black metal boxes. They were vented and from under the floor, tubes emerged and entered the underside of each box. Around the perimeter were separate fans and there seemed to be another extractor above. The tube work, pipes and cables seemed to go everywhere.

'Ah, this is tomorrow. Well, it's actually today, of course, but eventually, everything that you've just seen will be replaced with this.' Olivia knew she had to pay attention very carefully now.

'Wow, it's more space age, isn't it? What's inside them?'

'I can open it briefly, maintaining the ambient temperature is important, but I'll let you have a sneaky peek.' As he fumbled around for his key, Olivia took out her phone and took a photo. She pretended she was checking her texts, so the angle was all skewed. As he opened the door to one of the boxes, she managed one more photo before he turned round.

'This is the start of the fibre network. It's all connected underground, fully insulated and cabled. It's a beauty. Soon the whole city will be using this.'

'Oh, my word,' exclaimed Olivia, trying to chivvy him along with his excitement. 'Do you feel like you're working the Star Ship Enterprise, when you're in here?'

He smiled proudly. 'Yes, I do actually.'

'Well, Scotty, that's quite a responsibility you have then.'

Olivia didn't know what the quality of the pictures would be like, but she knew this was a vital component of plan B, based on what Elinor had told them. She looked at her phone, exclaimed how late it was and thanked the man for his incredible generosity. If she needed to come back, she had to make him feel very clever and proud. She had schmoozed as best she could.

Chapter Fifteen – The Operation

Elinor had not had a good night's sleep for years. She had struggled even more for the past few weeks and the last few days had been extra difficult. She was thinking about plan B throughout the day and couldn't switch her brain off when she hit the pillow. She had avoided evening alcohol, which Amanda said was quite worrying and she wasn't having caffeine after two p.m. None of that seemed to make a difference. Her brain was racing constantly.

Ed had arranged with her to meet Joel and Heena at Joel's office at the Civic Hall. After signing in at reception, getting her visitor's lanyard and being given directions to Joel's office, she couldn't help but take photos of the sculptures of past dignitaries, the carvings of the owls that were everywhere and the gold-framed paintings of some old handlebar moustachioed, mutton-chopped, Lord Mayors.

She spotted Joel's name on the door and knocked. Ed was already there, sat comfortably on a chair, and she could imagine him in his prime, right there. Joel and Heena greeted her warmly and she liked them instantly. These two were just how she expected some of her old six formers to be once they had settled into a career path. Full of life and the eagerness of youth, but developing adults with real drive for the future. They made her smile and welcome. Ed wanted Elinor to pass on her years of experience of engaging with a difficult crowd. The disenfranchised young people who didn't want to be in school, let alone be educated in something they had no connection with. Elinor explained that whilst there were indeed similarities between teenagers and old men, there were also many differences. Children weren't her colleagues, they had to be there. She had backup with the form tutors, heads of year and senior leadership teams. Joel and Heena's colleagues were set in their ways and didn't really have the same line management system. It would be more difficult to get this lot to change their ways than her teenagers. Elinor asked them both if there was anything specific that they wanted to push through, that way they could try to find something that might be the gateway.

'Well,' said Heena. 'Walls have ears, so I'm speaking quietly here. It has taken us far too long to just get them to use email properly. They still don't follow procedures and we've had all sorts of problems when they've replied to all, instead of just an individual. It's caused so many issues.'

'Oh God, yes,' added Joel. 'When Henry thought he had only replied to Matthew and told him that he thought Sandra was an interfering bitch, and we all got the email, including Sandra. That was horrible. He said it was true anyway and then blamed the email system, not his lack of professionalism. This is what we're up against Elinor.

They just come at you all pompous and pious and loud. It's like being railroaded.'

'I know exactly the sort of characters you mean,' assured Elinor.

'They don't mind having the internet for all their TV programmes and Sports, but they won't look to the future for the city and access for everyone rather than just those who can afford it,' added Heena. 'We just want to make sure that every school, care home, hospital, housing estate, community group and small business, doesn't feel left behind when it comes to technology and facilities. These blokes are only bothered about their vanity project park and ride scheme outside the city.'

Things were starting to stir in Elinor's mind. 'Legacy,' she said confidently.

'Pardon?' questioned Joel. Ed sat back and watched as Elinor came up with a game plan for the pair of them.

'They need to be assured that they will be remembered, for something grand. Something more important than a park and ride. They need to envisage that a big portrait of them will be painted and hung on the wall down these hallowed corridors. They need to imagine that someone might even go as far as to carve a bust of them and for the brass plaque to state that it was carved in honour of the great man who got this or that done for the citizens of the city. You have to make them feel grand and inflate their egos to bursting point. Then you also have to be prepared that they will take the glory for all your hard work, but if it's worth it, then you can do it.' Heena and

Joel looked at each other, then back to Elinor and Ed and smiled.

The time had run away with them. Ed promised to come back to Elinor with a list of the key proposals that Joel and Heena wanted to move forward. Then they could action some ideas to go back to the "crusties" with. She told them to start by making them think it was all their idea and the best thing since sliced bread and then to wave the glory and the end adulation right under their noses. These men were shallow, it just might work.

As Elinor walked through town back to the bus stop, her head was spinning with bumbling councillors and ideas for drawing them in hook, line and sinker. As the bus pulled away she put her head on her hand and stared out at the streets she had known all her life. It was glaringly obvious that some of the big council estates and tower blocks were still lacking in so many basic provisions; too much dense housing for a start, no decent local shops, no off-street parking, no safe play spaces. As the journey hit the big duel carriageway she saw the road works. CityFibre vans, on every corner. Piles of big purple plastic tubing. Then closer to home, the Open Reach vans were out. A man was down a hole passing cable underground to another man at the end of the street. Elinor lifted her head from her hand and stared like she had just seen her prey.

By the time Olivia had texted her photos to everyone and explained what she had seen, Elinor was back home. It was past two o'clock, but she needed the caffeine to help her stay focussed now. She got out a lasagne to defrost and then sat herself down at the kitchen table. Surrounding herself with her big sheets of paper and notes, she took the lid off her pen and started making notes.

Time ticked away and scribbles became sketches, which became plans, which became a plan of action. The rough drawings were put to one side and neater ones were created. The new big black boxes that Olivia had seen were obviously the next version of the exchanges. The second image inside one of the boxes meant absolutely nothing to her, but she knew that Harry and definitely Carol would be able to explain what she was looking at. Elinor wrote in capitals when she made lists and statements, she always had. It added clarity to listings and it made everything more affirmative. The lids of different coloured markers came off and went on as she swapped colours depending on the links. Elinor didn't know whether she was losing her mind or creating something meaningful, but she knew it looked awesome. Her stomach rumbled and she looked at the time. Four hours of knitting together the impossible. In the kitchen the microwave pinged and she put the lasagne on a tray and went back to eat it at the table.

The idea of being able to get things together at this side was beginning to fall into place. How it connected on the other side was just constantly out of reach. It was just not making sense at all.

It was dark when she reached for her phone. She wanted to let everyone know where she had got to, but there was still nothing concrete to give them. Elinor needed to know if there was anything that could link the other side to the living world, in any other way well before the loss of the landlines and the G networks.

'*Hi, Harry, sorry it's so late. I think I might have something possibly tenable. but I need your advice and expertise. When's good for you for a get-together please?*' Elinor pressed send.

She wasn't expecting such a speedy reply.

'*Hi, Elinor, we're just trying to wind down after getting the girls to sleep. I'm free tomorrow afternoon, only got a morning job.*'

'*Brilliant, is 1 OK at mine?*' It was. There was nothing more Elinor could do, certainly not without help and advice from Harry. There was another text from Harry.

'*Edie wants to come too and she's bringing cake.*'

'*Well, I'd be a fool to turn that down. See you both tomorrow X.*' After she had pressed send, Elinor realised it was the first time she had added an x to the message and hoped it was well received. Then she headed to bed and tried to read, then stared at the ceiling in the dark and waited for exhaustion to finally switch off her mind.

Harry had checked to see when Carol was back from her holiday and told her to suggest some times for a meet-up. '*Ay up, Oli, Stan here. Hope you've had a* bon vacance. *Just letting you know, we may need your help very soon. No rush, just let us know when you can face us again. Also, sad news, but good news too. Tom has passed on. He left a message for Elinor.*'

Carol replied straight away, '*Oh no, that's sad. I think, but then it is good too, isn't it? Re: putting our heads together, yep, but I've got to prep the site for walkers on Wednesday, so I'll let you know after that. See you soon, Stanley!'* A thumbs-up emoji had to do, but Carol wished there was a bowler hat she could have added.

'Welcome, welcome, come on in,' chirped Elinor as she opened the door to Harry and Edie. Edie was carrying an upside-down large Tupperware and Elinor wondered if she had stared at it for too long rather than at the faces of her new friends.

'Go on Edie, tell me what drug you've put in it this time?' Edie and Harry laughed.

'You know her too well already Elinor, you should see the size of our cocaine bill. She only calls it self-raising, cos it gets you high.' Edie tutted happily.

'It's orange and polenta cake Elinor,' explained Edie.

'And I can confirm that it's bloody gorgeous on its own or with cream, creme fraiche, ice cream or custard, or all of them together,' stated Harry, patting his stomach.

'You silly bugger,' tutted Edie once more, through a big grin.

When they were settled at the table and each had their brew and plate of cake, Elinor unrolled her latest sheet of ideas. 'What I want you to think about Harry is actually very scientific this time. As an electrician, you understand about making sure that volts and amps and ohms and all the rest can work with each other. You know where to put a breaker. You know where to put resistors to lower power and you know how the circuitry works.' Edie and Harry nodded and Edie looked at Harry with pride. 'So now I'm going to ask you about some things which may not be in

213

your skill set, but which you should be able to apply your knowledge to and give me some sensible suggestions and let me know when there's a definite impossibility.'

'Well, I'll do my best Elinor.' Harry was always happy to help, but he was now very puzzled.

'OK.' Elinor took a deep breath and Harry and Edie knew they were in for one of Elinor's big ideas. Harry offered his support.

'Go on lass, you know we have faith in your schemes.'

'Thank you, right, here goes.'

'When people go to hospital, they often get given implants for things. Never mind just getting bits of metal holding bits of them together. Like someone who gets an implant behind their ear, so that sound can go straight into the bone. Or someone who gets a pacemaker. There are people who are now getting chips put into their arms that are actually keys. They contain data that gives them physical access to computers and doors. Hell, there are those who get mechanical arms and hands fitted that they then control with their minds. So when I said I don't know how we link technology to nature, well we already do. I just hadn't put it together.' Elinor sat forward, took a huge bite of cake and made a glorious satisfying moan. 'Jesus that's good Edie.'

'Thank you, love, now what do we do next then?' After a slurp of tea and another bite of cake, Elinor continued. 'The big black boxes that Olivia snapped for us, are the next phase in fibre technology aren't they?' They nodded even though neither of them had even thought about it.

214

'And they link to underground technology that will end up at every property eventually. It's flawed, not everyone will have access, but that's what has been diminishing with the landlines anyway.'

'Right I get you, I think,' said Harry, now leaning into the table and demolishing his slice of cake at the same time. 'So, we need to link the black boxes and the underground to the exchange on their side, so it's upgraded too. And there's the sticking point for me, is there a way to link our system with the mycelium and the trees, so that we take it beyond our living fibre technology cables? Would that be enough? This is why I need you to think like your life depends on it, Harry.'

'Ooh right, I had better get my thinking cap on then, OK.' Elinor picked up her pen, waiting for Harry to bring up some words of wisdom. Both women looked at him intently, willing him to magically come up with the answer to all their problems. 'I think I need my sidekick to work with on this, but if we could make smaller receivers and tap into the fibre system and then link them to that mycelium, perhaps. But you said it won't travel through the air, so even if it worked and we got to feed into home internet or cable, most people would still be on their phones, so the connection would be lost at the last hurdle. But perhaps, it could connect a small distance, possibly?'

Elinor sat back on her chair. 'I know we are as close as we can be right now, but I think you're right, let's get Carol on the case too.' Edie moved forwards towards the cake and looked at Elinor. 'Oh yes please, just one more slice.'

Chapter Sixteen – The Big Leap

At the proposal meeting, Joel and Heena had used every trick in Elinor's book of persuasion. The mood at the end of the meeting was far more positive and there were definitely ideas on the table that some of the councillors thought needed more consideration. Joel had phoned Ed to say thank you and said if there was anything he could do for Ed, to just let him know. Ed said he would hold him to that. Back at home, he was wondering whether being told to contact Elinor Coates had in fact been all about helping Joel and Heena. 'She must have hit the right chord with them, Pat. Joel is buzzing with anticipation that they might actually get two items passed. That's an absolute coup for them.' Pat wondered if Ed was getting a taste for being back in the fray in some way. 'Not on your life! Even just going in there and spotting the odd familiar face, reminded me that I might not have made it to my age if I had stuck around longer. You can't breathe in that place. No, it's a young person's game now and Joel and Heena are welcome to it.' Pat was incredibly grateful to hear that.

The shift work was becoming normal for Olivia now. Trying to avoid the very early starts meant that she was limiting her workload, but she knew sanity was better than cash, especially when she needed to be completely alert and in the moment with her daughters. Her mum and dad were great at school runs and short notice requests, but she didn't want to rely on them and she didn't want to abuse that generosity. The girls could be exhausting and as much as she knew her parents doted on them, she knew that the girls were tiring them out more easily. She was contemplating a better job, but not until September. More importantly, the girls' birthday was looming at the weekend and that was priority number one. Nel and Erin would get what they were given and it would be perfect. There was no pandering to fickle trends or copying their friends, but it would be just the right side of special, based on what she had been listening to with the girls' conversations. They would have a superb day out with their mum, Gramps and Gran and the girls wouldn't have a clue, as it was a secret. They had already borrowed a large paddling pool and inflatable flamingoes. This would be waiting for them when they got back from Flamingo Land. Harry had put up the big gazebo at the back near the treehouse ready in case the weather wasn't fantastic. They could leave it where it was or drag it over the pool if necessary, but the girls would be wet anyway, so they wouldn't mind. Edie was making a flamingo cake and flamingo meringues. The events of the day would end with them watching Finding Dory as they couldn't find an animation about flamingoes.

After meeting with Elinor, Harry had been racking his brains for an idea about how to connect these two significant worlds together. He had jumped off his seat when he watched a Grand Designs episode that showed someone fitting a ground source heat pump. Then he calmed down when he saw them drilling into what looked like the earth's core to bring up heat. He made an audible gulp when he saw the cost. He would still tell Carol and Elinor about it though and he wrote it all down on a piece of paper. Carol had contacted him as she promised and drove down on Thursday morning. She was greeted by Edie and a late breakfast of a bacon sandwich, as Edie said a long drive always made her hungry. Then she asked if Carol had tried the cranberry biscuit recipe yet. 'I'm afraid they were a shadow of your supreme version Edie, I'm not sure if it was the different settings on my oven, the quality of the ingredients, or just a dodgy baker,' Edie said she would happily talk through it with her, just in case she had missed something off the recipe. Then Harry and Carol settled down to the task at hand. It took no time at all for Carol to say that she thought this was beyond her, but Edie was listening and Edie knew she had to keep her on task.

'Just give it your best shot Carol. You're writing the recipe now. As long as it does the job, that's the first big win, then let's take it from there. I mean, you did manage to improve that signal with your last job, so that's pretty amazing isn't it?'

'You're not wrong Edie, but crikey you wouldn't do anything this way with anything else would you?'

'No, we wouldn't, but perhaps we need more leaps of faith not fewer.' Edie was doing her bit and she had a knack of chivvying people along. Carol and Harry carried on trying to figure out what to do, where and how.

'Right, I'm having a thought and it might be a big one.' Harry spread his arms out across the table and picked up his pen and dramatically removed the lid.

'Have you been possessed by Elinor, love?' asked Edie grinning. She could see that her husband was getting excited about his work and she loved to see him enthused and smiling. 'Watch out Carol, he doesn't get like this often, you may need to stand back.'

Then Harry explained his brainwave. 'Elinor said that we can't use the transfer of signals through the air and I think she's right, up to a point. I reckon we might be able to get a signal from inside the home to a phone. Not if it's moved outside or further away, mind you, but just inside. I've said it before how crap our wi-fi signal is at the back of the house, in the basement, the garden and just because we've got thick stone walls. So to improve it we've bought boosters right?'

'Right,' Carol and Edie replied together. 'But if our swanky new fibre broadband is supposedly all about boosting better connectivity throughout our homes, you know, multiple appliances all working from it at the same time, shouldn't we also think that we might be able to get a signal from the other side to that underground connection and then to our phones, just like the landline, but with the last little hop, skip and jump through the air?'

'Christ Harry, you have been possessed by Elinor. I think you need to let her know what you're suggesting,' suggested Carol.

'Facetime her now.' Elinor appeared on the screen in portrait and after a bit of faffing about they had the screen working well.

'I've propped you against the Tupperware of biscuits, Elinor. I hope that's OK?' Edie was concerned that Elinor needed to be happy where she had been positioned. 'That's great Edie, I'm very comfy just there. Right Harry, what have you got for me? Fire away.' Elinor was excited that Harry had been so enthusiastic to tell her his idea. She knew she wasn't really in control of this next part of the plan and she would have to relinquish some authority again, just like when Harry and Carol went off to make the first booster.

As Harry explained what he had just told Carol and Edie, Elinor was nodding from inside the screen. 'This is amazing Harry, you're on my wavelength now. We have to treat the CityFibre and Fibre Broadband as the mycelium and somehow we have bring them together like an exchange, but I think that exchange needs to be on George and Gracie's side. I'm going to see if I can get this new fibre connected at my flat, what about everyone else?'

'If it means I can keep in touch with Mam, then yes, we can probably afford it, what do you reckon Edie?'

'It's a yes from me love, but will Gracie and George know what to do?' It was all enthusiastic conjecture and they knew it. Their excitement waned as they allowed reality to take over once more.

'Well look, I think this is an incredible suggestion,' said Carol trying to put a positive spin on the situation. 'I'll take a look at some of the gubbins that will be on the internet and see how we can get something into one of those huge junction boxes that they're fitting everywhere ready for fibre. It won't hurt and it will keep us moving forwards while we think of a better plan, OK?' Everyone seemed to sigh together and they watched Elinor seemingly lean back against Edie's Tupperware.

'It'll have to wait until after the twins' birthday though,' said Harry. 'That is going to take all our energy for sure. Then we're going to need a day off just to recover from that.' Carol and Elinor couldn't agree more. On the following Monday, they would get together for a plan of action and they would let Pat and Ed and Amanda know what was being planned.

Karen had just waved off a happy customer and put the forty-five pounds into her pocket. There was a bark from the front room and she went and opened the door. 'OK in you come. Your ladyship's dinner awaits. Give me half an hour and we'll get you outside.' Karen had not been able to quite shake off the memory of Pat and Ed and everyone else that night and the phone call from Tom. Although she was still convinced that this wouldn't end well for her, she had liked them all and wanted to know how this was playing out, so as the cards were still out on the table, she decided to ask about Pat and Ed and the others and what might be happening next. The whiskey tingled warmly on her tongue and she swallowed happily and separated the deck trying to tell herself that it didn't really matter. She was as casual about it as possible, almost as a throw away action, she shuffled and split the deck. Then she thought about the questions she wanted to ask. Was this bunch of friendly characters for real? What will happen next? Will they complete what they have been asked to do? After turning cards that were supposed to reveal the distant and recent past, she turned the card for the near future and quietly called out, 'fuck!'

Nel and Erin leapt out of their beds and ran into their mum's room and jumped on her bed, squealing. Olivia woke in a state of panic. It was only five-thirty a.m. 'Happy Birthday, darlings!'

'*Yay!*' they screamed, louder than she thought was imaginable. Although it may have been because they were right next to her ears. 'Well now, we had best go downstairs and see where your presents are and we need to see what you would like for your birthday breakfast too.' The twins charged downstairs and Olivia followed as spritely as she could after such a rude awakening. Ready on the table were two boxes, clearly labelled with each girl's name and wrapped in flamingo wrapping paper. Olivia watched as the pair of them ripped the wrapping to shreds. Their eyes were wide, and their grins were wider. Carol had suggested wrapping the presents and then putting them inside one box, to add to the surprise and slow them down. Between the discarded paper were two sun

222

print paper kits, out and about in the wild discovery kits, new hats with animal faces on, some sweets, – natural flavourings with no E numbers, and an underwater viewer for ponds and rock pools. Erin and Nel were very excited. 'Right we can take one thing each to Gramps and Gran's house to play with so you choose and I will carry them. OK, who wants pancakes for breakfast?'

'Yeah!' they yelled together.

The girls had put their hats on, been told the sweets were for later, not now and they could decide which craft kit they wanted to look at first. 'After breakfast I want you to get ready for an adventure. We will go and get Gramps and Gran and then we are taking you for a big surprise,' the girls squealed again. It was their day, Olivia loved them to bits and seeing them this excited and happy was still wonderful. It was however, very exhausting and it was still only seven thirty a.m.

The car pulled up at Edie and Harry's at nine. The girls weren't allowed to see the back garden or the cake, so Harry and Edie came straight out to the car. It was big hugs and cuddles and kisses all round. Edie squeezed between the car seats in the back with Erin and Nel either side and Harry rode shotgun. The clouds had thinned and a light blue warmth filled the air. Above them the red kites circled high on the breeze and eventually the sun broke through as they arrived at Flamingo Land car park.

Nel and Erin were beside themselves with childhood glee. 'Well you've played a blinder Liv. If we play our cards right, these two will run themselves ragged and sleep all the way home.'

'Harry, you know damn well, they're going to run us ragged and we'll sleep on the way home.'

'Very true, Edie love, but at least we're not driving. Liv, make sure you have an espresso before we leave.'

They took it in turns to go on a ride with the twins. Harry drew the short straw on the small log flume and looked like a giant inside the seating carriage. He also came off the worst when the inevitable splashing caught them off guard. Harry's larger surface area had him dripping wet, while the girls were saved from most of the tsunami by their granddad's bulk. Harry overdid the dramatics for the twins amusement and they laughed even more when Edie handed him a small tissue. They took countless photos of them all, including selfies and asking other friendly park goers to take the whole family shots. It was a very happy birthday, for all of them. They ate mediocre hot dogs and ice cream, that the adults endured, but the girls adored. In the early afternoon they headed for home and sure enough the girls fell asleep. So did Harry. He had pulled down the passenger visor to keep the sun off his face and Edie could see him in the little mirror. Then he started snoring gently. 'He's always slept like a baby.' 'He doesn't sound like one though mum.' They both chuckled and talked quietly so as not to wake them up.

Harry twitched himself awake and the women laughed at him. 'Have I been asleep long?' He yawned. 'Long enough to catch quite a few flies, dad. You'll not be needing any tea after that lot.' The girls stirred either side of Edie. There was a brief gentle wakening until they realised it was still their birthday and their energy returned. Mercifully, Olivia was just parking up as they realised they were back at Gramps and Gran's house and there were more treats in store.

In Edie and Harry's back garden, the girls stripped off and jumped into the water. The sun of the day had heated up the sides and the temperature of the pool. It was about a foot deep but it was a ten foot diameter. Despite leaves and the odd dead fly, the girls paid no attention and splashed around and each other. The little inflatable flamingoes just about managed to take the weight of an ecstatic six year old. 'Well as you handled the water so well earlier, Gramps, you can be lifeguard,' said Olivia. 'I have been called David Hasselhof in the past,' he joked and winked at Edie.

'I think you were called a "hassled oaf",' came back Edie, quickly and even Harry thought that was very funny, despite it being somewhat insulting coming from his own wife. Edie and Olivia laid the birthday tea table and over on the sideboard was a selection of little eats to have alongside the sandwiches and mini scotch eggs. Then Olivia stood at the patio doors with two towelling robes and called the girls and Harry in for tea. When Erin and Nel saw the birthday cake and the pink meringue flamingoes with upright meringue necks and black beaks, they yelled even louder. Edie grinned even more than her granddaughters. They had developed a hearty hunger after their water play and the sandwiches and little eats went down very quickly. In fact, they went down everywhere, and Harry made a mental note of where to get the vacuum out after they had gone. Photos were taken with them either side of the cake, blowing out the candles and greedily demolishing flamingoes. The girls hadn't wanted to take their food to the treehouse. Now they were six, they wanted to eat at the big table, because they were growing up. They set up Edie's phone for a picture of all of them, and Harry tickled the girls, just as the photo was taken.

After one more game of trying not to fall off the flamingoes, Nel and Erin were called back inside to dry off and prepare to go home. Finding Dory would be the sedentary end to their birthday and Olivia hoped they would fall asleep halfway through and then she could let them watch it the following evening again.

'Thank you so much, Mum, Dad. It's been bloody marvellous. Look at them.' Nel and Erin were still jumping up and down in the hallway.'

'It's been absolutely perfect Liv, I'll remember this one for a very long time.' Harry smiled warmly. Olivia hugged them both.

'Love you, Mum; love you, Dad,'

'Love you too, Liv,' they replied and then Harry knelt down to the girls.

'Come here you two, I love you so much, haven't we had a fandabedozee birthday?'

He kissed them in turn and blew raspberries on their cheeks as they giggled and screamed, 'Love you, Gramps!'

Edie gave them a huge hug each and said she loved them even more. After two trips to the car including a careful transfer of the birthday cake and other Tupperware secured sandwiches and little eat leftovers, the girls finally stopped jiggling in their seats and were strapped in properly. The final goodbyes and affirmation of love were called, then the door closed and the house was quiet once more. 'We are not going to touch any washing up or cleaning, or tidying, or sorting the garden,' stated Harry forcefully. 'We are going to sit down, with a cuppa and unwind and enjoy the calm, what do you say love?'

'I say you're a very wise man Harry Blackmoor and I love you.'

'Well now Edie Blackmoor, I think I love you even more.' And he kissed her. Then with mugs in hand they sat in the back garden smiling, tired and very happy, watching the inflatable flamingoes move slowly around the pool, caught on the early evening breeze as the red kites above them headed back to roost.

On Sunday, everyone went about their routines as though everything was perfectly normal. The Sunday shop, washing, catching up with family and friends, were all being ticked off everyone's "what to do on a Sunday" list. There was some gardening and a good walk and reading the papers, both online, for Elinor and in print for Pat. It could only have been more like a Sunday if someone had gone to church and someone else had made Yorkshire puddings. It was as though they instinctively knew to leave each other be, and have a day off from the spiralling strangeness that had engulfed them since the beginning of the month.

On Monday morning, Elinor was the first to let the recent events out of the box and take over her thoughts once more. She was so grateful to have Amanda to help her normalise it all. She was even more grateful that everyone else seemed so normal. Elinor knew that whatever happened next would be their last chance saloon. She had run out of any new ideas and had become obsessed with her mycelium connection and theory. Harry had been really useful, well everyone had and this last push would decide things either way. She felt a seriousness come over her, that she hadn't felt before. It wasn't like the final passing of Tom either. That had been closure. This sensation was unsettling and anxiety filled. It made her worry that everything could, of course, just come to nothing.

Harry was up and about, albeit a bit stiffly, after yesterday's emptying of the pool, bucket after bucket. Thankfully it was his day off from electrical jobs so he could take things slowly and he was looking forward to putting his head together with Carol's. He smiled to himself as he heard the Laurel and Hardy theme music again. Still grinning he walked into the kitchen as Edie was finishing washing up and she turned to smile at him. As she did so, Harry's face changed; the smile dropped instantly and he stared at her with fear in his eyes, but then she realised that he was staring right through her. There was one brief moment when his focus seemed to catch her eyes one more time and he called, 'Edie love, I don't feel...' Then he crumpled. His legs gave way under him and he slumped to the floor, heavily and completely. Terrified, Edie called his name and quickly moved over to him on the floor, removing her washing up gloves at the same time. No matter how many times she called his name, there was no response. She felt his pulse and could barely feel anything. Then she called 999. They talked her through CPR and she followed their instructions to the letter. She kept calling his name. They kept saying, 'Well done Edie, keep going.' It took an interminable amount of time for the ambulance to arrive and the paramedics to get to Harry. Edie felt like she was underwater. She couldn't hear properly, she was drowning in despair. As she locked up the house and followed Harry into the ambulance, she asked which hospital they were going to so she could call Olivia. It went to answerphone.

In the ambulance she held his hand. The paramedics were administering the defibrillator and it made her scream inside. Outside she was silent. Edie's world had just collapsed and she knew that Olivia's would too, as soon as she heard the message. Edie wouldn't leave Harry's side. Even when they told her that her husband had suffered a very extensive cardiac arrest and he wouldn't have known much about it, she needed to stay with him and keep him company and wait for Olivia. When Olivia burst into the room, she wasn't ready to see her dead father and her distraught mother and she hugged Edie and cried and cried.

Carol had been waiting for a text from Harry just to confirm what time she should get to his house. When he hadn't replied, she had phoned. Harry's phone was on the sideboard, alone in an empty house ringing loudly, with no one hearing. Carol thought the lack of response was very unusual and texted Edie, but there was no response either. So then, she texted Elinor, Pat and Ed, *'Hi, everyone, I've just tried calling and texting Harry and Edie and there was no reply. I was due to go round and plan our next steps. I know Harry was looking forward to it. I'm wondering if it's something to do with the twins or something. Not sure what to do next.'*

Elinor replied first, *'Let's wait a few hours before we get in touch, it could be anything. We can try and find out later on. Don't worry, Carol, I'm sure Harry will be on the case as soon as he can, regardless.'* They agreed to keep in touch.

Edie had gone numb. Olivia held her hand and a registrar and doctor talked through the details of recording the time of death and registering the passing of Harry Blackmoor for the coroner's report and general death certificate. She didn't want to leave him. She didn't want to leave his physical presence. She didn't want to imagine him in a cold room, in a drawer, by himself, without her keeping him warm. She didn't want to imagine trying to get into bed without him, without feeling his body next to hers, without ever hearing him breathe next to her again. She didn't want to imagine, never hearing his voice again, touching his hands or kissing him ever again. As Olivia managed to walk Edie away from Harry, a nurse came close and put her hand on Edie's back gently. 'Your husband's soul is elsewhere now. He doesn't need his body anymore; he's free now, he's at rest.' Both Olivia and Edie wondered if he was at rest though.

Olivia plucked up enough courage to text various distant relatives and some of Harry and Edie's old work friends and then she texted Pat and Ed and Elinor, Carol and Amanda. *'Hi, all. Dad died this morning. Mum and I are in shock. We'll be in touch when we're ready. Thank you xxx.'* The replies were simple. *'Oh no, so sorry Olivia. All my love to you and Edie and the girls,'* texted Pat first. Then Olivia realised she was going to have to tell her daughters, and she burst into tears again.

Pat suggested that their small group should have a few days of reflection and think about how they could support Edie and Olivia now. Pat volunteered to be the first one to get in touch with Edie and they were appreciative of her empathic ability to talk through things warmly, with the bereaved. Then they would decide what they should do next, now that Harry was dead.

Chapter Seventeen – The Leap of Faith

It was three days before Pat decided to contact Edie. She knew it was going to be one of the hardest calls to make. This little band of friends had been brought together through a situation created of death, but that did not make losing Harry any easier for Edie and Olivia, and Pat knew it. When Pat visited the patients at the hospice, they were strangers and that made it much easier. Edie and Olivia weren't strangers, they were now firm friends and Pat had realised just how much they meant to her. Pat phoned and asked if she could call round and Edie welcomed her with open arms. She let Edie talk and prompted direction delicately, asking how Olivia had told the girls. Apparently, they had yet to be fully aware that they would never see Gramps again, but Olivia and Edie talked about death and they talked about Harry and they looked through all the photos they had taken on their birthday and together they smiled and laughed and occasionally cried. They cried a lot more when the girls had gone to bed.

Pat let Edie make the drinks and still accepted the slice of cake that Edie had made for her visitor, knowing that Edie needed to do practical things to keep her occupied. It had been discussed between Edie and Olivia whether or not Olivia should move in and live with Edie. It would make things much easier and cheaper. Even though they weren't sure exactly when, Pat knew that Olivia didn't want her mum to live alone in the house with just the memories and silence. The twins had yelped with glee at the prospect of living with their gran, but mainly having their own rooms and the back garden and treehouse to play in all the time.

The conversation came round to the funeral and then Edie surprised Pat by saying she would like to speak to everyone about it very soon. Pat assured her that a funeral was a very personal choice and there was no need for any other interaction, especially as they weren't even actual family. They would follow her wishes and they would attend if she wanted them to and stay away if not, and do whatever Edie and Olivia needed. Without realising it, Pat even said that her and Ed would look after Nel and Erin for a few hours if she ever needed them to. She really couldn't believe she had just said that, but it came from a place of friendship and she meant it.

'Will you ask them all to come over tomorrow evening at about seven please, Pat? Olivia has said she can get the babysitter back for a few hours as the girls should have gone to bed by then.'

'Of course, Edie.' Pat gave Edie a very big hug and headed on her way. She relayed the conversation and Edie's request.

Everyone knew the possible emotions that would inevitably bubble up the following day. Pat said if Edie and Olivia got emotional, then no one should take it to heart if there was any anger. 'We let them do the talking and we wait in the pauses for them to have time to think about what to say. We don't need to second guess anything. They know that they mean so much to us now and have become our family.' The mood was understandably sombre and Elinor dared to say the next obvious thing. 'If it ends here because we've lost Harry, then so be it. You've all been amazing and I want to keep being friends with all of you.' Everyone agreed with that.

There were lots of deep breaths, wiping of eyes and trembling lips, as one by one everyone arrived and was welcomed in by Edie and Olivia. They sat in the dining room around the table and stared into the garden.

'Me and Olivia have been thinking and after talking to the funeral company we've decided to go with a woodland burial, Elinor. Harry seemed keen on your idea and thinking and well, we like the idea of a solid, sturdy tree growing above him, that is him. There's a woodland plot site just the other side of Ilkley Moor and we can buy a plot for the family. You get enough space for the adult tree, which means all of us can be buried together there over the years. If the girls don't want to that's fine, but I know me and Liv have decided we'd like to be under the arms of Harry's tree, with him.' That made everyone falter and gulp in tears.

'That's bloody marvellous, Edie,' said Ed, who was fumbling for a tissue in his pocket, but Pat handed him one sooner.

'I think we should do that too Ed, don't you?' asked Pat.

'Yes love, I do.'

'It was when you talked about the mycelium and how the roots of trees sort of talked to each other and helped each other and it just seemed right.' Elinor lifted her head from her hands. Her eyes were red.

'Oh, Edie, that's such a thoughtful thing to do, but none of this needs to have anything to do with us, it just needs to be what you and Olivia want and what you think Harry would have wanted.'

'It is, Elinor, don't worry about that. I'm hoping that he has found Gracie and helped her move on. He missed her so much.' Edie was starting to go and looked up to the ceiling and took another deep breath.

Edie turned her head. 'Harry would want us to finish this, Carol.' And she put her hand on Carol's knee. 'We'll all help you as much as we can, if you need to make anything else.'

'I'll do what I can Edie, I promise and I'm so pleased that this weird thing happened Edie. I'm still not quite sure what has happened exactly, but it's brought us together. Harry was right, I could have walked away but I didn't and it's the strangest feeling ever, but we had so many laughs and mishaps. We even called each other Laurel and Hardy, we had so many accidents.' There was chuckling and smiles and then Edie said it. 'I bloody love you lot and Harry did too.' They all began to cry.

'Fucking hell,' said Pat. Then followed it with an apologetic. 'Sorry.'

'No don't be sorry Pat, if ever there's a time to say fucking hell it's now,' replied Edie.

Everyone in the group left Edie's at the same time and Olivia said she would tell them when the funeral was. Carol promised to contact Elinor, and Amanda said she would be on speed dial to Russell. Pat and Ed reiterated the offer of looking after Erin and Nel and everybody said that was serious. When things had quietened down, Olivia gave her mum a massive hug and said she could go and stay with her if the house was too quiet. Edie declined with thanks and Olivia left for home.

Edie stood in the silence. 'I miss you Harry, God I miss you so much, love.'

Then she sat down and stared at the sideboard.

Karen was feeling very unsettled. The cards had delivered a message of sadness and melancholy. She couldn't rest and eventually phoned Pat. 'Hi, Pat, it's Karen, how are you?'

'Oh, er hi Karen, this is an unexpected surprise, I'm OK, thank you, how about you?'

'All fine here cheers.' Pat was unsure about Karen's voice; it didn't seem fine. Karen was unsure about Pat's voice; she didn't seem OK. 'What can I do for you Karen?'

'This is going to sound strange Pat, but has something horrible just happened? I read the cards the other evening and I wanted to know about what was happening with your thing and the results were really negative.'

'Oh, Karen, Harry died. He had a massive cardiac arrest last week. Edie was there for him, but it was too late.'

'Oh God, I'm so sorry. I knew it wasn't good, but I didn't know exactly what the outcome would be, or who it would involve.'

'It's been horrible and we've tried to be there for Edie. Please come to the funeral next week. I know Edie will be so grateful to see you.'

'Of course, I will Pat. Will you text me the details and I'll make sure I'm free.'

'Will do Karen, thank you.' When Karen put the phone down, she went into the hall and stared at the landline and the dog followed her expecting a walk. She leant down and gave the dog a big scratch under the chin. 'What the fuck is this all about, eh mush?'

Carol had a free week ahead for maintenance work at Barn End and invited Elinor and Amanda up, so they could escape the city for a night and talk through any final ideas of what to do next. She also hoped to persuade them to lend a hand with her next project. Elinor helped to load Amanda's car with Prosecco, overnight bags and their walking gear. As they left the outskirts of the city they chose to drive via the woodland burial site that Edie and Olivia had picked for Harry. 'Oh Mand, look. It's bloody gorgeous. You can see right across the river to the Cow and Calf.' This was where two large rock formations loomed large over the town. This was Ilkley Moor.

'Isn't that wonderful?' High up from the road a new wood was emerging. 'Let's just drive up a bit further and see what it's like. We might as well scope it out.'

'Good idea El. For a change, we are genuinely wanting to take a look and you can legitimately take some photographs too.' They parked up just through some gates and Elinor immediately spotted the big green box just by the verge. Inside was a small meeting place and a map of the site. Elinor took a photo of it and they walked around the path and up the hill. Spaced out around them were young saplings and small markers. The plates were small, but still lovingly inscribed. She looked at the road near the wood. 'Shame about the electricity pylon,' she said.

'I don't think the people of Ilkley would want to be without their electricity supply,' said a voice from behind them.

'Can I help you?' A man had come out of the small office by the gate, when he saw them looking at the site. Amanda spoke first.

'Oh hello, yes. Our friend is going to be buried here soon, and it seems like such a lovely thing to do, we wanted to find out a bit more and see it for ourselves.'

'Yes,' added Elinor. 'It seems very tranquil and I love the idea of creating a new woodland here.' The man was obviously well versed in discussing such a delicate situation, with calm and gentle seriousness. After talking them through how it all worked, he gave them a brochure, they thanked him and headed off to Carol's. Elinor took one last photo of the view across the valley.

It didn't take Carol long to show them around Barn End and they found themselves sat out round a fire pit soon enough, with a drink in hand, talking about Harry and Edie.

'I've just lost my right hand man, Elinor. Harry had lots of really useful suggestions when we were making the board. Now I don't know what's different or how we should change things.' Carol had lost faith in her own abilities and that was not like Carol at all. Carol's phone rang.

'Hey, you really can get a signal up here,' chirped Amanda in surprise.

'Hello Edie love,' said Carol surprised. 'What can I do for you?' Amanda and Elinor went quiet.

'Hello Carol, when you get a chance, could you come round before the funeral, I have a request.'

'Anything you need Edie, no question of it. I can get to you tomorrow afternoon, if that's good for you?' It was clear that Edie was not her usual self, but she still managed to offer her some tea, so that Carol didn't have to worry about food. Then she said her thank you and put down the phone.

'Oh, that poor woman, what is she going through right now?' Carol stared at her phone then stared out at the view.

'I really want to get this thing sorted, for Edie.' The weather chilled and a colder breeze whipped across the camping site.

'Let's not bother with the fire pit eh? It's perfectly warm inside,' suggested Carol. Then a barn owl swept low from a crop of trees across her field, to another. 'We can

239

come back out later and I'll show you the stars. We should get a good view of the milky way and if we're lucky, some shooting stars.'

'I think you're lucky enough Carol,' suggested Amanda, taking in the view with a deep breath. 'This is magnificent.'

They had been inside for a few hours until the blackness fell. There was no light pollution here. Nothing to get in the way of the starlight. Carol grabbed three big blankets and they headed back out with torches. On folding chairs, they sat back, pulled the blankets over them and stared up into the universe. 'Jesus,' said Elinor.

'Probably not,' replied Carol and they burst out laughing.

'Isn't it all fucking huge?' The milky way stretched across the entire sky. They saw the colours in it and they stared and stared, awestruck.

'I'm getting a stiff neck,' said Amanda.

'Me too,' said Carol. 'Shall we head in?'

'Yes please,' they both replied. They had all drunk quite a bit by now and as the ground was uneven, the undulations added to their instability as they walked back to Barn End and their drunkenness added to it even more. The laughing started and it echoed out into the hills and the night. A fit of the giggles lead to the inevitable howls and Elinor calling loudly that she needed the loo.

Inside the warm air of the house, Elinor asked for some paper and a pen. Carol was not short of stationery. Although she made no headway with any ideas, Elinor kept looking at the big sheet then turning back to the conversation. They polished off another bottle and the slurring of words became infectious. 'I need a coffee Carol, please,' said Elinor, aware that her face was beginning to ache from laughing and grinning. Amanda had told her latest tale of comedy capers at school and Carol and Elinor had high-fived each other in acknowledgement of leaving the profession. Amanda had replied emphatically. 'You buggers!' Which just made them laugh even more. Even when they tried to apologise, it fell on stony ground and Amanda called them both evil. Eventually Carol and Amanda headed to their beds, but Elinor sat at the table and stared at the empty white sheet in front of her. To begin with, she just doodled. Letting her mind wander along with the felt nib of a marker pen. Then she had one astounding thought. No matter how ridiculous, the leap of faith idea was formulating. For the next hour, Elinor scribbled and doodled, then redrew and refined, until eventually the largest sheet was drawn out, illustrated and annotated. She had sobered up and after one large glass of water, switched off the light and headed to bed.

In the morning, Elinor came downstairs and Amanda and Carol were already up. 'Morning, you two, how's the heads?' she asked, as she looked at her two friends, who seemed to be staring back at her strangely.

'We're fine El, more to the point, how are you, and what time did you stay up 'til, making this?' Amanda gestured to the paper on the table.

'Shit yes, I forgot about that. I'm not sure we're awake and alert enough yet are we?'

'Tea or coffee, and toast and yes we are awake enough. You need to explain this piece of art.'

On the paper Elinor had written in the very centre, as she usually did. This time it said "ROOTer" and was surrounded by bark to create the base of a tree trunk. From it she had drawn roots twisting away and branching out. The lines and arrows had turned into roots, they had life and form and they grew. There was a meandering wave of mycelium in orange that networked it all together. 'Either we are calling an art gallery, or you've drawn something amazing that might work.' Carol seemed to believe that this was possible. 'Come on lass, give it to us.' Elinor slurped on her tea, then took a big bite of her toast. Butter dribbled and she just managed to catch the marmalade with her tongue, before it fell onto her drawing.

'When Harry had mentioned about needing the booster to extend the signal of Wi-fi around their house, I realised that the first point of contact we have is the router itself. Then as I thought of it going into the walls, floors and cables and wires, I realised it was the root of everything, so I called it the rooter.' She pointed at the deliberate misspelling.

'I think we might be able to create, well sorry, I mean, I think Carol might be able to create.'

'Oh, here we go,' interjected Carol, smiling. 'Ha, sorry, yes. I think you can create a rooter. If we can put them inside the house, why can't we just put them directly into the ground too?' She pointed at one of the roots that had a small box and line drawn leading to the mycelium and a tree root, like a long spike. 'I have to believe that nature will do its part and work with us.'

'What about power?' asked Amanda.

'We can set up a small solar panel on the top of it if necessary,' suggested Carol.

'Actually,' thought Carol out loud. 'Perhaps we don't really need that to work forever anyway, but as a starter just to help get the signals moving. Did you ever see those kits for clocks where you just put the connectors straight into a potato?' Carol did a quick google search and showed Amanda what she was describing.

'Well that invention passed me by,' said Amanda baffled by what she was looking at.

'Oh, hell yes,' said Elinor, suddenly excited and animated. 'and there's an artist who created a field of glowing fluorescent tubes. All he did was put them upright in the ground, but underneath an electricity pylon. The current coming off the lines of the pylons is so great that it makes an earth through the tubes and they light up.'

'Now you're having a laugh?' questioned Amanda disbelievingly.

'Honest Mand look.' Elinor googled it and up came the image. 'See? Look, he's called Richard Box, and it's no bloody weirder or unbelievable than what we've all witnessed so far anyway is it?' Then Elinor went into the photos on her phone and selected the most recent one. She zoomed in on it and showed it to Carol and Amanda.

'Look what's right next to the Moor woodland burial site.' They were looking at the pylon.

'Fair play, but what do we do with that information? And what happens about connecting to inside and actually communicating? Sorry, I know I'm playing devil's advocate here.' Elinor thought for a moment. 'Look, Harry called me out on one thing that I said about the previous problems.' Elinor never liked to be wrong, but this was one time when she was more than happy to be. 'He told me that the distance through the air for a signal to get to a mobile phone might only be out of reach outdoors. He said that perhaps indoors, it might be enough to get from the normal router to a phone. We have to believe that he's right.' Elinor pointed to the last part of the image. I think we need to make a few rooters. Then we can have a few choices. We can put one near Harry's tree for a start. Would you be able to do it Carol?'

'It looks possible.' Then Carol started drawing and talking through what was vital and what might not be easy to get hold of. 'I need fresh air though to clear my head and to make way for a plan. I'll take you for a walk, then we can see where my brain is at.' They got themselves kitted out, they went to the loo one more time and Carol led them up the hill.

Edie had opened the door to the sideboard and looked at the phone. She delicately lifted the receiver as though it was a fledgling bird. She brought the receiver to her ear. There was no sound at all. No dial tone, no static. It was still plugged in, but there seemed to be no energy at all coming through it. She decided to phone Karen. 'Hello Karen, it's Edie, how are you?'

'Oh Edie, hello, I'm fine, how are you? What a stupid thing to say, I'm so sorry to hear about Harry. Pat told me. I had to phone her because the cards had told me something was up and I didn't know what, but I knew it was bad and then she told me and oh Edie, I'm so sorry.' Karen knew she had just blurted out a stream of waffle.

'It's OK, Karen. It's not easy at all. Look I wondered if you could do something for me please?'

'Of course, Edie, anything.'

'Well, our landline, my landline seems to have lost something, there's no real dial tone. The link and its usual noises, don't sound the same. I don't know if Gracie will call, or Harry, or if they can anymore. The line might not have enough power or something. Could you check yours please?'

'Sure, Edie.' Karen moved into the hall and lifted the receiver, the static was exceptional. 'Crikey could you hear that from your end Edie?'

'Yes, Karen, that's worse than ever. What do you think it means? Do you think I'll be able to speak to either of them again?'

'Oh, lord, I don't know love. I can ask for you though, I'll try.'

'Would you please? Just do your best. Oh, and please come to the funeral. It's at the Moor Woodland site near Ilkley on Tuesday at two p.m. Then everyone can come back here if they'd like.'

'I will Edie. Harry needs a grand send off and that's what he'll have.'

Then Edie called Elinor and left a voice mail. 'Hello, Elinor, it's Edie, would you do me a favour please and let me know what the signal is like from your landline now please? Now that Tom has gone. Thank you.'

Olivia arrived at Edie's with the girls. They undid their own seat belts and shot out of the car as soon as their mum had undone the child safety locks. They ran towards the house yelling, 'Gran, Gran, Gran.' Edie heard them and opened the door ready. Nel and Erin gave their gran an extra strong hug and lots of kisses and Edie held them tighter than she had ever held them before.

Chapter Eighteen – Into the Unknown

The wind had whipped up and was quite strong by lunchtime and the trees were thrashing their branches and sap green leaves. The cherry blossom from next door's tree was throwing up its petals like confetti across Edie's back garden and delicate pinks filled the air. Nel and Erin were playing in the tree house and Edie and Olivia were sat at the table discussing the final plans for Harry's funeral.

'Well, that's given me an idea for which tree we should choose Liv.'

'Yes, Mum?'

'Let's get a cherry tree. The blossoms are wonderful, the bees will love it and there's a possibility it could bear fruit too.'

'I like that, Mum, I think Dad would, too.' A big gust swirled the blossom like a vortex around the grass. The nearside tin can strained on its post by the house. The string couldn't hold out as it frayed against the raw metal made by the hole that Harry had created with his drill. It snapped and the length of it fell back into the grass and around the roots of the tree that the girls were playing in.

'Brring brring, brring brring.' Came the voice through the tin can in the tree house. The girls giggled and pushed their mouths close to the can.

'Hello,' they both yelled.

'Hello my wonderful ladies,' came the voice in response.

'Graaaamps!' they both shouted ecstatically.

'Just tell your gran and mum I'm sorting the exchange, I love you all.'

'Yay!' called back the girls and then only the wind made a noise. Whether the string broke before or after the call would never be known.

Olivia went to the tin can by the door to call the girls in for their lunch and saw that the string had snapped, so she walked over and knocked on the little door. Erin opened it, smiling broadly. 'Time for lunch girls, come on in.' They shot out down the slide and ran ahead into the dining room to where Edie had laid out their food at the table, on proper (plastic) plates. They settled themselves down cheerily, sloshing their juice and making loud lip-smacking noises as they drank and ate.

'So, what have the pair of you been up to out there today then?' asked Edie. Erin and Nel looked at each other and Nel turned to her gran. 'We've been talking to Gramps.'

Nel and Erin looked at their gran and then at their mum. The sincerity was clear. Olivia looked at her mum and Edie looked at her granddaughters. 'And what did he say, darlings?'

'He said he was sorting the "exange",' replied Erin.

'He said he loved us all,' stated Nel, knowingly.

'Well that's lovely isn't it? Now when you've had your lunch, you can have fifteen more minutes before we have to head home. Don't forget that you have to tidy up everything now, if you want Gran to let us stay here forever.' Olivia made everything seem perfectly normal. This was now the second time that Nel had interacted with a dead relative and that was not perfectly normal at all. The girls were finally learning about consequences of actions and they were taking things in. They still managed to leave a trail of chaos as they shot back out and up the tree.

'I believe them mum. I don't know how he did it, but I believe he called them.'

'I do too, Liv. The landline isn't functioning properly anymore and he knew they were here. Erin wouldn't have come up with a word she couldn't pronounce, not out of nowhere like that.' Edie took a deep breath. 'I've called Carol round this afternoon. I want her to get the booster thing back that they made. He was so proud of it. And I've asked Karen if she can find out from her tarot cards, if I'll be able to speak to Harry again.' Olivia held her mum's hand. 'I see Mum and I understand. If we know he is still working on trying to make things connect at their side, then he might still be on hold for us too.' Edie lost it. She had been keeping it together so well, but this was how close her emotions were to the surface. Olivia moved round closer to her mum and hugged her tightly.

'I know, Mum, I know.' They cried together and then got themselves together, as Nel and Erin appeared at the other side of the closed patio doors. 'It's windy,' they yelled together.

'They look like they're inside a snow globe.' Laughed Olivia, as she slid back the door and the cherry blossom blew in with them.

As Elinor, Amanda and Carol were on the return leg of their walk, they had been discussing how they would never have all met if those first calls had been missed. 'I know none of this makes sense, but I do kind of wonder if it's been just as frantic for Tom, Gracie and George? How did they come together in the first place and then manage to coordinate themselves? Especially in the nothingness?' Amanda was baffled by it all understandably and Carol and Elinor agreed. 'I'm trying to think of it like a big waiting room at a telephone exchange. I don't think that they have sat there twiddling their ethereal thumbs waiting though. Tom said it was like he'd just been woken up and was sensing things.

So perhaps, it's more like they were connected in a giant board at the exchange, and an operator said, 'I'll just put you through.' Let's face it, I don't think we are in any doubt that any of this is to be believed. We would be laughed out of town and straight into the farm.'

'Yep,' agreed Carol. 'That very first night that I met Pat, she asked me not to tell anyone as it wouldn't be believed, and she wasn't wrong.'

'I wouldn't mind meeting Karen,' suggested Amanda. 'I'd like to ask a few things myself and you say she's for real and seems nice?'

'She is, really down to earth and no messing about. We've left her some good reviews. I think we freaked her out more than the other way round. I wonder if she's been invited to the funeral. I hope she has. You'll like her Mand.'

They strolled back to Barn End and gathered their belongings together. Elinor's phone got it's signal back and she listened to Edie's message about her landline. Carol was going to drive behind them and go straight to Edie's to see what she wanted. 'Feel free to stay at mine tonight too Carol, then you don't have a night drive back.'

'I'll take you up on that Elinor, ta. Then I can get a big shop in, in the morning.'

They packed the cars and unanimously decided to have one more trip to the loo. Then as Carol locked the door behind them, they stood on the door step and looked down the valley. 'You lucky sod,' said Amanda and a curlew called from the sky.

When Carol arrived at Edie's she was greeted with a hug of lifelong friendship. Carol gulped silently and breathed deeply. As they sat at the dining table, Edie said that if it was possible, she would like to get their motherboard back, as a piece of Harry's recent history. The landline phone didn't work properly anymore. It hadn't made it's little pings and there had been no communication from Gracie. 'He loved making that thing with you Carol. I had to listen to him telling me about it in great detail. I smiled in all the right places and said how clever he was, and you too of course. Look, I even took a photo of him with it, before you fitted it. It was just as he left the house. Look at his face. He's like a school boy with a project he's just won first prize for.' Edie showed Carol the photo.

'Oh, Harry, you crazy man,' she replied, and smiled warmly from the memory of that night.

'Well of course we can get it back Edie, but I do mean we. I can't do it by myself. It took two of us to put it in and it'll take two of us to take it out.'

'Oh crikey, I didn't think that through.' Edie's phone pinged and she read her text message from Elinor.

'Hi, Edie, my landline doesn't seem to be working either now. Virtually no signal and I haven't heard it ping for a week.' Edie read it out to Carol.

'Well then, we should go and check on the board anyway. It should be easier to get it out than it was to put in, but you'll need to be wearing the right gear, it's rather tricky underfoot and Harry face planting into his toolbag is proof of that.' Then Carol woke Edie right up. 'Here's my suggestion, let's do it now!'

'Now? Flippin' 'eck, Carol, that's a bit imminent, isn't it? What about being spotted?'

'So what, Edie? No one goes down that path, it's hidden and if anyone thinks we're stealing anything, they wouldn't find anything missing. Come on. I'll get some of the basic stuff from Harry's shed and you get a good old coat, some gloves and sturdy shoes on. I've got my walking boots and coat in the boot. Let's do it.'

'Oh god, all right. Although I'm suddenly thinking that this idea has backfired a bit.'

'Come on, Edie, Harry will be watching and he's going to love seeing you wade into his world.'

Edie felt very self-conscious of how she looked and Carol told her she looked like she was ready for a hike from Barn End into the dales. Then she invited Edie, Olivia and the girls to visit her up there any time. Edie said she'd love that and seeing the girls out in all that space would be incredible. Carol suggested getting everyone up to Barn End, but they would need inflatable mattresses and tents and they could toss for who got the beds. Edie said she should definitely have a bed and be nearest the toilet. Carol drove them and parked up in front of the Sainsbury's and reminded herself to grab a bottle for Elinor's, later on. With a small toolkit bag in one hand, Carol lead Edie round the back of the exchange. 'Oh, good grief, it is tight back here isn't it?' They disappeared into the undergrowth. Edie didn't realise that she had just placed her foot inside one of Harry's footprints. Carol was thinking about the fun she'd had with Harry, and Edie was thinking about how quick everything seemed to have gone. 'It doesn't seem that long since you were fitting it does it?'

'Feels like only yesterday, Edie. Now grab hold of that side there and we should be able to pull out together.' In perfect synchronicity, they yanked at a door each side and as they moved the wood backwards and forwards, they both fell and were caught by snagging thorns and brambles. 'Well nothing changes that's for sure,' said Carol, pulling herself back up and feeling the snagging fabric of her coat. 'One more strong pull and we should do it,' she promised.

'One-two-three-pull!' And with that she let out a huge trumpet like fart. Edie cracked and couldn't keep quiet. Carol had to laugh too and the pair of them howled. Caught up, snagged and now Carol's loss of dignity had them creased over themselves, on their knees. Their tears were full of laughter. When they looked up, they saw that the doors were open enough and there was the motherboard. The LED lights were no longer working. It had done it's job and now it was redundant. 'Let's get this thing out and home eh Edie?'

'Yes, but only if you promise not to fart anymore.'

'That is a promise I will never make you. Come on, you hold it on your side while I start unscrewing this end.' Edie felt sad looking at the board and at the hard work that Harry had put into it. Then she remembered that Carol had just farted and started laughing again.

Once the board had come away from the inside of the junction box, they closed the doors, tried to cover it back over with greenery and headed out carefully trying not to look suspicious, even though two middle aged ladies had just backed out from undergrowth carrying an oversized circuit board. They loaded the motherboard and the tool bag back into the car and Carol nipped into Sainsbury's and grabbed a bottle of fizz, as she called it, then drove them back to Edie's for afternoon tea. Over homemade quiche and salad, Carol explained what they had been working on and Elinor's grand final plan. 'That sounds like it might work this time, Carol.'

'We hope so Edie. It does now seem to make some sort of sense. And Elinor thinks that Harry's suggestion for the connection to mobile phones might be right, so of course that remains to be seen, but it's all we can do now to get it done. I've got an idea about what I can make. Elinor wants to know if I can make a few, but I'll try one to start with.'

'Where will you put it, the first one?'

'That's the question, isn't it? Not too sure yet, but if one can go near the big new exchange that Olivia saw and perhaps one could go near Harry's tree when you've planted it. That would be a good start, what do you think? That would seem to make sense, wouldn't it?'

Then Edie made a suggestion and Carol knew she had to honour it, and she would only have until Tuesday morning. 'Could you put one in with Harry please?'

Carol looked at her and felt herself well up. 'I will do everything I can to make sure the first one is ready and that Harry can take it with him, Edie.'

'Thank you, love.'

They talked about the funeral some more. There would be a wicker coffin, so it would also biodegrade. Olivia would talk about her dad and at the site would be a large print of the photo they took at Flamingo Land, all together, with Harry in the middle, beaming; with his arms around Erin and Nel on either side of him and Edie and Olivia at either side of them. Edie showed Carol the photo and again, she gulped back the tears. Edie seemed to be settling into acceptance and was calm. Edie disappeared out to the shed and came back with Harry's big toolbox of everything. 'I know you might need some of this and I know he would want you to have it, Carol.'

'I think you're amazing Edie, I really do,' said Carol as she took the heavy box from Edie's hands and headed out to her car. 'I will get cracking on this straight away and I will get it done.'

'I know you will. Have a good evening and give my love to Elinor too.'

Elinor had got back in touch with Ed, who was pottering about in his garden, making way for spring planting. 'Hi, listen Ed, I need you to see if we can get some intel from Joel and Heena please? Do you reckon you can ask them for an update on what the council's plans are to get the CityFibre network rolled out?'

'I will ask. Joel knows he owes me one after your help and as it's you that's asking, he'll know he really does need to pay back. Is there anything specific that you need?'

'What I really want is a distribution map, Ed. One that shows where they are up to with laying the fibre. So we can see the coverage as it is now. At some point we shouldn't need to add anything, but it would be good to get a plan of what they want to have covered eventually and when the timeline is for achieving various sections, the order of play, if you see what I mean?'

'I do see exactly. Would you like me to see if he can get you what Open Reach are planning too? I know Virgin are a law unto themselves, but surely the town planning department need to know what is being dug up and where, especially in their own streets.'

'That would be superb, Ed.'

Ed got straight onto Joel, who said he would get straight down to the communication link at the civic planning department. This was an office that dealt with infrastructure for the city. He asked Heena to talk to the CityFibre company and it didn't take long to get what they wanted. They said they were looking at promoting the amazing work that was happening to connect the citizens with the latest technology. They told them that they wouldn't be forgotten for being the people that made sure no one was left on hold. They played the game brilliantly. Joel emailed Ed all the information he could. *'I'm hoping this is enough, Ed. We don't want to push our luck too far. Hope it's useful for Elinor. What is she using it for?'* Ed replied.

'Thank you so much, Joel. Not too sure, but she's doing some crazy art thing and turning all sorts of technology into some arty multi-nature artwork. I'm not sure what it will look like in the end, but I'm sure it will be amazing. Thanks again, speak soon. Ed.' Then Ed forwarded it all to Elinor. Then he texted her to let her know he had emailed her. Then he remembered how ridiculous this all was.

Elinor and Carol were mulling over Carol's drawings of small circuit boards that were miniature versions of transistor radios, but she had applied a two-way mechanism, so they could send a signal as well as receive it. Elinor had attempted electronics as one of her teacher training modules a very long time ago and it had driven her insane. 'I don't know how it all makes sense to you Carol. I got all muddled up being taught about gates. Not, nand and nor nonsense or something. And traffic lights, I think it was the traffic lights that did for me.'

'God you really are talking ancient stuff. That still plays a part, but everything is different now and some things are much easier than others, once you know the basics.'

'Well I'm glad someone does. Oh hang on, Ed is telling me to check my email. Looks like Joel has found stuff for us.'

They read through the information and looked at the plans. The main arterial roads from the city centre were being connected and laid first. Then the ring road was joining them all up together in a big loop, like a wheel with spokes. It would then follow that the bigger roads such as bus routes were the second phase, then suburb by suburb. The date for completion for these first two phases was due to be December, 2025. Full connection for every street was December, 2027. Edie lived outside the city boundary and Harry would be buried even further. Elinor knew it was vital that Edie had some connection. Elinor rang Amanda and Carol reeled off a list of things she hoped Russell would be able to get. Carol would go to the school, meet Amanda, then and they would see if Russell would let Carol take what she needed. Harry's funeral was only three days away and Carol had promised Edie. The urgency built up and they felt on edge once more.

Russell walked down the DT corridor and got out his keys to open the department and there was Amanda, with someone else, wearing a visitor's badge. 'Hi, morning Russell, this is Carol.' Russell was surprised, he wasn't even fully awake and he hadn't had a coffee yet.

'Oh... *er*... hi, Amanda, hi, Carol, this seems ominous.'

'Not at all, Russ, we are just in one heck of a rush and it's too difficult to explain. Is there any way that Carol can plunder your electronics cabinet please?'

'Er yeah sure, fill your boots Carol, it's only going to waste.' Thanks, Russell, much obliged.' He took them to the store cupboard and switched on the light. He pointed to the back and Carol's eyes lit up.

'Nice! Right let's get the pick-n-mix bag out.' Carol worked her way through the drawers. She selected everything and spares. Rolls of wire and blank boards. Rolls of solder, copper tape and more LEDs. Amanda tried to explain to Russell, but she couldn't tell him what was really happening.

'Carol used to be a teacher too Russ, she taught electronics, but her school chucked everything away. So she's trying to make something for her new project at her house in the dales and I mentioned about your stash. I don't think she'll need to steal anymore.'

'No, this'll do nicely, Russ, you've got quite an amazing shop here though, but this should do me. Thanks again.' Russell was perplexed by the two women in front of him. They were like two characters from a movie, with some kind of ulterior motive that he couldn't work out, but they were also charming.

'Well, good luck with it all Carol, and Amanda, you owe me a drink, don't you reckon?'

'I really do, Russ, I won't forget.' They said their goodbyes and Russell went to get his caffeine fix. Carol took off her visitor's badge and gave Amanda a hug. 'Good luck Carol, let us know how you get on and I'll see you at two on Tuesday.'

After loading the car up with her shopping, Carol headed back up to Barn End and by mid-afternoon she was sat at her kitchen table, which was now covered in electronics kit, soldering as carefully as she could and she was using Harry's soldering iron. She had been building a device that could emit and receive signals. It fit into a plastic container about the size of a Rubik's cube and out of one side was a length of copper wire, which she hoped would connect it to the ground. This would be for Harry. The second one she made was slightly larger and had a metal post sticking out from it. This had been adapted from a tent peg, so it could be plugged, or plunged, into the ground. On top of the box, with wires disappearing inside to the circuit board, was a small solar panel, the size of those used to illuminate lamps down garden drives. When Carol looked up from her table and stretched from hunching over for too long, it had gone midnight. Now she knew what she was doing, she made two more. At three a.m., Carol finally went to bed.

Chapter Nineteen – End of the Line

It was a Sunday night and Karen had just got back from walking the dog. She had been rushed off her feet with readings over the past two weeks and wasn't complaining at all, but she also knew she wouldn't count her chickens just yet. Karen had promised to ask the cards if Edie was likely to hear from Gracie or Harry again, so she sat down at the table, poured herself a whiskey and began to shuffle the deck. Her mind wandered a little. *Would Edie be contacted again? Would this group of people be in her life much longer? Would they succeed in their strange little quest to keep the exchange between the living and the dead open? Were they for real?* As Karen shuffled, she asked the questions over again. She heard the phone in the hall "ping" faintly, and she looked at the clock on the mantelpiece. It was just after seven thirty. Then she dealt out the cards into their usual formation and began to turn them over one by one and read them. Karen studied each one and sometimes she chuckled and sometimes she seemed quizzical. By the end, Karen was lost in her thoughts. According to the cards, this hadn't been a plot to bring her down. The people she had welcomed in, didn't work for the Inland Revenue. She leaned backwards, stretched and looked at the full layout of cards, now upturned and spread out on her table. 'Well you lot, what a gang you truly are.' Karen went to take another gulp of whiskey and realised her glass was empty. As she got up to pour a bit more, the phone in the hall rang loudly and the dog barked. 'Bleedin Nora! Right, which one of you buggers is it this time eh?' Karen picked up the receiver and the static was loud.

'Hello? Who's this?' She knew she was shouting. The response was just audible enough through the crackling sound.

'Hello, Karen, it's George. Tell them – they're nearly there. Tell Ed, well done, I love him and tell him I'm going now Karen, thank you.'

Karen shouted back, 'Thanks, George, is Harry with you?' But there was no reply. This time the connection was lost for good. The silence was unusual now. Karen put down the receiver and then picked it up again, but there was no dial tone and there was no static. Karen decided to call Pat, first thing in the morning.

'Morning Pat, it's Karen, is Ed there?'

'Hi Karen, yes, he's in the garden, shall I get him?'

'Yes please, then put us on speaker phone so you can hear this too.' Karen heard the phone fumbling and the sound of Pat calling Ed. She heard the nattering as they came back to the phone and then Ed said hello.

'Right guys, last night I did the tarot cards for Edie, then I got a call from George, Ed. He said to tell you well done. Then he said he loved you and you were nearly there and told me to tell you he was going now.'

'Oh that's amazing, thank you, Karen. Thank you.'

'It's OK, Ed, look, I'll see you both tomorrow, OK?' Pat gave Ed a big squeeze and Ed gave Pat one of his longest bear hugs.

Carol arrived at Edie's early on Monday morning. 'Crumbs, what time did you set off, Carol?'

'I couldn't sleep Edie, so I thought I might as well just get up and go. I'll shoot straight back as I've got a group who should be arriving just after three.'

'Well come in and have a coffee at least please.'

'I won't say no to that.' Carol rummaged in her bag and pulled out the small device that she had made.

'This is for Harry, Edie.' Edie stopped what she was doing and looked at it.

'Crikey, isn't it small? Especially compared to the last thing you made.' She looked at the copper wire that was coming out of one side. 'Do you think it'll work Carol?'

'I actually don't think we're in control of what does or doesn't work Edie. I think there's something else at work here, so it either will or it won't, but no one can accuse us of not trying.'

'That's so true. Olivia's coming round after her shift and we'll take it to the funeral directors. They can make sure he's got it with him ready, you know. I've got to take his best suit, shirt and shoes too. Olivia suggested his overalls, but, well, I'm sure he would rather be smart, especially if he does get to be with Gracie.' She smiled.

'It's all so daft and strange all at the same time, isn't it? Even if it doesn't work, I like the idea that he is holding something that connects us all together.' Then she finished making the coffee and opened a Tupperware of biscuits. 'I made your favourites.' It was the chewy cranberry ones that Carol had struggled to make herself.

'I think I forgot to add the golden syrup to the recipe I gave you Carol, two hundred mil, added to the melted butter.' Carol took one and then bit into it. 'Jesus these are good Edie. How much cocaine do you put in them? You could make these to sell you know. Seriously!' Edie smiled proudly. Carol finished her biscuit and Edie wrapped up the others to take with her. After the usual trip to the loo, Carol gave Edie a big hug and said she would see her on the following day at two. On her way out, Carol spotted the big motherboard, propped up next to the front door. There was something missing. 'What have you done with the insulator, Edie?'

'Oh, I've taken it off. We'll be having another trip to the Disco soon enough, and I want a certain little madam to put it back where it came from.' They both laughed, recalling the audacity and nimble fingers of Nel's sneaky theft. On the drive back, Carol wondered who else would be at the funeral. She thought she should just hang back out of the way, ready. It was going to be a very strange day that was for sure.

At the funeral, director's Edie had laid out Harry's suit on the table with a nice crisp ironed shirt. His shoes were next to his clothes, highly polished. There was no tie. Harry hated ties and she was going to make sure that they didn't do the top button on his collar up either. But Edie would not be part of that last ceremonial procedure. She did not want to see her husband's body, when it was not alive, without Harry still in it. She had asked the funeral director to place the small device in Harry's hand and make sure the end of the copper wire was firmly inserted between the folds of the wicker walls. The gentleman who she spoke to was very puzzled but promised her every request and Olivia drove Edie back home.

There were four big boxes and two bin liners by the front door and they contained Harry's other clothes. Edie had washed everything and ironed everything. Anything that was too worn had gone into the bin liners for the clothes bank, but the boxes were going to the British Heart Foundation charity shop. Olivia put them in the back of her car to take away with her. Edie told her about the boxes that Carol was making and Olivia said she could probably find a place for one of them, behind the big exchange where no one would see. They sat down at the kitchen table and Olivia talked about who was coming to the funeral the following day. There would be some distant cousins on Gracie's brother's side and some old work colleagues of Harry's as well as some friends from the street. Both Harry and Edie had been only children, so there were no brothers or sisters on their side. It was a tough call to decide whether or not Nel and Erin should go. But Edie had said that Harry wouldn't want them there just yet. Olivia agreed and said that in a few years' time, she could take them, preferably in spring when the cherry tree might be in blossom. The girls would go to school as normal and Olivia would get the babysitter to pick them up from school and look after them for a few hours before Olivia would get back home. When her daughter had left, Edie went into the kitchen and began making food for the wake. She spoke out loud, 'What would you like us to have Harry? I'll do you a selection of sandwiches and I can do slices of quiche. That's always easy to eat, finger food isn't it? And don't worry love. I've made sure I have the best selection of your little eats. That sideboard will be groaning with Gracie's Tupperware.' Then she stopped and cried.

It was finally Tuesday morning and Edie was up early. Olivia would be round as soon as she had dropped the girls off at school. The fridge was full of cling film-covered quiche and only the fresh sandwiches needed making up. The drinks were lined up on a side table with the glasses ready. Edie needed to keep busy, so she went out into the garden and tried to rake up some of the windfall of leaves and petals. Then she noticed that the tin can phone still had it's broken string, so she headed to the shed for some more. There, still pinned to the wall, was Harry and Carol's drawing for the motherboard. Carol had Harry's toolbox now, but the wall still had a selection of smaller hand tools, hooked to it, with shadows painted to identify which tool went where. She grabbed the ball of string and the big scissors and went back outside. Edie measured the original string and then remembered Harry's advice and measured it again. She knotted one end and as she was about to pull it through the first can, she saw the jagged sharp metal edges of the hole. On the wall in the shed was a pair of small pliers and she bent the metal over so that it could no longer catch and rub at the string. She checked the other tin can and did the same. Once she had strung up one tin, she carefully placed it in its holder inside the tree house then threaded the string through the hole in the treehouse wall. The string stretched across the small lawn back to the house and she carefully worked it through the other can, knotted it, and then set the tin on its hook. She gave it a satisfying twang and went back inside.

It was quarter to two and Elinor and Amanda parked up at the Moor Woodland burial site. Without realising it, they parked next to Karen. 'Hi, Elinor.'

'Hi Karen, Amanda this is the amazing Karen, Karen, this my friend Amanda.'

'Hi, I'm not sure about amazing, but you remembered my name, so that's a win.' The light humour broke down the severity of the imminent proceedings and they chatted together until they saw Ed and Pat drive in. Amanda waved and they parked up alongside them, just as Carol turned the corner. They greeted each other like old friends, realising it had been just over a month that they had actually all known each other. Thrown together by three ghosts, they still did not understand how this had all been orchestrated. They watched as other people turned up and they smiled at strangers but stayed grouped together. Then at the gate appeared a large black hearse. A big wicker coffin was laid in the back. It had a bunch of white lilies on the top and down the side were white floral letters spelling "gramps".

The group went silent until Ed spoke. 'Hello Harry, pal. Time to rest good and proper eh?' Pat squeezed his hand and pressed herself into her husband's side and he put his arm around her. The others took in deep breaths and then Edie and Olivia arrived in the car behind. They smiled at everyone as they got out. They held each other's hand as tightly as they could, for emotional and physical support. The coffin was carried by four pallbearers, two from the funeral directors and two from the site. They carried the coffin ahead of Edie and Olivia towards the plot where Harry would be laid to rest. There was the gentlest of breezes and the sky was very light grey. The cloud cover was high and the sound of birds in the trees and the swifts above them became the choir. Everywhere was green and fresh. There was no vicar or priest, there was no mention of God and Olivia readied herself to speak.

She talked of her dad, she talked of him as a boy and as a young man making excuses so he could go into Edmunson's far too often to visit a young lass he'd taken a shine to, behind the counter, called Edie. The group laughed at the thought. She talked of Edie and Harry's life together and her luck to have such a father, who made adventures come to life, because he made things for her. Then she choked. Next to her was the photo from Flamingo Land. Printed up large on a board, leaning against an easel. Harry was grinning out from the very centre, looking a bit wet, but smiling widely, with his hands around his granddaughters. She talked of Harry as Gramps and how she could not have raised her daughters without her mum and dad. At this point, everyone fumbled for their tissues. She spoke of Nel and Erin virtually living in the tree house that Gramps had made for them and spoke of the loss of them not having him around for longer. Then she spoke of a group of people who had recently come into his and Edie's lives. A bunch who had been kind and supportive of each other, who had become great friends, who shared a story of belief and blind faith, that they would remember for the rest of their lives. Elinor, Amanda, Pat, Ed, Karen and Carol fumbled and all grabbed an arm or a hand or a sleeve and held on tightly to each other. 'Fucking hell,' whispered Pat to Ed.

'Here here,' said Elinor.

Harry was lowered into the ground. Olivia and Edie were holding onto each other as the first shovels of earth went down on top of the coffin. The wicker creaked. Next to the easel was the cherry tree. It stood about two metres tall, young and slender, it's large roots wrapped in hessian. The woodland burial plot was not dug to six feet, just to four, so as the pallbearers changed roles they began to fill in the grave quickly. Then two of them took the cherry tree and undid the hessian, releasing the roots. When the grave was almost full they placed the tree in the centre and held it upright and continued to fill it in tightly. Eventually Edie and Olivia took over the final soil filling, until the tree stood firmly by itself. 'Rest easy Dad,' said Olivia and touched the trunk of the tree. They placed the white lilies at the base and the floral letters at the far end.

As people began to leave, Carol walked up to the grave, Edie turned round to watch, and then so did the others. Very delicately, Carol placed another small device just behind the base of the trunk, pushing in the small spike. Then she carefully tied a loose length of string around it and the tree. 'Well Stanley, let's hope this works eh?'

Everyone said their thanks to the burial site manager and pallbearers and the cars began to leave the grounds. Edie and Olivia drove home first, so they could be ready to receive guests back at the house. The others followed, but Elinor and Amanda held back. Eventually the sound of the last car disappeared and the choir of birds took over once more. Elinor looked up at the nearby pylon. 'You better do your thing and be bloody useful,' she called to it.

Amanda laughed. 'You tell it. Come on El, let's go and catch up with the others.' As they drove away, the breeze lifted and the white lilies and flowers quivered a little, then all went still.

Back at Edie's house the conversations flowed. Distant friends and next door neighbours told stories of Harry and his adventures with them. Edie hoped he was able to hear the outpouring of love. She wondered if Gracie was listening too, brimming with pride about her son and she hoped desperately that they were together, even if it was for the briefest of time and then she wondered if she would feel close to her Harry, ever again. She continued to hold it all in and smiled in all the right places. Carol reminded her about the offer to come and stay with Olivia and the girls up at Barn End and Olivia thought that would be amazing too. 'We can run them ragged in all the fresh air,' promised Carol. 'And if you think they're up for it, they could even camp outside.'

'Oh, I'm not too sure about that just yet,' worried Olivia. 'I wouldn't put it past them to just head off for a midnight walk in their pjs and disappear, carried off by owls.'

'Fair enough, but they can still stay up to look at the stars and go on adventures through the woods. We will tire them out completely.'

'I'm holding you to that.' Smiled Olivia. 'And if you're wrong, you have to take them again.' They all laughed at the probability of Carol not being able to run down the batteries on these two bouncing bunnies.

'I'm inviting you all to come and stay, if you like? Perhaps a big gathering will be just what we need?' Karen asked if she could bring her dog and everyone pooled together their camping resource suggestions.

Carol went back into the hallway and opened her bag. She brought out the third device she had made and took it to Edie. 'Would you like me to fit one of these here too Edie?' she asked. 'You might as well, Carol. There's a spot where you can see the internet cable go into the wall. Can you plant it in the ground next to it?'

'Of course.' Carol pushed the small spike into the ground and the plastic box sat on the grass with its little solar panel, catching the reflected light from the window.

Without seeing Carol's placement of the box, Karen had gone into the kitchen to help Edie tidy up some of the plates and glasses. Edie had hung a bin liner from the inside of the kitchen door for used napkins, foil and cling film. 'I think he's going to contact you Edie,' said Karen, in her clear and matter of fact way. 'The cards seemed to think that there was a conversation still to be had. It's as much as I can say really, but I do genuinely think so.'

'Thank you, Karen, I hope so too. Pass me the bin bag, will you?'

Olivia was about to leave and Carol remembered to give her the final box for the exchange. Olivia promised that at her next shift there, she would make it priority number one. Then after many goodbyes, Olivia left to go and relieve the baby sitter and said she would call her mum the following day. Amanda had asked Karen if she could book a reading and Karen was more than happy to oblige for later in the week, after she had checked her bookings, as she seemed to be very busy more recently. Relatives, friends and neighbours gradually peeled away, until Edie was stood once more in her kitchen alone. There was too much silence and so she clattered her way through the washing up, drying and putting away all the crockery, cutlery and glassware. Most of the Tupperware bowls were empty, but she decanted the leftover little eats into one container then burped the lid, chuckled, and put it into the pantry. She knew Harry thought that was funny too. The twins could have those tomorrow. She hoovered and polished, she plumped cushions and she made sure everything was exactly how it should be. Even though she knew there would be sticky finger prints covering everything by tomorrow afternoon, and she couldn't wait. There was nothing that would distract her today and Edie knew she probably wouldn't sleep either, so she went upstairs and opened the hatch and pulled down the attic stairs.

She switched on the light and even that reminded her of Harry, she climbed into the space and headed to the boxes of photos. Although she was planning on bringing them down, she realised that she couldn't manage it by herself. 'Oh Harry, I still need you, even for the smallest things.' It was taking all her resolve to keep in control. The tears had already flowed uncontrollably and even though she knew they would keep on flowing, for days, weeks, months and years, she just wanted to feel OK. As she pulled out the photo albums, she placed them close to the hatch so that tomorrow she could pass them down to Olivia. Then they would have a day of reminiscing, and it would be fun to show the girls pictures of their mum when she was six. On the shelf above was one of Harry's boxes. This is where he had kept a few of Grace's belongings. Edie moved the box near to the hatch too. Then stepped down the ladder, switched off the light and pulled up the steps.

Chapter Twenty – Land Line 2.0

Up on the hill facing the Cow and Calf, the Moor Woodland burial site was basking in sunlight. Harry's cherry tree was being gently caressed by a warm spring breeze. The tree's roots had begun to spread. They snaked their way through the soil, feeling outwards and downwards, towards nourishment, water and the wicker weave. The mycelium was spreading too. Thin threads networking and criss-crossing like the finest silk fishing net, reaching the roots of the cherry tree. The fine white tendrils had begun surrounding the wicker coffin. Gently, it would engulf the sides and find its way through the smallest gaps until it was inside.

Elinor was unable to focus on anything. Not only did the funeral replay in her head over and over again, the events of the last month were beginning to blur into a dreamlike fantasy that she was struggling to believe had actually taken place. She had played Tom's last message over again, just to remind herself that it had been real. She packed a small bag with some hastily made sandwiches and a Chilly bottle of water, went to the loo one more time and headed out to catch the bus.

'Welcome onboard the Number 36 bus,' said Harry Gration warmly.

And before she knew it, he said, 'Next stop is the Harewood Arms, get off here for Harewood House.' And so she did. If she walked her clockwise route, then after walking along the inside of the estate walls, she would get the big view of Harewood House first, the distant hills and the big sky. Then she would stroll through the woods, pop out at the far end and walk through Weardley, and after hopefully seeing the deer in lower fields, she could stop at the Muddy Boots cafe, where she first met Edie, Harry and Olivia, for a cuppa, an acrobatic display of red kites and the loo, before catching the bus back. She wasn't sure if she should tell Edie she would be close by. She was unsure if she would just want some space. Elinor set off walking. The grand house was small from this distance. Nature was bigger, vastly bigger. She felt wonderfully insignificant again. She held her head up to the sky and breathed as deeply as she could. The red kites were calling and once she was in the woods, there was only the sound of birds and squirrels. A flash of metallic blue shot past her by the little bridge, as a kingfisher darted by the waterside.

Ed and Pat had been having similar feelings and had decided to drive out to Brimham rocks. From the very top mound of land, they stared southwards and held hands. Facing south east they could see the unusual white domes of Menwith Hill, the American and RAF communications and interception station, that was a landmark for everyone around here. Especially as the big "golf balls" had gone from Fylingdales on the North Yorkshire Moors decades ago. 'I bet they haven't realised what communications have been happening right under their noses,' said Pat.

Ed laughed. 'Ha, yes. If the dead were so inclined they could be passing on quite a few top secret spy details couldn't they?' Then Pat laughed. Directly south from them was Harrogate and the information panel told them that over towards the west they should even be able to see York Minster on a good day.

'No chance, not without binoculars and especially with my eyesight,' tutted Ed. The unusual rock formations were crawling with families, children and the more serious bouldering brigade. 'This is just perfect isn't it love?'

'It really is. Can you imagine Nel and Erin running round here?'

'Oh lord, not on my watch,' said Ed with the anticipation of falls, cuts and bruises on his mind. 'I'd be a bag of nerves, wouldn't you Pat?'

'God, yes. I'm glad Olivia and the girls have decided to move in with Edie,' added Pat. 'Kids are an amazing positive reinforcement and a mind distraction too. Edie's house will be filled with life, not just the memories of death and that's what the future is all about.'

'You're not wrong there, Pat.' Then Ed grabbed her shoulder and pulled her closer for a kiss on the cheek.

Nel and Erin had run off to the tree house with the Tupperware of leftover little eats. Olivia had taken them their drinks and set them up with Finding Dory, again. Back inside her mum called down and asked her for help from inside the attic hatch. 'I'll pass them down and then we can go through them. See which we think the girls will like to see the most.' One by one the albums were handed down.

'Oh, now grab this last one. It's Gracie's box of things, that your dad kept.' Olivia had the box on her head at first, until she got the angle right. Then they brought everything downstairs. Edie moved everything from the dining table and popped it all onto the sideboard. Once all the albums and Gracie's box were set out, they sat down and began to look through the snap shot memories of their lives, with Harry at the centre of it all. They laughed and they cried again.

'Oh I've had enough of crying Liv. I'm exhausted from it. I don't want to feel like this for too much longer. I need something to do, something positive.'

'I know, Mum. Grieving has no framework or timescale. It has no controls. But I know you'll get through this with us. Once we've moved in, you'll be fully occupied and you know it.'

Edie smiled. 'Very true, love.'

Olivia took the lid off Gracie's box and inside was a mixture of small ornaments, postcards, her passport and some diaries. Edie looked at the dates. 'Seems like the very last one is from the year your dad was born. Bet he tired her out and she never had time to write things down after that.' She opened the last diary and turned to the date of Harry's birth, Thursday 19th of November, 1953. 'Thursday's child has far to go,' she said gently.

'Read it out to us, Mum,' asked Olivia.

Edie cleared her throat a little and took a sip of tea.

'Thursday, 19th November, 1953.

Baby Harry born at 4.20 p.m., this afternoon. Seven pounds nine ounce. He's gorgeous, but I'm not going through that again, whatever Peter says. I'm shattered and in pain. Peter waited outside and when he came in, he just started crying as soon as he saw him. What a softy! Mum has just visited. She was already telling me what I should do and giving me advice. Hope to be home by Sunday. Peter went off to phone everybody and when he came back, he said he'd get us a phone for the house, because he'd just spent five bob on calls using the phone box outside the hospital. Apparently, it's 2d for five minutes, but he only spoke to people for about a minute, and he got no change when he put the phone down. He was livid. I said it was a good idea, especially for emergencies and better than having to nip out to the phone box in all weathers. And it means people will be able to call us now. I'm absolutely Knackered.'

Edie and Olivia laughed at the idea of baby Harry and Edie agreed with Gracie that one was enough, then Olivia mentioned that she had no choice in the matter. 'Oh yes, sorry, love.'

It all seemed so present, like she could hear Gracie speaking, like it had only happened yesterday. She scanned through the days ahead. There was less written and Edie knew that with a brand-new baby, a diary entry was never a priority. Then she skipped forwards to Christmas week.

'Sunday, 20th December, 1953, Tom's invited us to his and Lynne's for a Christmas bash on the 27th at seven p.m. Will be nice to have a night out. Mum looking after Harry. Harry won't have a clue it's Christmas anyway, so we don't feel guilty. I'm going to nudge Peter to see if he'll get us a television like Tom's. Peter was impressed with it when we watched the Coronation. They've had an inside telephone for years already.'

Edie flicked forwards, just as Olivia asked the question. 'What were Elinor's neighbours called, Mum? It was Tom and who?'

'Wednesday, 28th of December, 1953, Had a very weird and wonderful evening at Tom and Lynne's last night.' Then Edie stopped for a nanosecond, looked at Olivia and then continued to read, 'George and Viv were there, too. The evening started really well, and we were joking about sharing Harry between us, so everyone could have a test run looking after a baby. Tom and Lynne refused point blank and said they would be happy to be Uncle Tom and Auntie Lynne, soon enough, but George and Viv seemed more keen.'

Edie went quiet as her eyes scanned ahead. 'Mum, what's the matter?' Olivia was puzzled. What had her mum just seen?

'Bloody hell, listen to this, Liv,' Edie continued. 'Then Tom said something odd had happened the other day and he needed to tell someone and as we're best friends he chose us. He said that his dad, Albert, had phoned their home phone and asked if they were both OK and he wanted to speak to them. Then the phone went dead. But Albert was killed in the war in '42. We thought he was joking, but he went white as a sheet telling us, and Lynne promised us it was real. On the way home Peter said he wasn't sure if we should get a phone fitted next week after all, and I said we bloody are, because I know he can be a skinflint sometimes. Still, it was odd. So, we all promised to keep it to ourselves and we will see what happens when we get our landline.' There were no more entries and no more diaries.

'Well now, this opens up a whole new story, doesn't it, Mum? Shall we tell the others?'

'Yes, let's, it does kind of explain how and why these three came together to get us. I'd like to see them all again anyway, sooner rather than later, too.' So, when they had agreed what to say, Olivia texted everyone, *'Hi, everyone, hope you are all good, Edie and I would like to invite you round for a catch-up; we have an interesting development.'*

Elinor replied straight away, *'Hi, Olivia, I'm ten minutes away from Edie's right now!'*

With that, Elinor was invited straight round and found herself sitting at the dining room table once more. Harry could just have been in the other room, but he wasn't.

Elinor couldn't believe what she was reading as she scanned the diary entry. 'Jesus Christ, no wonder they all found each other. They were friends in life and they were going through something that may have been similar to us. Tom and Lynne had no children, so they chose me, I suppose.'

Olivia looked out towards the garden and the treehouse. 'Mum, you're going to need to write all of this down for Nel and Erin, aren't you? Just in case.'

'I suppose we should, not just me though, it's all our story, isn't it?'

Just then Olivia recognised a noise, a vibration coming from the sideboard. Not from inside it where the old landline had been, but from on the top, where Edie had placed her phone. She picked it up and passed it to her mother. "Caller Unknown" it said on the screen. The vibrations continued. 'Answer it, Edie,' said Elinor knowingly.

Edie swiped the screen and held the phone out flat, so they could all hear. 'Hello?' she spoke tentatively.

'Hello, my darling,' Edie stood up without even realising it. His voice sounded like it was underwater, on a different plane, unworldly.

'Harry, oh God, Harry, I, I, er, is it really you?' Edie's eyes were filling up and Olivia stood up and held her mum. Elinor stayed sitting down, put her hands to her face, fixed her gaze on Edie and began to cry silently.

'Yes, love, I love you so much. Tell Olivia, I love her, too, and Nel and Erin. And say thank you to everyone, I think we did it. Say thank you to Elinor and Carol.'

'I love you so much, Harry, I miss you so much.'

'I know, love, I've got Mam and we're going now, Edie. Don't rush love, take your time and hug everyone for me. I love my cherry tree.' And with that, the call ended.

Chapter Twenty-one – The Party Line 2.0

Edie, Olivia and the girls walked back up the hill towards Barn End from the stream. They were completely drenched. Whilst looking in the rock pool near the little waterfall, using the girls' underwater magnifying telescope, it was Edie who had slipped and it was Erin and Nel who went to rescue their gran. Olivia had gone to lend a hand and then she slipped. They had stared at each other and just decided that wet through was wet through, so they sat there splashing about until Edie said her bum had gone numb and the girls thought that was hysterical. Carol spotted them walking up and got the kettle on.

Edie, Olivia and the girls were staying in the caravan that Carol had added to the site and there was a large frame tent that Elinor and Amanda had just spent far too long trying to put up. Carol apologised that they were short of some tent pegs, but as they had been used for the device posts, everyone agreed that was a fair swap. Karen was staying inside the house on a camp bed in the little room that Carol used as her office, so she could keep the dog inside at night. Pat and Ed had Carol's double room and Carol took the single. The laughter was loud and happy.

Once the wet clothes had been swapped for dry, they were hung out on the line and everyone convened around the top grassed area that Carol was now calling her garden. Elinor and Amanda had been up earlier in the Summer, to help Carol dig and prepare some beds, for the hardiest of plants. Edie had brought an amazing selection of homemade cakes and biscuits and Elinor had made the biggest lasagne ever. Pat and Ed had loaded their car with enough bacon, eggs and sausages to feed an army at breakfast time and there was no shortage of Prosecco and wine.

It was Ed who called Nel and Erin over to the group as they were stroking the dog incessantly. 'Girls!' he called, cheerily.

'Yes, Uncle Ed?' they replied loudly.

'Me and Auntie Pat have got a present for you.' The dog was released from petting duty and relieved to have a rest, then it laid down in the grass and just put its legs in the air, exhausted. Nel and Erin ran back up to the group. Out of the back of Ed's car, he pulled a very long bag about eight feet in total. Out of the top of the drawstring end were some wooden poles and canvas.

'What is it?' asked Erin.

'Well open it up and see, and then see if you can guess,' suggested Pat, more excitedly than she expected herself to be. The bag of bits was too heavy and cumbersome and Amanda found herself offering to help.

'Thanks, Auntie Mand.' And slowly they drew the contents from the bag. Even the adults were unsure what it was. Then Nel read the words on the side.

'Tee pee?' She giggled.

'What is a teepee?'

'Well!' declared Elinor. 'It's something I'm going to need very soon.' Everyone laughed and agreed this was inevitable, but Erin and Nel looked on puzzled.

'I think Uncle Ed and Auntie Pat will need to help you make it now, don't you everybody?' suggested Edie and everyone agreed very loudly.

It was not as easy as it looked. No sooner had one pole been erected, then another bit collapsed. The audience watched the show. 'To me, to you!' called Karen and the group laughed more and filled the air above them with happiness. Pat and Ed were doing their best and the girls were running around them offering help and advice.

'Ooh, its like watching Witness, but without Harrison Ford and on a penny-pinching budget,' suggested Carol.

'But does that make us the Amish Community?' asked Olivia.

'Nope, more like the "Ar kid community",' offered Karen.

'Please someone, make a Yorkshire version of that, please!' And the group of friends looked at each other and the landscape around them and laughed even more. Eventually Ed and Pat managed to get the teepee into place and secured the guy ropes. The girls shot inside followed by the dog and a cheer went up at Barn End.

When the evening came and night fell, the girls were eventually extracted from the tent and the dog only came out when the smell of warm food filled the air. They sat round the fire pit, glasses in hand and bottles close by, as darkness surrounded them. They watched the owls fly low across the field and they watched bats flitting and twisting as they hunted for the moths that had been gathering around the outdoor lights. Nel and Erin had long sticks with marshmallows pierced on the ends of them. They hung them over the pit and watched as one after the other caught fire and fell into the flames. So, Karen offered to help them out, and suddenly, Auntie Karen was the flaming stick lady and the girls were very impressed. Nel and Erin put on their little head torches and ran off down the field. From where the adults sat, the twins became fireflies.

Pat knew only one person could mention the missing member of this incredible bunch and eventually Edie spoke.

The blackness was pinpricked with billions of stars and Edie looked up at them and then around at the group. 'I just want to say, that even though I can't deny I would rather be at home with Harry right now, if this is in some way the recompense for losing him, you know, well, if it's that I've gained you lot and got to know you, well, I think I'm still very lucky. Harry would have loved to be here now. So I just want to say thank you for being wonderful too.' There was an understanding and gentle mutterings of agreement and thanks in response.

'Well, I think that we all deserve a pat on the back, don't you?' said Elinor. 'This has been the strangest, most ridiculous and amazing experience, but I still think we have one more thing to think about.' Amanda looked at her sideways.

'For God's sake El, are we not done yet? Don't you dare get a big sheet of paper out now and your pencil case of Sharpies, don't you dare!' As everyone laughed, they also looked towards Elinor and wondered what she was about to say.

'I think we need to agree on something and make a promise if that's even possible. If, when we're dead, if we're needed to create some sort of new exchange, can we agree to come back together wherever that is and see what we can do?' They looked at each other and then at the two bright torch lights dancing back towards them.

The End